Winter's Roulette:
The Frank Brennan Adventures

WINTER'S ROULETTE:
The Frank Brennan Adventures

A collection of novels by
Dana McSwain

WINTER UNSCRIPTED

Brennan's Lament

BANGKOK VENGEANCE

Webb House PUBLISHING

Winter's Roulette by Dana McSwain
Copyright © 2020 by Dana McSwain

Published by Webb House Publishing, L.L.C.
Lakewood, OH 44107
www.WebbHousePublishing.com

Cover by Timm Bryson, em em design, LLC

ISBN: 978-1-7352860-1-3 (print)
ISBN: 978-1-7352860-3-7 (eBook)

www.danamcswain.com

This book is dedicated to the cinematic genius of:
Tango & Cash, The Kurgan, *Raw Deal*, *XXX*,
Timothy Dalton, Geena Davis in *The Long Kiss
Goodnight*, *The Saint*, *The A-Team*, Sean Bean in
Goldeneye, *Airwolf*, Don Johnson, *Tales of the Gold
Monkey*, *Riptide*, Marion Fucking Ravenwood,
Simon & Simon, Ricardo Montalban, *Miami Vice*,
Knight Rider, Timothy Lambert, *Magnum P.I.*,
the entire cast of *Big Trouble in Little China*, and
that one episode of *Moonlighting*.

WINTER UNSCRIPTED

CHAPTER ONE

...

Frank Brennan, veteran Hollywood action hero, barely glanced at the script for *Armed Assault Force VI: Fast Force* and threw it back at his agent.

"Nope."

"Come on, Frank. One more. Just one more."

"I told you no six months ago, and I meant it. No. I'm not doing this shit anymore."

"It's a guaranteed two-million-dollar paycheck. Do you have any idea what that means to me, Frank?"

Frank fixed his agent with the steely glare that had stared down big-budget Hollywood drug lords, fascist dictators, and terrorists.

"Your ten percent means dick to me, Travis, if I have to go through another surgery on my rotator cuff. I'm done. I can't do this action hero shit anymore. Too many miles on this old car."

"Jesus, you're not that old, Frank," Travis said. "The studio is willing to CGI the big fight sequences, and your double can do all the close-up shit you can't do anymore. It's easy money, Frank. Come on."

"Okay, hear me out, Trav. *AAF I*, I did all my own stunts—"

"Which was stupid, by the way, Frank," Travis interjected.

"Considering the budget at the time, it was expedient. I've done less and less of my own body work since then and still came out of the last four movies with months of rehab after surgery. No. I am done. I did my time, and now I want to do something else."

"Ah, yes. Dramatic work." Travis sighed and scratched his head violently. "You're nuts, you know that, Frank? Why don't you just do one more action film for old Travis and then retire to that boxing club you own? That's very 'Frank Brennan'. Forget the drama."

"You're my agent. Do your job. Get me some dramatic scripts, and stop shoveling this action hero horseshit in my lap."

Travis sank his head into his hands and heard the thundering of hooves as his favorite cash cow ran off over a cliff. No way anyone was hiring Frank to do dramatic work. He was done, washed up. A mediocre actor who was all looks and no chops.

Still.

Travis perked up. Still, he could use Frank to square some other deals, pay back some of the favors he owed. Ride this cash cow one last time into the horizon.

He sat up and smiled, then reached into his desk drawer and pulled out a folder. He tossed it to Frank.

"You holding out on me, Travis?" Frank growled.

"Take a look."

Frank scanned the pages, then looked up, his dark eyes somehow darker when he was angry.

"You're kidding."

"Hear me out, Frank, before you say no."

"Give me one good reason I'd do a romantic comedy, Travis. Before I shove this script up your ass."

"I'll give you three. One, Joel Truman is box office gold. Every single one of his four rom-coms has made over seventy-five million worldwide. Two, he's already cast Meg Thomas as the female lead. Three, I'm sure it's not lost on you, Frank, that Meg's daddy dearest has written and produced nine Academy Award winning dramas. You do the math. Joel is looking for an older man, chiseled good looks, darkly handsome, believable as former special ops. That's you, baby."

Frank scratched his jaw and looked at the script again. It was barely a script, more of an outline. And it looked terrible. One trite stereotype after another. *Alone on the Range*, directed by Joel Truman, written by Alex Winters. He'd heard of Joel, everyone had. Wunderkind director, made it big with his first movie, a quirky rom-com called *The Russian Samovar* about a couple in Detroit.

Alex Winters? Never heard of him.

He let out a deep breath and added another verse to the catechism of hate he liked to mentally recite when he was with his agent.

"Make the deal. I don't know what you're getting out of this, Travis, but if I humiliate myself, I will make it my personal mission to see you in hell."

Travis smirked at him. "*Armed Assault Force IV: 4 Score.* I love it when you quote yourself, Frank."

"Go fuck yourself, Travis. Who is this guy Winters?"

An amused expression fell over Travis's smarmy face. "Go see for yourself. I'll get you a meeting with Joel this afternoon."

"You're a slimy bastard, Travis."

"Tell Alex I said hi," Travis said with a smirk.

Frank strode out of the office and jumped into his black Jeep Rubicon. *A romantic comedy. I gotta be out of my mind,* he thought as he drove crosstown to the studio. *Out of my goddamn mind.*

CHAPTER TWO

· · ·

Alex Winters chewed on her pen and for the ten thousandth time, wondered how the hell she had wound up here with Joel Truman. *Simple. You ghostwrote a lame rom-com as a joke, and next thing you knew, Joel optioned it and made you a screenwriter.* The bushy-haired director, who looked about as commanding as a pimply-faced sophomore, was pacing in her basement office at the studio. She looked around her bare bones, windowless office and realized that even though she'd made it all the way to Hollywood from Detroit, you'd never know it. She sighed and tried to focus on what Joel was rambling on about.

"It's kind of brilliant, actually, signing someone like Frank. It's sideways, it's out of the box. I like it. That's my brand. The quirky unexpected," he shouted, arms waving. Joel always got worked up when talking about his brand.

Alex threw her pen down and bit back a snort. *There is nothing unpredictable about what we do here, you putz. We make the visual equivalent of SpaghettiOs.*

"Refresh my memory, Joel. Frank who? Frank O'Hara from that shitty mime vs. spy nightmare InterStudios shot last year or the other Frank from all those direct-to-streaming Amish buddy cop flicks?"

"You know, I still think I could have made *The Mime Who Knew Too Much* work. InterStudio's casting is for shit. Rob Bourne would have been perfect as a French Canadian assassin mime. What that guy *can't* do with body language! Right, Alex?"

Alex flinched at the mention of Rob Bourne: actor, pretty boy, and her first foray into learning why not to mingle with the talent. Instead of rising to Joel's bait, she countered, "Focus, Boy Wonder. We were talking about this Frank guy you just cast. Amish Frank or Mime Frank?"

With a groan, Joel rummaged about in his backpack—*Jesus Christ, Joel, you're twenty-nine, not nine*—and pulled out a manila envelope. He reached inside and began tossing 8x10 glossies on her desk. She grabbed one and spun it around.

"Frank *Brennan*?" Alex tried and failed to keep her voice from ascending an octave.

Joel, busy shadowboxing, didn't seem to register her reaction.

"You bet your ass I signed Frank Brennan. Frank "Armed Assault Force" Brennan!"

Veteran star of umpteen action hero movies, Frank Brennan was a household name. Tall. Dark eyes. Black hair, eternally scruffy, lanky and muscular, absurdly good-looking in a grizzled sort of way. If you liked that sort of thing. She flipped the picture upside down and pushed it away because, unfortunately, she *did* like that sort of thing. *Great.* She put her head in her hands and thanked God one more time for the attention-hogging director across from her who let her avoid the talent and hide down here, sending lines up with runners. Joel was a putz, but he wasn't all bad.

"Fine. Frank. So run through what you want one more time so I can get started."

"A cattle rancher. Ex-special ops or something, you decide. City girl, recently widowed, crashes her car in a ditch outside his Big Sky ranch, breaks her leg. Kindly rancher takes her in while Goober-like local mechanic fixes her car, nurses her back to health, lots of local color shenanigans, it-girl bullshit, borderline butch best friend—that's what we brought Tilly Masterson on board for, she gives great hot lesbian—rides off into the sunset. Got it?"

Scribbling fast, Alex nodded without looking up. Pretty standard. She'd have this done in a day, tops.

"You're a gem, Alex."

"Yeah, yeah. Get out and let me work. And have someone bring me more donuts," she said, gesturing to the empty box on her desk. "I'm out."

She waited for the door to slam, and then hazarded one more peek at the pictures of Frank Brennan. *Really dark eyes. Jesus, look at those forearms. Maybe he's gay. And stupid. Yes, that's it. Let's focus on him being a half-witted homosexual and forget about Mr. Commando.* With a grimace, she swept the pictures into her trashcan, and began scribbling again. Not even a day. She could crank this shit out in a couple hours.

CHAPTER THREE

· · ·

"Come on in, it's open."

Frank heard the soft voice mumble through the basement office door. He opened it and walked inside. The room was almost totally empty, little more than a supply closet. The walls were bare; the lighting a septic shade of yellow. The floor, however, was crowded with towering piles of steno pads, notebooks, and loose sheets of paper. Sitting at a battered metal desk parked in the exact center of the room was a girl—a box of donuts open in front of her—scribbling away on a notepad. She looked about twenty, her chestnut hair haphazardly arranged in a messy bun on top of her head, a Bjork t-shirt on her not unimpressive bust. She looked up at him, brown doe eyes glazed over with boredom.

"Hey. Can I help you?"

"Alex Winters?"

"In the flesh. And yes, I'm female."

"What?"

"That's usually everyone's first question. And you are?"

"Frank. Frank Brennan."

"Ah! The talent. Why are you slumming it down here, Mr. Brennan? Shouldn't you be topside with Joel in Xanadu?"

He furrowed his brow. "You *are* the screenwriter?"

"Yep. Donut?"

He cringed. "No. Thank you."

"They're fresh, I swear. Joel is a little prick most of the time, but he does not skimp on the craft services." She picked one up and dunked it in her coffee, then took a bite. Through a mouthful—*that explains the mumbling*—she said, "Mmmm, Bruno's makes the best donuts."

"Yeah, no thank you. I'm Paleo, so no donuts."

"Right. It's all Paleo this year. Caveman diet. I've heard of it. Sounds miserable."

He bristled. *What was her problem? And how had she shifted the conversation to his diet? And was that a framed picture of a hissing cat on her desk?*

"It's not the caveman anything. I don't eat anything cultivated or modified, only . . ." He trailed off.

"What cavemen ate?" She smirked.

He smiled at her thinly. "Let's start again." He glanced back over to the cat. *That cat looks about as easy to deal with as this chick.*

"By all means."

"I just wanted to talk to you about my character's story arc."

"Right," she said slowly.

"I mean, I have a loose script, but I want to see the final draft. I want to make sure my character is sufficiently sympathetic. You know."

"Right," she said again, stuffing another donut in her mouth.

He stared at her in mute horror as she finished it in two bites.

"How on earth do you eat like that?"

She licked her fingers off. "I only eat donuts and coffee when I'm working. Brain food. Carbs." She shrugged.

"How are you not as big as a house?"

She stared up at the ceiling for a moment and considered his question. "Tapeworm?"

Frank shifted uneasily in his chair and tried to regain control of the conversation. "Anyway, the way I see it, my character's motivation is based in his childhood. His hometown. Local boy scarred by warfare, looking for a reprieve, a rest—"

"I'm going to stop you right there." She gave him a perplexed look before she continued. "You've never worked with Boy Wonder before, have you?"

"No, I have not worked with Joel. But he assured me we could give my character a little dimension. You know, let me stretch my acting chops a bit."

"What Joel says and what Joel does are two different things, Frank. Let me tell you how this is really going to work. You get an outline. You sign up. You show up. We stumble around for a while, Joel makes changes, I write lines daily, we adjust on the fly, it all comes together in a big mess of stereotypical, one-dimensional tropes. We all go home, you get paid, music swells, run the credits."

"But—" Frank's face screwed up in annoyance.

"Listen, I hate to be the one to tell you, but Joel sold you a bill of goods. This is my fourth film with him, all rom-coms. There is no story arc. People want pre-digested, non-Paleo movies, Frank. You know that. They don't want to hunt it down and kill it and eat it raw; they want it inserted into their stomach with a funnel. So that's what we give them. With a big budget and lots of soaring music. Your job is to bring in the ladies with your ..." she gestured at him, "all that business, and look sufficiently dramatic and hot. My job is to pull it all together while Boy Wonder worries about his percentages."

"But my character is ex-military, right?"

"Sure."

"Will that be reflected in the storyline or in costuming?"

She shrugged. "Listen, your character is a truck driver with a chiseled jaw who meets a small-town widow in Portland—"

"What? That's not what I signed on for at all!" Frank snapped.

"No wait, that's the one we're doing next." She shuffled the papers on her desk, and finding what she was looking for, started nodding. "My mistake. Your character is a cattle rancher ... oh yes, I see, former SEAL who falls for a ..." she shuffled through her papers. "Joel hasn't really decided yet. Probably widowed city girl but he tends to change his mind, so I'm waiting until he calms down before I commit to that. He's kinda hyper."

"You're kidding me."

"Nope. Welcome aboard. Your job is to stare into the sunset and flex and smolder. I'll think up manly, desperate things for you to say."

"This is bullshit. I'm going back up to talk to Joel."

"You do that. Tell him steerage class says hello. And to send more donuts if he wants his pages by tomorrow."

Frank stormed out the door and slammed it behind him. He stopped in the hall for a moment, fuming. *I hate you, Travis, you sleazebucket.* Then he took a breath and opened Alex Winters' door again. She was scribbling like he'd never even been there. He cleared his throat.

"Forget something?" she said, without looking up.

"How old are you?"

"Thirty-four." She flashed him a peace sign. "Not that it's any of your business. We good here?"

"Do you even know what you're doing?"

"Ask Joel." She rolled the pen through her fingers, all the way to her pinkie and then back again. "Tell me, Frank, how old are you?"

"Forty-six, princess."

"Aren't you a little old to play a knight in shining armor, grandpa?" With that, she went back to her scribbling and a fresh donut, ignoring his enraged face.

He slammed the door again and stormed down the hallway.

"Grandpa"? What a bitch. The first woman he'd seen in years who literally surpassed gorgeous, and she was a raging bitch. Figures.

On the other side of the door, Alex threw her donut at the wall. It slid down and landed on a pile of crumpled papers. *"Princess"? Who the fuck did this Brennan think he was?* She peeked into her wastepaper basket and saw him smoldering up at her. *Shit.* It had taken every last ounce of resolve inside her to pretend she didn't know exactly who he was and avoid those absurdly sexy brown eyes. She kicked the wastebasket across the room with one boot and picked up another donut. *What an asshole.*

CHAPTER FOUR

. . .

"So, first let me introduce our cast and crew for *Alone on the Range . . .*"

It was the first day of shooting, and Joel loved to treat it like the first day of kindergarten. *That's it, Joel. Make everyone say their names and one random fact about themselves. Jesus,* Alex thought.

"We have Frank Brennan, the powerhouse behind *Armed Assault Force I* through *V* as our steely-eyed cattle rancher, Rob; the illustrious Meg Thomas as the big-city widow, Kate, running from a tragic past straight into his ex-special forces arms; Tilly Masterson as the doomed land management officer/best friend, Sarah; and Tim Lewis as the everyman local mechanic, Walt. It's romance, it's comedy, you'll laugh, you'll cry. That is, if I do my job right." *Cue the canned laughter.*

Alex wasn't listening. Instead, she studied the principals of *Alone on the Range.* Meg Thomas was beautiful, in a fragile, wasted, anorexic sort of way. If things went the way they usually did, she and Brennan would have a high-octane romance that would hopefully not implode until the movie was done. Tilly Masterson, cast as Sarah the land management officer, was obviously already infatuated with the sweet young thing they'd hired to play the waitress in the diner. Alex had seen them making out on every conceivable surface already. Poor Tim Lewis, cast as the Goober mechanic, would watch everyone pair off, try to hook up with an extra, and fail. It was a trope in and of itself, really. Fascinating.

But not fascinating enough to stick around and watch. Mary Li, her best friend on set, would fill her in on all the juicy details like she always did. Meg was already acting the part of the waif-like widow, one of those actresses who has no personality of her own so she camouflaged that by becoming every role that came along. Brennan looked annoyed by something; he seemed to be standing as far away as he could from the rest of the cast, like they were contagious. Weird. If he was true to trope, he should have been playing grab-ass with Meg.

If she had her way, she'd write it differently. Tilly would not die at the hands of the poachers; she would leave the land management bureau and open a diner that served only pie with the hot waitress. Meg would slowly realize the rancher was not her type and fall in love with the non-traditionally good-looking older man Goober. Yeah, Meg and Goober Tim made more sense. That girl had daddy issues enough to fill a whole bookshelf. And Goober was a good guy, warm and caring, and he wouldn't care that Meg was a bit of a flake. She let her eyes dart over at Brennan, standing away from the rest of the cast. He didn't look like he wanted to be paired off with any of them.

Alex jumped out of her reverie when she heard her name.

"And last and almost least . . . ha ha ha . . ." Joel loved to laugh at his own jokes. "Let me introduce you to our intrepid, long-suffering screenwriter, Alex Winters. Plucked by Yours Truly from obscurity for no more than a game of Skee-ball and a slice of pizza. Take a good look because Alex rarely leaves her basement lair. You may never see her again, but we are all at her mercy. Wave to the nice actors, Alex."

Alex curtsied and waved sarcastically all around, then flipped Joel off. The whole cast burst out laughing, and with the ringing sound of it in her burning ears, she turned and stormed away. *He always has to mention the pizza. Joel, you prick.* She was almost to the studio door, a short sprint down the basement stairs to safety, when a voice called her name. She turned slowly on one heel, fists clenched at her side.

"Yes?" It was Brennan. *How did he sneak up on me that fast? I didn't even hear him coming.*

He held his hand out to her. "I'm sorry we got off on the wrong foot. Let's try this again. Frank Brennan."

She shook his hand, eyes wary. "Alex." Maybe he wasn't a complete asshole. She swallowed hard. "Alex Winters." She pulled her hand from his and waved it in the general area of the distant cast and crew. "Well, good luck with all this. Break a leg." She turned to go.

"Alex, wait."

She spun back around, one hand holding the studio door open.

"What?"

"If you have a minute, could we talk about some of my lines?"

Son of a bitch. He was sweet talking her. She idly rubbed the tattoo behind her ear and smiled sweetly at him.

"No," she snapped, and slammed the door in his face.

The door to Alex's office flew open, slamming against the wall as it did. Two weeks into filming, and Alex didn't even have to look up to know it was Brennan. *Again.*

"Is there a reason you're singling me out for special treatment, Frank? I mean, I'm flattered, but how about you spread it around?" She reached across her desk and surreptitiously slipped the framed picture of her cat, Poppy, into her desk drawer. *No way I am giving Frank more ammo against me. Hack screenwriter cat woman. Oh, God. That's exactly what I am.*

"I can't believe Meg isn't down here five times a day nagging you about her lines. Isn't she?" Frank said.

Alex's only response was a snort.

"Not even Tilly? Tilly's a high-caliber actor. No way she's okay with this shit."

"Nope. Tilly doesn't care because she's in lust and just signed on to play the lead in that foreign film about the Holocaust after this shit show. Meg spends all her time in costume and makeup and consulting her astrologer. You're literally the only soul who schleps down here. Not even Joel bothers. He texts. Or sticks angry notes in my donut box, if he really wants my attention." She rubbed her eyes and threw her pen down on her desk. "What's your problem this time, Frank?"

"This is my problem, Alex." He held out the paper in his hand like he was on stage and read aloud, pitching his gravelly voice as high as he could to mimic Meg's.

"I lost my whole family when our locally-sourced gluten-free sushi food truck exploded. And ever since then, I've wondered if I could ever move past the smell of gasoline and raw tuna. It wasn't until I came here to your ranch that I learned the smell of manure was what I needed to drive the past out of my nose." He let go of the paper and let it fall to the floor at his feet. "What the actual fuck, Alex?"

"Those aren't even your lines, Frank! Those are Meg's! I don't see her down here bitching about it!" She stood up so fast her chair flipped behind her.

"No, they're not, *Alex*, but I'm the one who has to stand there and listen to her say them with a straight face! How the *fuck* am I supposed to do that?" he yelled.

"You're the actor, Frank! Act!"

"You're the writer, Alex! Write! Something other than this manure you keep spreading!"

She glared at him for a long moment, and he braced for her to scream back. But she didn't. Instead, a smile began to crack on her face. It burst forth in a laugh that she'd obviously been holding in.

Frank tried not to smile at the sight of her laughing and failed. Alex laughed with her whole body, her ever-present scowl vanished, and he found himself delighted. "Oh, well, as long as you're amused, Winters." He tried to wipe the mirth from his face but instead felt his grin widen and heard his own rueful laugh mix with hers.

She was bent over her desk now, breathless, tears of laughter streaming down her face. Through choking breaths, she sputtered, "You are literally the first leading man to call me on any of this shit."

Frank stared back at her, incredulous. *You sneaky little devil. You're doing this shit on purpose.* He bent and picked up the paper. "Alex?"

Wiping tears of laughter off her face, Alex managed, "What, Frank?"

"You have a sick sense of humor. I like that in a writer. Hell, I like that, period." He ran a hand through his hair, a mischievous look appearing in his eyes. "Tell you what, cubbie. Just for you, I will make it my personal priority to nail this scene so hard it screams my name."

Alex stared at him, all laughter gone, and croaked, "Sounds great."

He left with a grin, shutting the door carefully behind him, and Alex sank into her chair, her legs rubbery. She slid open her desk drawer and peeked at the 8x10 glossy she'd pulled from the trash.

Shit. He's not gay or stupid. And goddamn, he really has a way with words.

CHAPTER FIVE

· · ·

A hand gripped Alex's shoulder and spun her around. It was Frank, a grim look hatcheting his rugged face.

"What now, Brennan?" Alex said, wrenching his hand off her shoulder. "And didn't your mother teach you to use your words, not your hands?"

Frank shook his head, giving her a rueful smirk that did not reach his determined eyes. "You've got a quip for everything, don't you, Winters? My trailer. Now."

Without an explanation, he turned and stormed away. Alex followed him, trying not to look like she was either slightly terrified or following him. She took her time, stopping at craft services and, with a smirk, loading up a plate with a half-dozen powdered sugar donuts. She climbed the steps to his trailer and knocked on the door five times, humming to herself and balancing the plate on her notepad.

Shave and a haircut.

He broke into her ditty with a barely restrained, "Get your ass in here."

She sighed and opened the door. "The response is 'two bits'. Is that what haircuts cost you back in the day, Frank?"

She slid into the banquet table across from him and dumped the plate in the middle, a smug smile on her face as the powdered sugar flew up in a cloud and landed on his black t-shirt. His lips raised in disgust as he brushed it off, ignoring her comment.

"So, Miss Winters—" he began, his voice thin and measured.

"Alex. Just Alex."

"Just out of curiosity, what is Alex short for?"

She shook her head. "Nope. Nothing doing."

His head jerked up like a hunting dog catching a scent. "Oh, I see. Someone doesn't like her name? Let me guess. Alexandra?"

She winced. "Stop it. Why did you drag me in here? What's your complaint this time?"

"Maybe all your little schoolgirl friends in Pasadena called you *Lexie*? Am I close? Or maybe *Allie*?" he teased.

"One, I am not from Cali. And two, no."

"No, what?"

"Just no, *Francis*."

His jaw clenched. "*Touché*."

She pointed at her chest. "Wordsmith."

"Yeah, about that." He reached behind the banquet and pulled his script out of a gym bag. "What is this shit?" He threw them across the table at her.

She didn't pick them up. "Those are your lines for this afternoon. In which your ex-military cattle rancher Rob tries to teach the fish-out-of-water city girl Kate to ride a horse, they end up in a bale of hay, then they French for a while, until she feels survivor guilt because of the freak accident that killed her whole family and stumbles off hilariously into a cow pie because of her broken leg, all the while being heartbreaking, charming, and sexy."

"It's bullshit."

Alex shrugged. "It's a workable trope for this set up."

"You keep saying that. *Trope*. Like it excuses this predictable, one-dimensional garbage you keep feeding me. I mean, even on *Armed Assault Force III: Armageddon*, which had almost no budget, we had great lines."

"Give me one example. I'm a bit fuzzy on *AAF II* through *V*."

He stood and put a pen in his mouth like a cigar, clenching it in his even, white teeth, his five o'clock shadow making the angles on his face sharper.

"I can smell it, Chief. The winds of revolution are blowing across this bloody battlefield. The winds of freedom." Then he mimed throwing a grenade and slumped back into his seat.

Alex started drawing in the powdered sugar dust on the table, biting her lips so she wouldn't laugh. She finished her sketch, a little hangman, then finally looked up and met his eyes.

"This is what we do around here, Frank. Joel is a trope dealer, and I am his backroom chemist. I make the product. Blue-haired indie girl, con man with the heart of gold, hooker with the heart of gold, popular guy/nerdy girl, odd couple, rich man/poor girl? Any of this sound familiar?"

"I'm not stupid, Alex. I know this is a rom-com. But can't it be smart and sexy, too?" He paused, considering. "Listen, I've done action all my life. I can't do it anymore. Too old."

She raised her eyebrows.

"Shut it, cubbie."

She smiled.

"And I thought I'd try something like this, sorta get my feet wet, and try to do some more serious acting." He ran his hand through his hair, slicking it back from his face.

Alex took pity on him. "We don't do serious here, Frank. I hate to break it to you."

"Well, yeah but . . ." Frank picked up the papers and rifled through them, his muscular arm reaching across the table and brushing her arm to grab a pair of glasses. He slipped them on and gave her a dark look, daring her to comment.

Alex bit her lower lip, less from wanting to tease him about the glasses and more because of what they did to his already handsome face. She tried to look back down to the drawing she'd done in the donut dust of a hang-man, but she was riveted by the way one lock of his black hair had fallen over the front of his spectacles. *He does this for a living, Alex. He's professionally sexy. It's not real,* she told herself firmly.

Frank found what he was looking for and began read-ing aloud to her in a flat, mocking tone.

"You're so strong. Stronger than any woman I've ever met. And so different from every woman I know. I want to be alone, need to be alone, but damn it, woman, you've blown into my world and burned it all down." He looked up at her.

She could feel the flush blooming across her face. He smirked at her, no doubt thinking it was embarrassment at the lines she'd written. She had barely heard him. Another lock of hair had fallen, and she'd reclassified him from "professionally sexy" to "mercenary."

"Did you want me to change something?" she asked, pinching herself under the table. *Get your shit together, Alex.*

"Well, considering her family died in a fire, maybe at least that line." Frank grinned at her. "Wordsmith."

Shit. Him and his chiseled jaw. She was getting sloppy. She reached out and snatched the papers from him. She read the pages two times through, all the while he stared at her in silence. A third time and she forgot he was even there as she plucked a pen from her hair and began crossing things out, rewriting the whole scene. When that didn't please her, she flipped the whole thing over and began rewriting the afternoon shoot cold. He was right. The whole scene was a new level of bad. Lost in her work, when he spoke, she jumped, her eyes flying up to meet his in surprise.

"Hello? Alex? Remember me?"

"Sorry. Occupational hazard." She slid the handwritten lines across to him, blurring the hangman as she did. He took them but only glanced at them.

"Where'd you learn to do that?"

"Do what?"

"Write." He leaned back in the booth and stretched again, arms rippling. *Mercenary.* She needed to get out of here.

"Around. I did some ghostwriting a few years back. It turned into a scriptwriting gig. And here we are."

"Do you write anything else?"

"No," she said pointedly.

"Nothing? You don't have a diary you scribble in at home?"

She made a face at him. "Let me ask you something, Frank."

"Shoot," he said, now reading the pages, glancing up at her.

"Where did you learn to do *this*?"

"Act?"

"Yeah, specifically act like you're interested in a no-talent screenwriter to get your lines changed?" she spat at him. With that, she rose, grateful that the interested look on his face had been replaced once more with anger. That was easier to process.

"I think we're done here, Winters."

"I was on my way out anyway. I'll go give Joel the new pages."

"Don't you need these?"

She tapped her head. "It's all up here. Keep your pages."

She hoped he didn't see her legs shaking as she exited his trailer, pausing after she shut the door to lean against it until her heart stopped racing. It was horrible and thrilling to be in such close quarters with him, but he was too magnetic, too unaware—*of course he's unaware, you half-wit; he's way, way out of your league, sunshine*—of how he affected her. She fled down the stairs and went to find Joel, determined to put Frank Brennan and his eyes far, far from her mind.

Inside the trailer, Frank read the new lines. It was still trite, but it was good. Really good. He tried speaking them out loud. They sounded good, sounded like him. It was as if Alex had picked up on his phrasing, his mannerisms and injected them into the scene, cutting the saccharine sweet with something darker and more intense. Something sexy and unpredictable. And she'd done it in ten minutes flat. *She really is a sneaky little devil.*

CHAPTER SIX

. . .

"No. Listen, I am not saying this shit. I have *some* self-respect left, surprisingly. No."

"Frank, listen. It's just this one scene," Joel said. "We have to get it in the can today. I've got a whole crew waiting, we are already over budget—"

"I don't give a fuck about your crew and your budget. You're not the one out there humiliating yourself. I am not saying this garbage. Where is that deranged screenwriter? Where is Alex?" he demanded.

"No, *you* listen, Frank. My name is on this thing, too. And it doesn't matter how stupid it is or how embarrassed we are; all that matters is the box office take and my percentages. Every day we go over budget is literally money out of my pocket. Get your ass out there and do your job and stop being such a fucking *prima donna*. And stop hassling Alex; she's just doing her job." Joel's voice shook, the tremble in his almost adolescent voice belying his blustering words.

Frank stepped into the much smaller man and smiled at him, his teeth barred like a shark. Joel took a step back into the sound booth wall as Frank reached out with one quick hand and brushed a fleck of imaginary lint off his scrawny shoulder, making Joel cringe.

"Don't hit me, Frank."

"I'm not going to hit you, Joely. Where is she?"

"Shit." A beat. "Fine." Joel threw the script down on the floor, hitting Frank's tactical boots. "She just stepped outside to take a call or something."

Frank leaned in even closer, eyes nailing Joel to the wall, and pinched his cheek. "Atta boy. See? That wasn't too hard, was it?"

Before Joel could answer, Frank spun on his heel, fists clenched, and strode toward the soundstage doors, kicking them open with one foot. A flash of light entered the room, the outside bleached into negative, then vanished as the black doors slammed shut behind him.

"Take five, everybody. Shit, take the whole goddamn day," Joel yelled as he stormed off in the other direction, toward his trailer.

"Motherfucking 'you complete me' bullshit," Frank muttered to himself as he stalked through the ever-shifting sea of extras, PAs, and golf carts blocking his way. He'd gone about ten feet when suddenly the entire lot seemed to notice, almost as one, Frank's wrathful march, and they parted for him, scurrying out of his way, leaving him a direct path to the object of his search.

She was huddled up against another soundstage wall, her back to him, looking like some goddamn college kid in her baggy cargo pants and complicated t-shirt tank-top business she wore every day. His step faltered, once, as he found his eyes skimming up and down her, from her flip-flops—ankle bracelet with bells on it—*Jesus fuck*—up her completely camouflaged legs, pausing at the way her loose cargos hung off her hips, running back down those baggy pants, imagining what was hidden inside. Then he stopped completely as she ran one hand through her long chestnut hair and pulled it back away from her ear. She had a little tattoo behind her left ear, and he found himself squinting at that tiny patch of skin, trying to discern what it was. His brow furrowed as he felt the beginning of an unsettling shift in his mind. He had a sudden flash of his father kissing his fingers when his ma came out of the bedroom in a new dress. *Why the fuck would I think of that?* Frank gritted his teeth and crossed the five feet separating him from Alex, the sea of onlookers reforming behind him at a safe distance, a silent congregation breathless for the show.

He could hear her now, her voice tight and pleading. *What the hell?* he thought. *Alex? Crying?* He paused, hand hovering just behind her shoulder blades when he heard her say, "No, please don't hurt her. I'll do anything." He drew his hand back, followed abruptly by his whole body, not wanting to interrupt her, in time to hear her sob, "No, no, no! Please don't! You sick son of a bitch!"

Someone was threatening Alex? But why? What the hell did this dumb kid get herself into? He felt his anger toward her shift, the Formula One gearbox in his mind punching through all eight gears straight into rage at whoever was threatening her. It was one thing for him to do it. That was professional. This, whatever it was, sounded personal.

"Alex," he growled.

She spun around, the phone still at her ear, her face a blotchy mess. He fought the urge to wipe the tears that dripped off her chin and instead dug into his pocket for something, anything, for her to wipe her nose with. He came up with a Starbucks receipt and handed it to her, digging deep as well for something consoling to say.

"You're a fucking mess, Alex," is what came out. *Great, Frank. You're really nailing this rom-com shit.*

She ripped the receipt from his hand and tossed it on the ground, using her shirt hem instead to blow her bubbling nose.

"What do you want?" she choked.

His face screwed up in a blend of concern and disgust, thrown by this new, fragile Alex.

"I . . . uh . . ." he started. "Well, the thing is . . ." He searched his mind for the angry speech he'd recited between the soundstage and here and found it had vanished entirely. "Are you all right?" He heard the sea of onlookers shift behind him as they wandered off in a swell of disappointed murmurs at the lack of excitement.

She cleared her throat and wiped her eyes, emotions short-circuiting across her face, until she bit her lower lip and nodded, as if she'd landed on a decision.

"Frank," she whispered, "I need a favor. Please."

He leaned in and bent down to her. She smelled like donuts and lemon, sugar, and something vanilla. *Jesus, she even smells like carbs.*

"What kind of favor?"

"All this army tactical crap?"

He placed his arm on the wall next to her and leaned in even closer, scanning the lot to see if anyone else was watching.

"Like, can you really do all that guerilla stuff you pretend to do?"

"Maybe," he whispered. "Why?"

"Someone's got my best friend. They're holding her." She fixed him in her gaze, her liquid brown eyes wide and afraid. "I want you to help me break in and get her out. Please, Frank. You owe me. Sort of."

"Shouldn't we call the police? Alex, what's going on?"

"No. No police. I can't explain."

"Did the kidnapper say that?"

"No," she said, shaking her head. "I can't contact the *police*, Frank, that would be crazy. Look, will you help me or not?"

"What the hell have you gotten yourself into, Alex?"

"They warned me, and I didn't listen. It was stupid. There, I admit it, Frank. I'm an idiot; are you happy? Listen, Mr. Big Nuts Commando, if you help me spring Poppy, I'll rewrite anything you want, no questions asked. The whole script if you want. Even if they fire me. I think I can get in and out myself, I just want you there in case I need," she gestured up at him, "all of this business."

"Anything I want?" He grinned down at her.

"Anything. Within reason."

He let her stew for a minute, enjoying having her right where he wanted her for a change.

"Just tell me this—are there Mexican drug lords involved?"

"Of course not. Don't be ridiculous."

He pretended to consider, even though she'd had him at 'please'. "Fine. I'll do what I can. I'd hate to think all that training for *Armed Assault Force I* through *V* was for nothing. Where are they holding your friend?"

She scrambled in her pants pocket for her pen, then stooped down and picked up the receipt that fluttered at her feet.

"Turn around," she demanded.

He turned and felt her use his shoulder to write on, the pen digging through his shirt into his back. Finished, she spun him around and stuffed the paper into his hand.

"Meet me at this address at midnight. I drive a purple Prius. I'll be waiting out front."

"Of course you do," he groaned. "Purple Prius. That's so you. And no, you won't be waiting out front. You'll wait a block away. There's your guerilla lesson number one."

"Are you going to meet me or not, Frank?"

"I'll be there, princess."

CHAPTER SEVEN

...

He cut the headlights on his black Rubicon a quarter mile before his nav system said he'd arrived at the destination. She had not been waiting as he'd ordered a block away. Typical. He'd dressed for the occasion: black pants, black turtleneck, tactical vest, boots laced up to his knees. For added protection against whatever Alex had gotten herself involved in, he'd painted his face black, and forgoing his sidearm, slipped a machete around his waist and a SEAL knife on his thigh. He knew how to handle both—and well—but he was hoping that a terrifying guise would help him avoid any confrontations. He didn't really want to tangle with anyone not paid to let him win.

He groaned as he pulled up behind her car. Alex was leaning against the hood of her purple Prius, her athletic form all that he could make out against the glare of her headlights. He slammed his Jeep into park and leapt out, silently, leaving his door ajar and rushed up beside her, grabbing her by her wrist. She jumped and screamed, her other hand flying up and catching him in the jaw. He used his other hand to clamp down across her mouth, silencing her, then yelling himself when she bit him.

"What the fuck, Frank?" she hissed.

"Do you want them to know we're here?" he hissed back. "What the fuck are you doing waiting here, lights blaring, advertising yourself. 'Hey, bad guys, here comes Alex and her buddy Frank!'" He glanced down at her feet. There was a large rectangular box there with a handle on top. "And you never, ever bring the ransom money, babe. I learned that filming *Armed Assault Force II: Bangkok Vengeance.*"

"Frank?"

"Alex?" he replied thinly.

"What the hell are you dressed up for?"

"What do you mean, what am I dressed up for?" He glanced back down at her feet. "Wait. What is that?"

"It's Poppy's cat carrier. Did you call me 'babe'?"

His eyes traveled up from the cat carrier to her face, then looked over her shoulder at the building in front of which she'd parked. The offices of LA County Animal Control.

"Alex?"

"What?"

"Is your best friend, Poppy, by any chance, *your cat*? That hissing beast you have framed on your desk?"

"Of course she is." Alex wrenched her hand out of his and began talking fast. "That's why we're here. It's just . . . I'm putting in fifteen-hour days filming this stupid piece of shit film, and Poppy likes a bit of fresh air. So I leave the kitchen window open, and Mrs. Reilly in 2B *hates* Poppy and calls Animal Control on me. They've taken Poppy in *five times*, and the animal control officer said the next time they are going to *euthanize* her, and I know you hate me, Frank, but she's all I have. I am literally that sad. Laugh if you want, but please, please, Frank, help me."

Frank took a step back and crossed his arms, nodding.

"I see." He cleared his throat. "You dragged me out here in the middle of the night to break into the animal shelter and rescue your cat."

"Well, sure. What did you think we were doing?" Alex said over her shoulder, as she hauled the carrier over to the six-foot fence. She hopped up on top of it, climbed the last few feet of fence nimble as a middle-schooler, then hopped over to the other side, landing solidly on her feet.

"Can you toss the carrier over on your way? She's going to be in a bad mood. Frank, are you coming or what?"

"I cannot believe this, Alex. You really are batshit."

"Maybe I am. But I'm not the one dressed up like I'm LARPing *Call of Duty*. And Frank?"

"Yes, Alex?"

"I think you can leave the machete in the car."

"Hold still, you big baby."

Frank winced. Alex grabbed him by a fistful of his hair and jerked him back.

"This is happening, Frank. Whether you want it or not."

"Why do you have to be so rough, Alex?" he complained.

"Aw, come on, Frank. I thought you liked it rough." She finished dabbing his face with alcohol, her nose screwing up as she did. "Well, female audiences give guys with scars top points for sexy. You're going to be really, really sexy if you don't let me clean these scratches."

They were back at her apartment, Poppy slumbering on the kitchen counter, while Alex tried to clean the myriad wounds that crisscrossed Frank's face and arms.

He looked up at her ruefully from the chair. "I can't imagine why I thought your cat would be less of a pain in my ass than you are." Then, for reasons he could not fathom, he winked at her. But she was too busy fussing with a cut on his arm to notice.

She shrugged and replied, "I guess your tactical gear doesn't work against cats, huh?"

He rose, pushing her away. "All right, all right, enough fussing." He stretched; his arms seemed to span the small kitchen as he did. "Off to bed with you, young lady. You've got a long day of rewrites to do tomorrow." He crossed the room and flung himself on her couch, unstrapping his knife as he did and tossing it on her coffee table. "And take that damn beast with you in case she wakes up and decides to finish the job. Jesus, you two look like twins standing there like that."

"What are you doing?" she asked, clutching the hissing Siamese cat to her chest.

"Don't get your panties in a knot, Alex. It's two in the morning, and I'm beat. I'll sleep on the couch and be out of your hair by dawn. And don't worry, your chastity is safe with me." He considered winking at her again, but she was staring at him this time, her expression unreadable.

She nodded. "I know that, Frank. You'd never let me forget it." She ducked her head and headed back into the darkness of the hall. Her voice floated out to him, "There are blankets in the cedar chest. And pillows."

"Alex, I'm—" he started to apologize.

She cut him off. "Thanks, Frank. Good night."

Her door slammed shut, and he had no idea if she heard him reply, "Sweet dreams, Alex."

He drove his fist into the couch, cursing. *Why did she set his teeth on edge like that, every time?* Just when they were almost getting along, she had to freeze up, throw down, and complicate everything. He pulled his shirt out of his pants, unbuckled his belt and threw it on the floor, then sat up and unlaced his admittedly ridiculous boots. *She is in there laughing at me.* He threw the boots against her door with two satisfying thuds, hoping to get a rise out of her, but she didn't respond to his hair pulling. Darkness came from under her door; no sound at all.

He crossed the room and lifted the lid on the chest, grabbing a blanket, when his eyes caught the edge of something deep under another blanket. Papers. He started pulling blankets out, one after another, glancing back at the door in case she came back out. There, at the bottom of the giant chest, were six bundles, manuscripts by the look of them, each four-inch-thick bundle tied in twine and bearing the name Alexandra Winters.

He pulled the one off the top and sank back down into the couch. He read the first page. Then the second. A blink of the eye and he was ten pages from the end of the gripping thriller, dawn approaching, having not slept at all. He finished the book and sat staring at it for a long minute, thinking. He cocked his ear to her door. Silence still. Moving quickly, he replaced all the manuscripts, including the one he'd read, and selected another one, the largest one, and slipped it into his vest. He replaced the blankets and slipped quietly out her front door, taking the stairs down two at a time. He stopped abruptly at the door to the second floor, a devilish grin on his blood-stained face.

He pushed the door open and walked down the hall until he found 2B, the placard on the doorframe reading "Reilly, Marge". He knocked three times, the staccato report echoing in the empty hall, then hooked his thumbs into the arms of his vest. He rolled his shoulders and then planted his feet broad and square, arranging his face into the dead-eyed thousand-yard stare that had landed him an action hero franchise.

A middle-aged woman wearing a hideous red fleece robe answered. She clutched her robe to her chest when she saw him, as if worried he'd ravish her. *Not likely, Marge,* he thought.

"Who are you? What do you want?" she gasped, taking in Frank's face and gear, his broad shoulders completely obscuring the hall, his eyes glittering black as his hair.

"Let's just say I'm a personal friend of your neighbor, Alex Winters. And I would take a dim view of you calling the cops on her again. Do we understand each other, Marge?"

She stared open-mouthed at him like a terrified fat fish.

"I'll take that as a yes." He pivoted and walked slowly away, laughing silently to himself as he heard Marge slam the door and lock it. He texted Joel from his car and told him he was taking the day off, pleading a fever, then drove slowly home. As he drove, he made a mental list of all the things he'd learned about Alex that night. It was somewhere between *climbs fences like a monkey* and *doesn't take any of my shit* when a grin crossed his face. A grin that grew to a genuine smile that burst out of him in a loud barking laugh.

He spent the day reading her book and added to the list *one hell of a writer,* all while another list, one he didn't dare admit to himself, grew longer and more intricate. That list started with *my lips on her tattoo* and ended with *her saying his name, Frank, softly.*

CHAPTER EIGHT

• • •

"*Y*ou're calling *me* down here to your secret laboratory, Alex? That's a first."

Frank shut the door carefully behind him and stood waiting across the room, uncertain how to proceed. *If this was Armed Assault Force IV: 4 Score, I would just stride over there, and she'd fall into my arms. I suck at this shit without a script. Also, Alex is not a Bangkok prostitute sympathetic to the revolution. She'd probably gouge my eyes out.*

She barely glanced up at him when she waved him over.

"Good. You're here. Pull up a seat. Let's get to work."

"Work? Oh, no, no, no. Rewriting this piece of shit is your job, remember? My job is to stare into the sunset and smolder." He crossed his arms over his chest and gave her a smug smile.

Alex peered up at him through her eyelashes. *Oh God, he's brandishing those forearms at me. How many push-ups can that man do?* she wondered. *He can push up off me as much as he likes.* She shook her head, trying to clear the image of him sprawled on her couch last night, not seeing the bemused expression on his face.

"No what?" he asked. "Why are you shaking your head?"

"Oh," she stammered. "Nothing. Never mind. Anyway, you are going to help. How the hell am I supposed to give you what you want if you don't ask?" She went back to scribbling, ignoring his shock. "I rewrote the scene of the car crash, so it's more like Kate's totally oblivious that Rob is not interested in nannying her uppity city ass. And I added some scenes with Rob and his bestie Sarah, mostly about her vendetta against the poachers and his futile attempts to get through to her." She tossed a sheaf of papers to him. "Here, have a look. We can start switching things around until you're happy." She looked up at him cautiously. "But not too happy. We are tiptoeing dangerously out of the formula. Too much and Joel will lose his shit and the whole thing will fall apart."

He reached into his shirt pocket and pulled his glasses out. As he did, Alex spun in her chair away from him, mentally reciting a Hail Mary. She recited it four times, driving the image of glasses on a rugged face and sexy push-ups from her mind.

"Alex? You fall asleep over there?"

She spun back around. He'd slipped his glasses off. *Thank you, Blessed Mother.*

"Well?" she said shortly.

His face lit up. "I love it. Nice job, kid. It's still cheesy as fuck, but it's got an edgy sarcasm woven in. I can live with this."

"You're happy, then? We're square?"

He settled back in his seat and seemed to ignore her question for a while, scanning the bare walls, studying the continents of paper that littered the floor.

"Tell me something, Alex." He fixed her with his gaze. "If you could do anything you wanted to right now, what would it be?"

I would shred your clothing from your body and wrap my legs around your head like a boa constrictor. Sorry, Blessed Mother.

She cleared her throat. "You mean with the script?"

He nodded. "Of course, with the script."

"Why?"

"Just answer the question, Winters."

She twirled a length of her hair around her finger, biting her lip and thinking. "Fine. What the hell. Okay, so I'd turn it on its head."

"How exactly?"

She reached into her drawer, past the picture of Poppy—and the picture of the man sitting across from her staring daggers at her—and grabbed a notebook.

"It's all here. I wrote most of it out already, but I mean, now that you're involved, I'd want to change a few things. Based on what we've been doing here."

He narrowed his eyes but remained silent.

"I do this for all of Joel's films. I give him what he wants, then I rewrite the whole thing how I'd do it."

"Outstanding, princess. So run it through for me from the top."

She stood and started pacing, running her hands through her long hair and working it up into another sloppy bun.

"Okay, so the whole rancher/widow thing is tired as fuck. But what if the widow was a catalyst to wake up a tightly knit small town? What if the rancher has secretly been in love with his best friend, the land management officer, for years, but she has an obsession with her job and this ring of poachers that threaten not only her, but him, too. She thinks she's protecting them both, but she's really just pushing him away, hurting him. And the widow is so oblivious and spoiled until she gets to know the small town and falls in love with Goober, the mechanic. I'd rewrite Meg's lines to be way more comedic. She has great comedic timing, but she keeps getting cast as an ingénue. And then a poacher stake-out goes horribly wrong, and the land management officer gets wounded and tries to run away to draw the danger away from the rancher because she thinks she can handle it on her own, but he finds her and they go out guns blazing." She finished in a rush, stopping at the end of her circuit of the room to face him.

"Guns blazing, huh?"

"Well, figuratively speaking. I mean, I don't want to kill them off. I think they deal with all the poachers and then . . . well . . . I don't know exactly how it ends."

"Come on, Alex, you have to have an ending. That's what audiences go for. You can't have all that sexual tension and then not deliver."

She shrugged. "I'll figure it out. Sometimes it's best to let these things develop on their own. You can't force it. I mean, that's probably the only good thing about working with Joel. He lets me figure it out."

"One more question. Why am I not making this movie?"

She threw herself into her chair. "Because it's weird and kinda dark and the right characters don't end up with the right partners. No one would make that movie." She shrugged and tucked the notebook back in the drawer.

He leaned back in his seat and crossed his arms again.

"What if you and I rewrote the scene with the widow and the rancher and changed it so it's the rancher and the land management officer?"

"I don't follow you. Is this for Joel's version or mine?"

He shook his head and stood up, walking across the room to lean against the wall. "Doesn't matter."

She tilted her head at him. "Go on."

He looked up at the filthy light fixture that barely broke the gloom in the room. "They are getting ready for the stakeout, lots of sexual tension, they might not live to see the light of day."

She started nodding and before he knew it, she had a pen in hand and was scribbling away.

"Right. It's night; it's in the abandoned barn. All hope is lost. She's busy polishing her rifle and he's trying to tell her how he feels but she is just so caught up in the poacher shit she doesn't hear him. But it's gotta be simple, Frank. I don't want to insist on it. I want it sparse and wrenching." She drummed her pen on her desk, biting her lip and thinking.

"I think I'm in love with you," Frank said simply.

Her head snapped around to him. "That's perfect! It's simple, it's terse. It's just like him." She nodded furiously, her pen flying across the page. "He says that to her, lays it all on the line, and it's just crickets from Sarah. Then we cut the scene, and it's a total gut punch to the audience."

She finished writing and beamed up at him. His face was lost in the dark of the room.

He pushed away from the wall and headed to the door. "A total gut punch." He turned the knob and pulled the door open, the light from the hall washing over him. Without looking back at her he said, "Sounds like you can take it from here. Thanks, Alex."

"Frank?" she called out.

He turned and stepped back into the room, trying to keep his face from looking hopeful. It wouldn't have mattered; she didn't look up.

"I'll slip a few new scenes in on Joel tomorrow. You better be ready to bring your leading man A-game, buddy."

He shut the door firmly behind him, trying hard not to slam it. *Goddamn it, Alex.*

CHAPTER NINE

...

The shoot ran late. The rest of the cast had needed time to learn the new lines, and the whole while—hours—Alex stood outside the soundstage, leaning against a wall chewing her nails, her eyes locked on the soundstage door. When it finally opened and Frank walked out, her heart stopped in her chest.

He walked over to her, his hair blacker than the night sky, his face unreadable. He stopped in front of her and leaned his arm up over her head on the wall, his other hand running a path through his ink-black hair. She let one slow breath out from between her lips; a bit more pressure, and it would have been a whistle. He winked at her, his face too close to her. She could smell him, some sort of sweat, boot polish, and Asian cologne cloud that followed him wherever he went. She licked her lips, imagining she could taste him. *I bet he tastes like Thai food and sex.*

"Can you stop 'manspreading' at me, Frank, and tell me how it went?"

"I'm not 'manspreading,' Alex. I just came over here to talk to you. I'm just standing."

"Sure you are," she said, sliding down the wall away from him. "Are you even *capable* of standing like a normal human, or do you *at all times* have to be posing for a shoot?"

He slid his hand off the wall and shoved both hands in his pants pockets.

"Better?"

No, she thought. *That is not better. Now you look all scruffy and chastened. Jesus Christ.*

"Give. How did our new scene go? The one we worked on."

His face lit up like moonrise, his black hair falling over his unshaven face, fake blood and bruising from the fight scene with the poachers creating a lunar landscape, a gradient of black and white she wished she could map with her tongue.

"I wish you would have come inside, Alex. It was amazing. The whole scene with Rob's best friend—the land management officer, Sarah—and the poachers? It was intense. I could feel the words deep in here," he grabbed his broad chest with one hand, "you know? Like I *felt* it. I knew how he felt about the land and his family. It felt real, raw, and a bit unpleasant, but real. I surprised myself, you know? I didn't know I had it in me."

I did, she thought, saying out loud, "Good."

He looked up at the sky for a minute, then took a step toward her.

"It got me thinking, though."

She slid another twelve inches down the wall. "Thinking what, Frank?"

"Well, this whole story, right? Cattle rancher and city girl? Joel's story, not ours."

"Yeah?" *Ours?*

"It doesn't wash. There's nothing real there."

"Well, this is Hollywood, Frank. We don't deal in reality."

"No, I get that. But what if we talked to him. Showed him your version. How great would this story be if he was really . . ." He stopped and stepped closer to her, looking around to make sure no one was listening.

"How great would it be if he was really falling for his officer friend? Not some starry-eyed city girl who likes the way he looks on a horse. But a real woman who understands him. Someone who might actually care about him, flaws and all, and not some romantic notion of who he is?"

Her throat went dry. She pushed away from the wall and backed away from him. "Doesn't work like that. Not in the movies, not in real life. You're asking me to commit professional suicide. It's one thing for us to joke about it with my pretend script, another to try to talk Joel into it. Won't work."

"Sure it will. No man wants to spend his life staring admiringly at some it-girl and her flights of fancy. They want someone real, an actual woman, who's clever and funny. Keeps him on his toes. We could go talk to Joel, together, and sell him on it. We wouldn't have to substantially change the rest of the story."

"That's not the way this trope works, Frank. The officer is nothing. She's a footnote. A scrappy little-sister-best-friend who will fade away while he spends his life adoring the ditzy widow and her hot ass."

"Why can't we rewrite it? Make it what we want."

"Because it's absurd," she said, tears springing to her eyes. "At the end of the day, guys like Rob want a hot trophy wife like Kate, not a prickly, girl-next-door who eats too much grease, laughs too loud, and swears too much. That trope doesn't exist."

He took a step back and jammed his hand back in his pocket. "Maybe if she just gave him a chance."

"What are we even talking about, Frank?"

"Nothing, Alex. Nothing at all." He stepped back again, his face lost in shadow. "See you tomorrow, kid."

"'Night, Frank."

Stupid. Stupid, stupid, stupid. I'm an idiot, she told herself over and over, tears streaming down her face as he walked away, in the dark. *I think Frank Brennan just asked me out, and I'm too terrified to take him up on it.*

CHAPTER TEN

. . .

Frank walked purposefully across the lot, determined to get in his Jeep and drive until he'd shaken off whatever had possessed him to emote like that.

Like a goddamn schoolboy. Every time. And every time she shoots me down. What am I even doing? She's not interested. At all. She thinks I'm old, dumb, and useless. Goddamn this film. Maybe she's right. I am too old for this shit.

"Hey, Frank, glad I caught you." Joel came jogging over to him at the gate.

"Yeah, Joely, I'm just heading out. Can it wait?" he asked guardedly.

"Ten minutes, tops. Meg is looking for you; she wants to run through some lines for tomorrow. She's having kittens about some bullshit. Can you please go talk to her? Ten minutes, I'm sure you'll have her sorted by then."

He turned back and stared across the darkened lot, calculating the chances of running into Alex on his way to Meg's trailer. She'd probably left for the day. Or she was already ensconced in her basement lair. Unless she was still leaning against that wall, those big sad eyes clawing his chest to pulp. He groaned.

"Fine. I'll give Precious a few minutes, and then I'm out."

Joel clapped him on the back. "Frank, you're a lifesaver. You know how these young actresses are. Fragile, needy. You're the perfect guy to handle her."

"I thought that was your job."

"Hey! I'm doing you a favor."

"How so?"

"Listen, a little birdie told me you want in Daddy Dearest's next big thing. Go cozy up to her, make sure your name is on her lips when Daddy asks who helped her through this. Take more than ten minutes if you need to, you know what I mean?"

Frank stepped into Joel and pointed one finger at his face.

"You're a sleaze, Joel."

"Aren't we all?"

Without responding, Frank strode off in the direction of Meg's trailer. *Ten minutes with her majesty and then I gotta clear my head of this Alex shit.* The walk to Meg's trailer took him past the wall Alex had been leaning on. She was gone. *Of course she's gone, stupid, you're not even a blip on her radar.* He paused there for a moment and ran the scene over and over again in his mind, trying to find the mark where it all went wrong, tried to rewrite his lines twenty different ways so the scene ended differently. But it was useless. He wasn't a writer. He was an actor, a washed-up action hero without a script or a plot, and he had no idea how this movie ended.

———

I need to go home and drink myself unconscious, Alex thought as she cut across the lot. *And put Frank Brennan and his goddamn everything out of my head.* She stopped her anger-fueled march to kick the back of a trailer, wincing and grabbing her foot when it connected with the hitch.

"Son of a bitch!" she hissed, hopping on one foot.

"Now, I wonder what would make a nice girl like you kick my poor innocent trailer, Alex Winters."

Alex's head jerked up at the face smiling at her from behind a lit cigarette in the dark lot. "Mary Li, you scared me."

"You scared me, with your muttering and kicking." She tossed her a pack of smokes. "Here. Tell Mary Li all your problems. The doctor is in."

Alex caught the pack easily, tossed it from one hand to the other, then underhanded it back to Mary Li. "Got anything stronger?"

"Oh, honey. It's a man. I knew it. I haven't seen you this rattled since we shot *The Russian Samovar.*"

"It is not a man. It's a . . . a . . ." She let out a frustrated scream and kicked the hitch again.

"If Frank Brennan isn't a man, honey, no one is. Come on inside. I've got a bottle of whiskey just for this sort of thing. We'll get you feeling better in no time."

Alex followed her inside the hair and makeup trailer, trying hard not to stomp her feet like a toddler. She did feel immediately better once the door shut behind her; the womblike cocoon of Mary Li's domain felt cozy and safe, just like her friend.

Alex threw herself into a makeup chair, tossing a wig to one side. "Is it that obvious?"

Mary Li cast her a sympathetic glance and poured an extra ounce of whiskey into the tumbler. "Only to me, sweets. I know you pretty well. I think everyone else, including Frank, thinks you hate him. Like, on an elemental level." She handed her the cup. "Drink up, baby girl. I have never seen someone so determined to be unhappy as you are."

"I was perfectly happy. Writing shitty scripts for Joel, hanging out with you and Poppy; my life wasn't so bad. And then Mr. Dreamy Eyes Commando breezes in here, strong-arms me into writing for him. Starts dragging really great stories and dialogue out of me, even though it's not even remotely what we do here . . ."

"And being handsome and gruff and chasing you like an angry puppy wherever you go?"

"Yes, especially that."

"He does have dreamy eyes, that one. All dark and piercing."

"I thought you were helping. This is not helping." Alex slumped in the chair and held the now-drained glass against her forehead. She rubbed her other hand on the evil-eye tattoo behind her ear.

Mary Li noticed the gesture. "Listen," she said, "I don't know what that tit Rob Bourne did to you when we filmed that first movie, but that little pissant does not deserve this much space rent-free in that pretty little head of yours." She topped off Alex's glass and tucked her friend's hair behind her ear to reveal the tattoo. "Or on your skin."

"I'll tell you what he did. He flirted with me, he led me on, and I lapped it up like an asshole. Then he humiliated me in front of the cast and crew. And I got this tattoo to ward off handsome leading men and their serpent tongues from tricking me again into being an idiot."

"And you think Frank is like that."

"Well, no. He's an opinionated ass, but he's not cruel. He's not unkind. He's sort of . . ."

"A gentleman? Honey, he's rough around the edges, but that man has a code. And hurting someone like you would break it."

"I think he tried to tell me that tonight."

"Well, what are you going to do about it?"

Alex shrugged. "Nothing?"

With a snort of disgust, Mary Li plucked the glass from her hand.

"You are going to go find him, ask him to take you somewhere far away from this fairyland, and see if there's something there for the two of you. Even if it's just coffee." She pulled Alex from the chair and pushed her in the direction of the door. "You're going to put your big girl panties on and stop hiding in that basement of yours with your notepads and your donuts and your big sad eyes. I think a little Frank would do you some good."

"What if it doesn't work out?"

"Then you can come back and kick my trailer some more. Now, scoot."

CHAPTER ELEVEN

• • •

"Frank, thank *God* you're here!" Meg wailed. "I knew you wouldn't abandon me in my time of need."

Frank jammed his hands in his pockets and let out an exasperated breath. *God, she literally can't turn it off. She really thinks she is a big-city widow. She better not fucking think I'm her rancher.*

"What's the problem, Meg?"

Meg sauntered down the stairs of her trailer, still in her clothes—Boho skirt, cowboy hat, quirky sweater, and glasses, but noticeably minus the cast on her leg— from the day's shoot, lines in hand.

"I'm really nervous about tomorrow."

Frank's brow creased in confusion. "Tomorrow?"

"It's just, I've never kissed a much older man, not on screen anyway. I mean, unless you count my father, and I don't."

Frank stared up into the night sky, mentally reciting a catechism of hate for his agent, as Meg continued rambling incoherently.

"Not that I made out with my *dad*, that's ridiculous. Although, this is all acting, it's all about the *craft*, right? I mean, it's not *sexual*, so I *could* make out with my dad if the *work* called for it. And it is all about the work, isn't it, Frank?"

"I'm not following you, Meg. Get to the point."

"I want to run through the kiss scene for tomorrow's shoot. You know, Rob and Kate's first kiss? I don't want to do it cold for the first time in front of the crew and get it wrong.

"You've gotta be kidding me. You are an actor, right? You've done love scenes before, haven't you?"

"I mean, sort of. I've done like teenage first kisses, stuff like that. But this is a man and a woman's first kiss, and I'm certain I won't get it right. And you're so experienced and confident with these things, Frank."

"You have kissed a grown man before, haven't, you Meg?" he said shortly. "It's exactly the same."

"Frank, please. Just one or two run-throughs, and we'll be able to get it on the first take tomorrow, and you won't have to stand around making out with me all day. Deal?"

Shit. When you put it like that, Precious. He tried not to grimace as he barked, "Fine. One run-through and I'm leaving."

She hurried across the front of the trailer, pages fluttering. "Oh, thank you, Frank! You won't regret this. Okay, so scene opens, Kate's just finished painting the sunrise, and she's leaning back against the log cabin, just soaking in the dawn."

Kill me, Frank thought. *God strike me dead.*

Meg arranged herself in what she considered to be an alluring posture.

"Okay, and then you get off your horse and say, 'I wish I could write a poem about the way the sun hits your hair. But I'm just a simple cattle rancher. I'm better with my hands'."

Alex, I am going to kill you. I thought we took that line out.

"Didn't we take that line out?"

"Not according to my dailies. Come on, Frank."

Frank slid his hands from his pockets and rubbed them together, rolling his shoulders, trying to get into character.

He looked at Meg. *Ugh.*

"Give me a minute, would you Meg?"

"Take all the time you need."

Frank closed his eyes. He'd had a sex scene in *AAF III* with a skeletal freedom fighter with skin as leathery as a turtle that had repulsed him even more than Meg did. So he did now what he did then. He scanned his mental inventory of hot babes, looking for one that he could pretend he was kissing. But instead of Rita Hayworth or Jane Russell, Alex popped into his mind. His blood began to race; he could feel beads of sweat break out on his upper lip. Alex, leaning against the building. Pushing him away. Her hair falling over one shoulder. Her breasts full above that narrow waist, old concert t-shirt riding up so he could see the pale skin underneath, her high, tight ass in those sloppy cargo pants. Jesus, those lips of hers, the way she was always biting them. He wanted to bite them; he wanted to ruin those lips. He tried to find another face in his personal scrapbook, but they all seemed to have vanished under the burning gaze of Alex's liquid brown eyes.

His eyes flashed open, the intensity of his imaginings superimposing, for a brief second, Alex over Meg's simpering form. That fraction of a second was all it took. He rushed at her, grasping her by her upper arms, his lips on hers before the startled squeak could escape, his momentum slamming them both into the side of the trailer, the aluminum frame groaning and creaking. He forced his tongue into Meg's gaping mouth, his hands slid to her back, gripping her shirt and holding her tight against him. He pulled her hair back and bent her into his demanding arms, then bit her lower lip. He scraped his unshaven jaw down her cheek to her neck, pulling her shirt from her shoulder, and that was when the illusion shattered.

"Jesus Christ, Frank!" The world went white for a second, a ringing in his ears as Meg smacked him upside his head, sending him stumbling back. "What the fuck was that?"

He looked up at her, bewildered. Her face was red and blotched from where he'd savaged her; her shirt was half-torn. But instead of looking terrified, she was annoyed.

"Frank, it's supposed to be a closed mouth, tender, sweet kiss—look, it says so in the script—and then he makes her breakfast and drives her to PT in town for her foot. That was not tender. That was rapey. God, is that how you old guys kiss?"

Embarrassed, Frank put both hands up and backed away. "Jesus, I'm sorry, Meg. I don't know what came over me. That was my fault. Listen, I better go. I'm not feeling like myself."

"I should say not. Maybe you're coming down with something. I hope it's not strep. I had strep once and something in my antibiotics made me actually gain weight. I gained like three pounds. Ugh, I hate antibiotics. You should see my doctor; he does amazing things with *kombucha*. Do you want me to get his number for you?"

"Sounds great, Meg. Tomorrow. Give me Dr. Kombucha's name tomorrow, okay? I'm gonna go home, get some shut eye."

He hurried to the parking lot, face red and ashamed. *Jesus fuck, what is this woman doing to me? First she's got me rescuing cats, now I'm molesting my cast mates. It's no good,* he told himself. *No good at all.*

But as he crossed the dark lot, all he could think of was how good, how right it would have been, could have been, if it had been Alex.

CHAPTER TWELVE

. . .

Alex jogged through the lot, scanning between trailers, looking for Frank. *I can do this. I don't know what I'm going to say, but I'll know when I see him. Either that, or I'll stare at him until I die of smolder. Either way, I'm going for it.* She did a full lap of their area of the lot. Nothing. She slowed her jog to a walk and headed back to the main sound stage, where Frank's trailer was.

"Hey, what are you doing out of your pit?" Joel's voice called to her from the studio door. The floodlight shone down on his giant puffy hair, making him look like an adolescent clown.

"Oh, nothing. Hey, I was looking for Frank." She paused, trying to think of something plausible. "You know how he's been on my ass about his lines."

"I know. What a dick. Tip of the hat to you for how you've been handling him."

"He's not a dick. He's just . . ." she trailed off, wishing she could bite the words back.

Joel narrowed his shrewd eyes at her. "Going soft on me, Winters?"

She shook her head. "Not a chance. Anyway, I had something he'd asked for. Seen him around?"

"Yeah, I saw him about a minute ago, over by Meg's trailer."

He was still here. She turned and started to sprint away, stumbling and falling flat on her face when she heard Joel's next words.

"Yeah, he was banging Meg up against her trailer. He's into some rough shit for an old man." In true Joel form, he neither acknowledged nor offered to assist her up after her fall.

She scrambled to her feet. *I have to get out of here before I start crying. I cannot let Joel see me cry.* She took a deep breath and turned back to Joel, forcing a wry smile and a snide laugh that hurt so badly she wished she could die.

"Took him long enough," she growled. "I figured those two would be going at it on day one."

"Want me to give him those papers?"

She looked at him bewildered. "What papers?"

Joel cocked his head at her. "The papers you were taking him."

Shit.

"Oh, forget it. It can wait. At least until he's done banging Meg. See you tomorrow, Joel." She turned and walked away slowly. *I can cry as much as I want when I get home. Not a moment sooner. Not here.*

"'Night, Alex. Sweet dreams."

———

Alex stumbled through the parking lot, sobbing and choking. *Okay, I can cry in the parking lot. Parking lot is safe; there's no one here anyway.* She ran down two wrong aisles before she remembered where she'd parked her Prius that morning. Finally catching sight of a flash of purple, she broke into a sprint toward it, tears blinding her. She ran twenty feet before she slammed into something large and wall-like, with arms that grabbed her to break her fall.

"Hey, hey, hey, Alex?" Frank's voice broke through her pounding ears. "What happened? Who's chasing you? What's wrong, honey?"

She wrenched his hands off her arms and pushed him away from her, hard. He stumbled back into a grimy old Volvo.

"What the hell, Alex? What was that for?"

"You stay the fuck away from me, Frank."

"What did I do?" He reached out for her again, recoiling at the look on her face.

"I am done with your needy bullshit, Frank. You want to be a dramatic actor? You want to ride me into the ground to do it? You think you can snap your fingers and old Alex comes running. Well here's a news flash, asshole. You're not a dramatic actor. You're a hack. A joke. You're just a washed-up has-been who is exactly like every other dickhole leading man I have ever met. You stay away from me. You don't like your lines, you talk to Joel." She stood there, shaking, horrified at the things she said to him but too heartbroken to stop herself. *I thought you were different. I thought you really liked me.*

He stood up from where he'd slammed into the Volvo, straightening his shoulders and shoved his hands deep in his pockets. His face was dark, sunken into something worse than angry. He leaned forward and spat his response to her through gritted teeth.

"You're the worst writer I've ever met. You couldn't write your way out of a garbage bag. You think you're sarcastic and clever, but you're really just a bitch."

With that, he turned and walked away, every ounce of his concentration channeled into keeping his stride casual and uninterested.

You think I can't act, Alex? Well, you just saw the performance of my life.

CHAPTER THIRTEEN

...

The mood on the set went from slightly off to flat-out uncomfortable. Frank and Alex pointedly ignored each other, refusing to speak directly to one another, even going so far as to send notes via runners while sitting five feet away.

Edits flew back and forth between them; even Joel backed slowly away from the verbal game of mumblety-peg they were playing. The tone of the scenes, under the weight of her edits and his acting, shifted from light-hearted and quirky to dark and intense. No one, from the director to the gaffes, knew quite what to do with the depths Frank was plumbing with his delivery, and they for damn sure didn't know how to mark the raw undertones of the new pages that Alex tersely delivered day after day.

Three weeks went by, the days grew longer, the takes grew exponentially as the cast and crew tried to keep up with Frank and Alex's new pace, and Joel's lips disappeared altogether. One morning, Frank found a text message from Joel, sent at three in the morning. Not a good sign.

Frank, no scenes today. Meet me at my office at 9. Sharp.

When he arrived, late, unshaven and agitated, he found Alex waiting on the couch outside Joel's office. Her hands were clenched contritely in her lap. She kept folding them and unfolding them in a hypnotic rhythm. He took a seat next to her and leaned over, placing one hand on her hands.

"Stop that," he said, his voice low and firm.

She turned to glare at him. "You don't have anything to be worried about. You can't get fired. They fire screenwriters all the time."

"He's not going to fire you. He's just gonna yell at you. Buck up, cubbie."

"When I want advice from you, I'll . . . I'll . . ."

"You'll what, princess?"

"I'll blow my goddamn brains out," she finished.

He stared at her, face blank as he tried in vain to be offended. His sudden bark of laughter made her jump.

"You take that attitude in there and Joel will not only keep you on set, he'll kiss your ass."

She whirled away from him but he thought he caught the edge of a self-satisfied smile color her face.

The minutes ticked by as Joel kept them waiting. Fifteen minutes. Twenty.

"Kinda feel like we're waiting outside the principal's office in fifth grade," he elbowed Alex's side, "not that you'd know anything about that."

She didn't reply for a long moment and then whispered, "In sixth grade, Mary-Margaret O'Brien and I snuck up onto the roof of the convent house next to our school to smoke. The door got jammed, we were stuck up there for hours, and they had to call the firemen to get us down with a ladder."

"Illicit rooftop smoking? You?" he asked, delighted.

She nodded, still staring straight ahead. "Finished the whole pack." She turned then, eyes dancing.

"Why, Alexandra Winters, you naughty thing. What was your penance?"

"I think I'm living it now," she replied wryly. "What about you?"

"I, too, attended a parish school. Our Lady of the Blessed Sacrament. Sister Rose Terese had it in for me from day one. So I started shortening things."

"What do you mean, shortening things? What things?"

"The flag. Took a half-inch off a week. She didn't notice till Epiphany. By then the stars and stripes was a postage stamp. Her chair legs. Took a quarter inch off every other week, that's tricky business. By Easter she was about six inches off the ground." He flashed her a crooked grin.

"That's a hell of a long con for a junior high boy, Frank. I'm impressed."

He shrugged, brushing his hand across his mouth in case a smile tried to escape. "Try third grade."

Alex sputtered a dry surprised laugh.

The doorknob to Joel's office turned.

"Here we go," he whispered out of the side of his mouth.

They both looked down at her lap, as if realizing at the same second that his hand was still covering hers. He slid his hand across her leg and hoped Joel didn't notice they were holding hands.

"Alex. Frank. Step inside," Joel said, using what he must have thought was his grown-up voice.

He shut the door firmly behind them and took his seat at his desk. He waited for his two guests to take a seat in front of him.

"Joel, I—" Alex started, her voice cutting off as Frank kicked her.

"Shut up, Alex. Don't start apologizing right out of the gate."

Alex flushed and kicked him back.

"Well, I'd like to thank you two for so succinctly illuminating the reason I brought you in today. The reason I canceled a whole day of shooting." Joel paused and steepled his fingertips. "So what you two are going to do today is watch all the dailies. Start to finish. Every single godforsaken inch of film we have shot on this cursed project. And when you are done, we are going to talk. Do you want to know why we are doing this?"

Alex shook her head.

"Yeah, Joely. I do want to know why you're wasting my time," Frank said.

Through gritted teeth, Joel replied, "Because tomorrow, I have to go show something, anything, to the producers, who have lost all faith in this project. The people who pay the bills and your salaries. And I have no idea at this point what the hell to tell them." He reached over and hit play on the wall monitor and stalked angrily out of the room, hitting the lights as he did, and slamming the door.

Over the next two hours, Frank and Alex sat through the rough cuts of a movie that started off trite and sweet, a movie that slowly degenerated into something dark and disturbing, something decidedly hostile and unromantic. A movie that started out following the prescribed formula, handsome cattle rancher falling for strong independent woman, and seemed to career sideways into some kind of complicated relationship between the cattle rancher and the scrappy land management officer. The rancher and the officer seemed to be trapped in an intricate mating ritual involving arguing and prodding each other, passion clear in every exchange, all the while the intended romantic interest, the woman, seemed with each passing scene more insipid and scatterbrained. The edits that Frank had asked for and Alex had delivered fatally skewed the tired trope into something unpredictable and exciting. In short, studio suicide.

When it was over, Frank stood and clicked off the monitor. Joel entered the room a second later, as if he'd been listening with his ear to the door. Alex stretched and yawned; she looked drawn and pale. Frank wondered if he looked the same. He certainly felt it. The whole viewing was upsetting, on a variety of fronts.

"So I think you see my problem. Your feud has taken a simple romantic comedy and twisted it into something, something . . . I don't even think there's a genre for this. This is not a love story anyone in their right minds would pay to see, let alone pay to make."

"Joel," Frank started, "listen, I think that . . ." He stopped abruptly as Alex kicked him again.

"Don't apologize, Frank. It may not be the material they wanted, but it's a vastly better story than what they deserve." She leaned forward, lips drawn up in a sneer. "I have written trope after trite dumbshit trope for you on the last four movies you've made, Joel. All with actors half the caliber of the man sitting next to me. You don't like the lines? Too bad. I can't write any less for him. I can't diminish his performance with stale, predictable shit." She sat back in the chair, ears red and face forward.

Frank felt nailed to his seat by her unexpected words, his hands clenched on the chair arms.

"Good for you, Frank," Joel spat. "You've found someone to take the fall for your indulgent acting spree." He stormed back to the door. "They're going to make me fire you, Alex. Even if they don't, I don't see how we can finish this. But if by some miracle we can, if they don't pull the plug on the whole thing, you two better figure out a way to work with each other. I'm done nannying you." With that, he slammed the door.

Alex sat frozen, her entire face pink with embarrassment.

Frank scratched his jaw, uncertain how to break the unbearable tension that had fallen over their side of the room with her outburst. "Looks like Joel finally grew a pair," he said softly.

That did it. Her flush faded, and taking a deep breath, she turned to fix him with those mirthful brown eyes. "And am I mistaken, or did Mr. Junior Director just kick himself out of his own office?"

Frank laughed. "He did at that."

Alex stood abruptly and crossed the room to the large bank of windows. "He's right, you know. We have made a mess of this."

Frank inclined his head. "Did we? I think we're improving it."

"Don't sweet talk me, Brennan." She cleared her throat. "Okay, let's have it out."

"Have what out?"

She gestured between them. "This. This whatever it is."

"Okay, Alex . . . where do you propose we start?"

"Why don't you tell me what your problem is with me, and I'll tell you what my issues are with you. Then maybe we can stop letting it color the movie. And we leave it all here in this room and walk out and hope to God we get another chance tomorrow. Finish this piece of shit and then never cross paths again."

He flinched at the "never".

"Fine," he said shortly. "Ladies first." He leaned back in his chair and crossed his arms over his chest.

"I meant what I said the other day."

His eyes narrowed at her.

"I mean, I said it in the worst possible way, but—"

Frank cut her off. "Well, you are a wordsmith, *Alex*. I think you said exactly what you meant to say. I believe you described me and my career as a 'joke'."

She bit her lower lip and shook her head. "New rule. No interrupting."

He let his breath out of his nostrils, flaring them as he did, and nodded once.

"I was angry with you and hurt—why doesn't matter anymore—but I chose the worst possible way to tell you how much I admire you. I really do, Frank. I said those things because I care. And because I think you have the talent to be a great dramatic actor. It would be so easy for you to just ride that action hero shit until you are too old to throw a grenade, but not you. You're brave enough to try something new. Something really hard. That has to be terrifying at your age."

"I'm not that old, Alex," he said, bristling. "Why do you insist on thinking I'm too old for—" He shook his head. "Never mind."

"I said no interrupting." She cleared her throat and continued. "But what I *should* have said is that you can't dream half a dream. It's all or nothing. You want to be a dramatic actor. Fine. I think you have more than enough ability to do it. But you can't wade in. You have to dive in. You don't get there by working with Joel. You have to take shitty jobs that don't pay, you have to chase good writers and coaches, you have to burn every other thing down to the ground and chase only this one thing. You can do it, Frank. And I think you are selling yourself short. I know you are. Because you're scared of looking stupid."

He stared at her in silence, the moment stretching out uncomfortably. "You done?"

She nodded.

"Then have a seat. My turn."

She sat down, but instead of leaning against the windows like she had, he placed one hand on either side of her, gripping the chair, and leaned in, bringing his face level with hers. He stared at her until she stopped searching the room for somewhere else to look and met his gaze steadily. He could see her heart pulsing in her neck.

"Are you going to kiss me, Frank, or are you gonna let me have it?"

He bit back the words he wanted to say and said instead, "You're like the pot calling the kettle black, babe. You think I'm a sellout? What about you, Alex? You're screenwriting for the lowest common denominator, writing trite crap, when I know, *I know* you can do better. And it's not just the new pages, Alex. You can *write.* You have a goddamn gift. And you keep it locked up in a box while you barely scrimp by selling cheap words and selling yourself short. Who's the chicken shit now?" He stood and let out a deep breath he'd been bottling up, adding, "And by the way, you apologize too much. You need to cut that shit out."

She visibly paled, her lips forming words that never emerged. Finally, she said, "What are you talking about?" She sounded too calm.

He backed away from her and sat on Joel's desk. *Way too calm.* "All right, I read two of your books. I found them in the chest, the night we rescued your cat." His lips rose in a wry smile at the memory.

"You read my books," she repeated dully in that same too-calm voice.

"I still have one in my house; I'll get it back to you. Alex, they are brilliant. Stunningly brilliant. They could be bestsellers. Hell, they could be blockbuster movies. What are you sitting on them for? Why are you writing garbage crap for Joel when you are capable of so much more?"

"You *stole* my books," she repeated again. She rose out of her chair and advanced on him, fists clenched at her side. "You. Stole. My books."

Frank slid across the desk and dropped to the other side.

"Whoa, whoa, Alex. Calm down. I *borrowed* them. Right after I rescued your cat. Let's talk about this."

She began circling the desk as he backed away, trying to keep the desk between them.

"What, you've been laughing at me all this time?" She picked a stapler up off the desk. "Maybe sharing it around with the crew?" She threw the stapler at him.

He threw up a forearm to deflect it but it connected with painful accuracy on his elbow. "Goddamn it, Alex, no. Not laughing. Put the phone down. Alex, do not throw that phone at me."

She threw the phone at him. It tangled around his neck and chest like a bolo, then she lunged across the desk, arms swinging. He grabbed her easily and pinned her arms to her sides and clutched her to him, the tangled phone wrapped against his chest and neck.

"Alex," he said into her ear. "They're good. Your books."

She stopped struggling. He drew back a few inches and looked at her.

"Really good. No lie." He felt her arms go limp, so he let her go and stepped back. "Why won't you try to sell them, Alex?"

She sighed and wiped her eyes. She let out a long, shuddering breath and said, "Probably for the same reason you won't do live theater. I'm afraid of being laughed at."

"Aren't we a pair?" He raised his hand to her tentatively and chucked her on the chin.

She reached over and unwound the phone from around his neck and let it fall to the floor. "Who would have thought it, huh?"

"We good?"

"Yeah. We're good, Brennan."

Frank glanced down at his watch. "Wanna grab a pizza, Winters?"

She shuddered. "No. Never pizza. Anyway, it's not Paleo, Slim Goodbody."

"I'll make an exception. Don't you like pizza?"

"Let's grab some cheeseburgers and I'll tell you all about it."

Frank turned and crooked his arm out. "Lead the way, babe."

"Don't call me babe, Frank."

"*Alexandra.*"

"*Francis.*"

"Goddamn it, Alex."

She smiled and slipped her arm through his. "That's better. We sound like us again."

CHAPTER FOURTEEN

• • •

Alex watched in mute horror as Frank dissected his cheeseburger until it was nothing more than two meat patties and a smear of mustard, a pile of buns, cheese, and condiments discarded on one side of his plate.

"Mustard isn't Paleo, Frank."

"Sure it is. Mustard seeds are. The rest of it is sort of Paleo. It's like, water and vinegar and stuff."

"Why, Frank Brennan. Are you fudging your action hero diet? For shame. What if the caveman police find out? Will they take away your rugged good looks?"

He looked over at her, surprised. She looked down and busied herself with her napkin. Frank reached over and grabbed a French fry off her plate.

"Hey!"

He jammed the fry in his mouth. "God. I haven't had a French fry in nine years."

He reached back for more.

She smacked his hand. "Get your own."

"I just want a few of yours."

"Jesus, Frank, you sound like a woman. You specifically said you didn't want fries, now you're going to eat all of mine."

He darted a hand in and grabbed another handful faster than she could block him.

"Wow. You've got catlike reflexes, Brennan. I thought that was all CGI."

He shrugged and jammed the rest of the fries in his mouth. "Okay, out with it. Tell me the pizza story."

"It's the most embarrassing story ever."

"So what? We're best friends now, right?"

"Are we?"

"Something like that. Quit stalling."

"Well, I came to Hollywood when I was twenty-five, right?"

"Okay . . ."

"But it's the *how* part that's embarrassing. Joel knows and Mary Li. But no one else."

"I'm flattered. Spill."

"Well, I finished school, couldn't get a job, and I'm working in Rochester, Michigan, as a barista. Shut up."

"I didn't say a word."

"That was probably the year you got your AARP card."

"Smart ass. Continue."

"Anyway, this guy that I went to high school with, the guy who sold that first movie to Joel, he knew I liked to write. I mean, everyone did. He bumped into me at work and asked me if I would ghostwrite this idea he had for a rom-com. At first I said no because he's a douche, but the more I thought about it . . ." She trailed off.

"This is the embarrassing part, right?"

"Well, he offered me five hundred dollars, and I was flat broke. And he's not that bright. And I thought, I'll write it and interject a bit of my sarcasm here and there and make his predictable tropetastic rom-com a snarky sub-trope and pay him back for mildly sexually assaulting me for a slice of pizza. Take his money and run. But next thing you know, he actually sells that piece of shit to a publisher. Joel options it and hires me to do the screenplay because he liked my style. And now I'm here. So it's poetic justice because he's still back in Detroit. I think he made like twenty grand off it, probably spent it all on Fireball at the party store."

"Whoa. Back up, Winters."

"What?" she said, taking a gulp of her water.

"You know what," he said, snatching another fry.

She avoided his gaze and took a big bite of her cheeseburger.

"Let's jump back to 'mild sexual assault and pizza.' Give me an address, Alex. I've got my machete in the Jeep."

"I bet you do." She put a hand on his arm and looked up at him. "That's sweet. I might take you up on that."

He put his hand over hers and gave it a squeeze. "I thought I was too old to play a knight in shining armor."

"*Touché.*" She pulled her hand away. He leaned back and stretched in his chair, his t-shirt riding up to reveal his ridiculously flat stomach and just the edge of his boxers. *Oh my God*, Alex thought. *Why? Why me?*

"Okay, Alex. So your rom-com con went sideways on you. How is pizza involved?"

"Okay, sophomore year in high school. My friend Jen calls me up and asks if I want to go to Chuck E. Cheese with her and her boyfriend Dylan."

"Chuck E. Cheese?" he said wryly.

"Shut up, Frank. Anyway, I said yes because I wanted to get out of the house and play some Skee-ball. But when they come to pick me up, they bring Dylan's douchebag friend, Mark, with them."

"Mark is the pizza molester?"

"I'm getting to that. So we go to Chuck E. Cheese, I avoid Mark at all costs, play a few wicked games of Skee-ball, everything is going fine. But then they all decide to order a pizza. I say forget it because I only brought enough money for Skee-ball and I didn't have enough to pay my share."

"This is already the saddest story I have ever heard. Have you written this screenplay yet? You could call it *The Sad Skee-Ball Diaries*. It's got a Razzy written all over it."

She threw a French fry at him. He caught it and wrapped the rest of his mustard-crusted patty around it, then shoved it in his mouth, grinning at her.

"I take it back; your caveman diet looks amazing." She slipped her patty out of the bun and dropped a handful of French fries on it, rolled it up like a burrito, and took a bite.

"You've been in LA for nine years and you're still eating like that?" he asked, delighted.

"I guess this place never stuck." She put her hastily made burrito down. "Anyway, back to the pizza. They're all eating pizza and I'm just hanging out and Mark slides a piece of pizza over to me and says, 'Here have a slice.' So I ate it."

"That's it? That's the pizza story?" he asked, one eyebrow raised.

"If you'll let me finish, Frank, I ate it and then on the car ride home he pinned me against the car door, slid his hand up my thigh, and tried to grab my crotch, all the while whispering, 'Come on, I bought you pizza.' He may have gotten a handful of tit; I was too busy barfing in my mouth."

Frank stood up, pushing his chair back so hard it fell over. "We can be in Detroit in four hours by plane. Or two days driving if you want me to bring the machete. I'll hold him down for you. It'll be just like *Armed Assault Force II: Bangkok Vengeance*."

She flashed him a mischievous smile. "Sit down. We're not machete-ing anyone."

"Pity," he said, righting his chair and sitting back down, closer now.

"I smacked the shit out of him right then and there. And then ten years later, when he asked me to ghostwrite his lame rom-com, I did. As a joke. A sick, twisted joke that likely only I would find funny."

"That sounds like you. Amazing," Frank said, shaking his head.

"I think you mean 'embarrassing'." She shrugged. "That's why I stick with Joel. I fell into this. I have no real talent, and I mean, it's all blind luck in this town. I'm hiding out, hoping no one notices I'm a fraud."

"Fraud? You're not a fraud, Alex. You're like a cat; you'll always land on your feet. I don't believe in accidents. You made your own way here because you're smart and clever, maybe not the traditional way, but you did it all on your own. Don't give Pizza Molester any credit. You done mangling that cheeseburger?"

She nodded, and he stood, throwing a handful of bills on the table. He held a hand out to her, and she took it as she stood.

"Thanks for lunch, Frank."

"You're welcome, kid. I won't even molest you for it." He winked at her and she burst out laughing. Encouraged by her gales of laughter, he pulled her to him in a bear hug, his chest tight and full when she hugged him back, her sparkling laughter in his ear. "If getting molested for pizza by a douche from Detroit got you all the way to Hollywood, where on earth would getting sexually assaulted by the former special ops team leader of *Armed Assault Force I* through *V* get you?" he said, laughing.

She pulled away from him slowly, raising her eyes to his, the laughter between them draining away. He cleared his throat and arranged his face back into something offhand and nonchalant. She straightened his shirt where she'd rumpled it and took another step back.

"Well, anyway. That's the pizza story. We better go."

She turned and led the way out and he followed, trying to figure out how to get that moment back.

CHAPTER FIFTEEN

. . .

"Come on, Winters. Let's go sweat those cheeseburgers off." He shifted the Rubicon into park and flung his door open.

She glared at him.

He laughed and patted her thigh. "You'll be fine. You may even like it. Give it a chance."

"Are you forcing me to exercise, Frank?"

"Consider it payback for making me rescue your cat in the middle of the night."

She looked down at her cargo pants and boots. "I'm not actually dressed for this."

"That's okay, kid. You won't need clothes."

He watched as her face went white, then red. She smacked his hand away from her and scowled at him.

"What the hell is that supposed to mean?" she hissed.

He cast a sidelong glance at her and fought the urge to reply, *Whatever you want it to mean.* Instead, he said,

"Let's just say I think it's an activity you and I could do well together."

She gulped.

"You chicken, Winters?"

She stared out of his Jeep at the shuttered boxing club. "But it's closed."

He pulled his keys from the ignition and jumped out of the Jeep.

"I've got a key. I know the owner."

"Is that too tight?" Frank said, whispering in her ear.

"Mmnoof urfgh ommmgh," Alex said, her mouth too full to reply intelligibly.

Frank rolled his eyes and plucked the mouth guard from her mouth, dropping it in the bucket.

"I told you, you don't need that, Winters. I'm not going to hit you in the head."

"Says you."

"I am a man of my word, Alex. Don't you know that about me by now?" He jerked the ties on the boxing glove and released her hand.

"How's that feel?"

She raised one glove-clad hand and hit him in the chest with it.

"Like the world's heaviest marshmallow."

"Wimp. Give me your other hand, princess."

She raised her other hand obediently and glanced down at her clothes. She was wearing one of his old t-shirts and shorts, a weight belt tied tight around her waist to hold them up in lieu of a proper belt. She was barefoot because none of the shoes at the gym were small enough.

"There," he said, chucking her under the chin. "Now you're going to learn how to box. I bet you take to it like a duck to water."

"What if someone comes in?"

"Nobody is coming in today. My gym. My rules. We're closed today."

"You own this place?"

He shrugged. "Maybe."

"Don't I need a helmet or something?"

He groaned. "Shadowboxing, Alex. Nobody is getting hurt. And you already look ridiculous enough in that getup."

"It's all I could find in the locker room," she said.

"That's okay." He turned and walked away from her to the other side of the ring, calling back over his shoulder, "Not exactly gonna ring anybody's bell like that, but you look kinda cute."

That's it, she thought. *I am done.* Alex sank into the stool in her corner of the boxing ring, her eyes filling with tears. He didn't notice her defeated collapse, and for a second, she entertained the notion that he would keep walking and never come back and leave her to drown in this horrid pain she was choking on. But he didn't. He turned around and saw her slumped there, heartbreak raw on her face.

"Alex?"

"I can't do this, Frank."

"Sure you can. It's just punching air. You got this."

"Not this. *This*. I can't do this whole thing. The whole montage of cute. You and me hanging out. You being so fucking wonderful. Laughing, fighting, flirting. And then humiliating me, hurting me, leaving me behind while you ride off into the sunset. I've seen this movie. I know how it ends."

"What are you talking about?"

"This! Me! I can't fake it anymore, Frank, I can't pretend with you. I can't breathe when you're around. Your fucking scruffy face, that goddamn lock of hair that keeps falling in your eyes—what the fuck is that, anyway? Does your barber have a state license in *sadism*? The way you walk; the way you're always leaning in on me. That stupid, fucking cocky grin, and I cannot handle your eyes, just *stop* it with them already. And you're so wonderful even when you're being horrible, especially when you're being horrible. You were right, I *am* a mess. I am so in lust with you, my legs are fucking rubbery with it. I hate myself. I loathe myself. I don't think I could get up from this stool if the whole building was on fire. So just do it already. Let me down easy, tug on my hair and tell me I'm a cute girl but I'm not your type, and let me be in peace already, Frank. You're too good of a man to torment me like this. You're too good of a man to *hurt* me like this."

She let out a shuddering breath. Not once during her whole speech did she look up, focusing instead on his bare feet, feet that blurred now into nothing.

She didn't see him walk on silent feet across the ring to her. So caught up in her own misery, she didn't see him standing over her, uncertainty, tenderness, and blind panic on his face. He stared down at the blubbering girl, thinking he should console her, trying to find the right words to make her know that he would never hurt her, and that for all the things she'd listed he'd done to her, she'd done no less to him.

Instead, he reached down with one hand, gripped the front of his old t-shirt, and hauled her up to her feet. He jerked the boxing glove off her left hand with his right and let it fall to the floor next to her bare feet.

"God, Frank, do you have to be so rough?" she mumbled.

He pulled her closer to his face, but she still didn't look up.

"I think you like it rough around the edges, Winters." He held his breath, wondering what she would do; the moment stretched out unbearably as she hung there in his grip, until he realized she was holding her breath, too. "Alex, look at me."

She raised her eyes. His were dark, penetrating. Hers were ravenous and feral. Sweat dripped down her brow, and he gingerly wiped her face with the back his hand. Then he pushed her against the turnbuckle and kissed her, softly at first, her pliant mouth timid against his, and then hard when he felt her clutch him back, her legs wrapping around him and pulling him in to her. He let out a low moan in his throat as she clenched both sides of his head, pulling at his hair, kissing him hard enough to bruise, their teeth clicking together, then she pushed herself back off the turnbuckle and sent them both tumbling to the ground. He hit the mat with a grunt then rolled them both over, ripping the other glove from her hand.

"God, I've wanted to do this ever since I saw you shove that donut in your mouth." He lowered his mouth to hers again and pulled at her bottom lip with his even, white teeth. "Every time you bite that goddamn lip of yours, I wanted to fuck you twenty different ways till Sunday."

She pulled away from him, eyes twinkling. "Jesus, Frank," she said, ripping the weight belt from her waist, "that's practically Shakespeare."

"I'm sure there's a fancy, poetic rom-com way to say that, Alex, but I'm not that guy." He pulled his shirt over his head with one hand as she raised her hips. He used his other hand to pull her shorts down, and she wiggled them off the rest of the way.

"Just so you know, even at my age, I've been imagining this for so long, well . . . I don't want to disappoint you or anything, but I feel like a fifteen-year-old in his dad's car on a Saturday night."

She smiled and bit her lip. "Today's only Thursday, Frank. Take all the time you need."

She tugged the waistband of his shorts down, her hand grasping the length of him, eliciting a groan that seemed to emanate from both of them. He pushed her shirt up and buried his face in her breasts; his tongue found her nipple and circled it, the edge of his teeth grazing her.

"Tell me, Alex, is this *manspreading* or *smoldering*?"

With a grunt he pushed into her before she could answer, her back smacking against the mat. Then he froze, his face dropped down to hers, and he whispered, "Please don't move. Just give me a minute, okay?"

She looked up at him, his eyes closed tight, his expression feverish and lost, and she wondered how she'd ever had the strength to push him away. She pushed against him once, just the barest movement of her hips, gripping every rigid inch of him deep inside her.

"Goddamn it, Alex," he hissed, reaching up to grab the ropes with both hands.

He collapsed across her, and as he did his lips found the tattoo behind her ear. He heard her whisper his name, *Frank*, and he whispered back a promise. "Alex, I'd never hurt you."

"Frank, wake up." She shoved him. "Come on, old man. Wake up."

"Quit nagging." He raised his head and smiled, his eyes still closed. "What do you want?"

"I'm hungry."

He put his head back down and pulled her across the mats toward him.

"Let me guess. Donuts?"

She wrapped her arms around him and rolled him over, straddling him. "Pizza. Go get me a pizza, Frank."

"What about me? I just burned off a couple thousand calories and nearly had a stroke. Caveman diet, remember? Besides, I'm sleeping."

She slid down his legs and took him in her mouth, her tongue tracing the part of him that was clearly not asleep. "You seem pretty awake to me," she whispered, swirling her tongue around his tip, then taking him deep in her throat.

His hips jerked and he groaned, "There's a defibrillator on the wall. Jesus God, woman, I am not a young man." She drew back, tightening her lips around him as she did, and then crawled away across the ring. He scrambled after her, grabbing her by her hips and dragging her up onto her hands and knees, his chest warm against her back.

"What if I promised you that you could eat the pizza off my belly, Frank?"

"Well, that's a different thing entirely. That's very caveman."

"Go get my pizza, Frank."

"In a minute. I'm busy."

CHAPTER SIXTEEN

· · ·

"That's why I told you off that night," she said. They were lying sprawled across the boxing ring, the side of his face resting on her inner thigh. An empty box of pizza lay nearby and her breasts and belly were still stained with red sauce, as was his face. He raised his head and put a kiss where his cheek had been.

"What night? You tell me off almost every night."

She flicked his hair down over his face and blushed. "I meant, that night in the parking lot.

"Oh," he said, putting his head back down. She could feel his breath on her. His lips were a fraction of an inch from where she wanted them to be. It was distracting to say the least.

"Could you move your head? I'm trying to talk to you and you're distracting me."

"Nope. I'm comfortable." Another kiss, higher this time. She tried to squirm away but his hands on her hips held her tight. "Very comfortable."

She let out a long, shuddering breath.

"I thought you were . . . Well, Joel said . . ."

He raised his head again. "What did Boy Wonder say?"

"He said you were banging Meg up against her trailer and I figured it was to get her dad to give you a role in his next big drama."

Frank pulled away. He slipped one hand from her hip and, making a fist, rested his chin on it, low on her stomach. He reached up with the other hand to slick the hair back from his face.

"And you believed him?"

"Well, I mean . . . I thought you liked her. I mean, she's beautiful."

"Alex, let me make something clear. I did not, nor would I ever, bang Meg Thomas. Did I kiss her? Sure. But we were working on the scene."

"Really."

"Really. I'm not interested in girls."

"If you're trying to tell me you're gay, this is a really weird way to do it, Frank."

Another kiss, higher this time, his tongue making lazy circles. She stopped squirming and arched her back, sliding down, driving herself into his face. He pushed her back up.

"I didn't say I'm into guys. I'm not into *girls*." He raised his head again. "Little waifish dingbats. I'm into women."

He planted a kiss on her left hip, his lips trailing a path to her right.

"Women with curves."

His lips slid back over to her belly button, his beard scratching her.

"Women with tight asses," his hands clawed at her as he buried his face in her neck, pulling her down to him, driving into her.

"And soft in all the right places."

He kissed her breasts, cupped them.

"Women who yell at me." He grabbed both of her hands and pinned them over her head.

"Women who swear like a trucker." He kissed her nose, then drove into her again, harder this time, insistent.

"What about you, Miss Alexandra? What kind of man are you interested in?"

She struggled to free her wrists but he held them firmly with one hand, even as his other hand traced the lines of her face.

"I'm interested in retired action heroes who know when to shut their pretty mouths and finish what they started."

———

Frank and Alex sat in his car the next morning, holding hands over the gear shifter and staring at the studio. She turned to look at him, wondering what he was thinking.

"You still have pizza sauce in your beard, Frank."

"Outstanding." He raised their hands to his mouth and kissed her. "So now what?"

"We go to work. Same as always."

"But what about this?"

She slid her hand from his and smoothed her hair back. "Oh, well," she cleared her throat and took a deep breath. "We can keep this quiet. It would look terrible if people thought you were banging the help." She forced a shrug. "It's fine."

He fixed her with an annoyed gaze. "It's fine," he repeated.

"Sure."

"Right." He jumped out of the Jeep and strode around to her side, ripping the door open. With one smooth movement, he hauled her out and threw her over his shoulder, the good one, not the one that had required two surgeries after *Armed Assault Force III: Armageddon*.

Alex drummed her fists on his back as he carried her, kicking and screaming, across the back lot. Extras, PAs, and the rest of the cast all stopped in their tracks to watch their progression.

"Morning, everyone!" Frank bellowed. "Don't mind us. Just taking the most beautiful girl in the world and the love of my life to her office. Somebody bring her a dozen old-fashioneds. Let me tell you, she is *hungry* this morning."

Her screams turned to laughter as he kicked the door of the studio open, jogged down the stairs to her office, and deposited her on her desk.

"How was that? Was that 'fine' enough for you?"

"Goddamn it, Frank," she said unconvincingly.

He kissed her nose. "I think you're working late tonight."

"I am?"

"You are. There are a couple things I want to check off my to-do list in this room. Wall, desk, floor. Wall again."

"Fine," she said, laughing as he darted in for another kiss. "Get out. I have a meeting with Joel in thirty minutes. I need to clean myself up."

CHAPTER SEVENTEEN

...

"What do you mean, *fired*?" Alex screamed.

Joel continued to lounge at his desk—a repurposed pinball machine, *God, what a douche*—unperturbed by her screaming, nonchalantly tossing a baseball around.

"Joel, you prick. After all this time, after every single piece of shit scene I delivered for you, you're firing me? Why? I thought you said the producers were fine with the changes."

"Oh, everything was fine until I saw your little walk of shame this morning. You're literally rewriting this whole movie for Frank Brennan because you're fucking him. Not cool, Alex." He continued tossing the baseball back and forth between his hands.

"That is not true." She took a deep breath and willed herself to stop screaming. "I'm rewriting it for *me*. I can't write your shit anymore, Junior."

"This is exactly what I mean, Alex. You've lost your professional perspective. Listen, Alex. I can't very well fire Frank Brennan, Captain Freedom. The studio would have my head. But I *can* fire you. This story is ridiculous. I'm replacing you and trying to salvage this before it turns into a bigger disaster than it already is."

"You are a piece of shit, Joel." She stood. "Fine. I'm out. I'll walk across the street to WorldCom Studios and have another job in an hour. And you can eat a dick."

Joel fixed her with his weasel-like gaze. "Oh, I wouldn't do that, Alex." He paused to toss his baseball up in the air and catch it. "I made some calls already this morning." He threw the ball up again. "You let me down, Alex. What is it they said in those old movies? You'll never work in this town again? Don't let the sun set on you?" He shrugged. "Something like that. I'll ask Frank. Didn't he have a line like that in *AAF V*?"

He tossed the ball up again, but Alex snatched it from the air.

"Hey!" Joel yelled, scrambling back from her in his chair.

Alex tossed the baseball back and forth in her own hands. "No, Joel. I think Frank said something like, 'I'm going to make it my personal mission to see you in hell'." With that, she slammed the baseball into the top of his pinball desk, shattering the brittle glass and setting off the jackpot.

———

Alex stormed to the parking lot, jumped into her car, and floored it though the studio gates. *Fired.* Her mind scrambled, trying to remember how much she had in savings.

Trying to think if she knew someone, *anyone* who would take her on. She scrolled through her mental list of people in the industry who owed her favors, but they all owed Joel five times more. And God only knew what sort of damage he'd done on the phone this morning.

Think, Alex. Maybe ten thousand in the bank. Enough to go back to Michigan, get an apartment. Maybe even get her old job back. *Frank,* she thought to herself. *I can't even talk to him. He's going to be all kind and worried, but there's nothing to be done about this. He's under contract. He'll finish this out with a new writer, and I can't involve him in this. This is my problem, not his. And it's early days with us. I can't expect him to get involved in this. I mean, maybe we could make it work. Cross-country relationship. Failed screenwriter barista and Hollywood action hero. Yeah, right.*

She rolled down the window and let the air send her hair flying. *Where am I even driving? Am I looking for a tall cliff to jump off, or a stunning panorama to make a vengeful speech on? I don't even know anymore. I don't know how to end this story.* She focused instead on the feeling in her chest, surprised to discover it was relief. Like the release of pulling out a splinter. She was glad, in a way, to be done with Joel. She really had nothing to lose now. *But what about Frank?* a little voice in her mind whispered. She considered calling him, but it was too damsel-in-distress. *I'm not that girl,* she told herself. *Not me. No, I'm the girl determined to be unhappy.*

Just then, her phone rang. It was Frank. *Goddamn it, Frank. But thank you, Blessed Mother.*

She pulled her car over and answered.

"You heard?"

"I heard. Where are you?"

"I just need some time, Frank. I can handle this. I'll be fine, but I need some time to think. I'll come back tonight and clean out my office after everyone goes home. I can't face the crew, not like this. We can talk then. Okay?"

There was a long pause on the other end of the line.

"Fine. But I need one thing from you."

"What?"

"I want a copy of the script you and I wrote."

"Why?"

"Do you trust me, Alex?"

She answered without thinking. "I do. I really do."

"I'll get the copy out of your desk, and I'll meet you tonight in your office. And Alex? Don't run off on me. I hunted down fugitives semi-professionally for the last twenty years. I'd just find you."

"I don't need you to rescue me, Frank. I can handle this. I have no idea how, but I'll figure it out."

"I know that, kid. But I have my own scores to settle."

"Is that from *Armed Assault Force I*?" she asked, trying not to cry.

"No. It's from 'That Pencil Dick Trash Talked My Girl.' There won't be a sequel."

"I love you. I heard you that night. But I just—"

"I know. Guns blazing?"

"Guns blazing," she whispered.

CHAPTER EIGHTEEN

· · ·

Frank was waiting for her in her office that night. She pushed the door open and screamed when she saw him leaning against the far wall, dressed in his tactical gear again.

"Jesus, Frank, you scared the shit out of me," she sputtered. "And before you ask—no, we are not machete-ing Joel."

He pushed away from the wall and wrapped her in his arms. She burrowed into his special ops vest. It felt nice.

"Hey, Alex."

"Hey yourself." She looked up at him. "What are you all dressed up for?"

"I thought we had a hot date tonight."

She pulled away and gestured around the room. "I don't know. I have to clear all this out before that little tit confiscates it. And it's been a long day."

"I wouldn't worry about Joel, princess." He gave her a mischievous smile.

"Oh, Jesus. You killed Joel."

"I did better than kill him. I got him fired."

"You got Joel fired?"

"You didn't think I got a five-film franchise by being a nice guy, did you, Alex?"

"You didn't have to do that. And it doesn't matter anyway. They won't hire me back."

"They won't?" He winked at her.

"What did you do?" she whispered.

"I took your script to the producers. They fired Joel on the spot. I had almost nothing to do with it. They not only reinstated you as screenwriter, they want you to co-direct with Seth Greenbaum."

"Seth Greenbaum? But he's big time indie. He's, like, a *real* director."

"Yes. Just like you're a *real* screenwriter."

Alex slumped to the floor. "Not fired."

"Co-director." He smiled down at her.

"You didn't have to do this for me."

"I didn't do anything for you. You did this all yourself. I just put your story in the right hands. It's all you, babe."

"You know what I think, Frank Brennan?"

He pulled her to her feet. "What do you think, Alex Winters?"

"I think you're a nice guy."

"No, I'm not. I'm a mean old man."

"Tell me you didn't do this for me."

"I didn't do it for you."

"Bullshit. You can act better than that. I've *seen* you act better than that."

He tilted her chin up to him and kissed her softly on the lips. "I did it for us."

CHAPTER NINETEEN

$\bullet\ \bullet\ \bullet$

Alex stumbled out of the makeup trailer, bouffant-ed and tucked and shellacked to within an inch of her life. *Mary Li really outdid herself this time,* she thought, looking down at the red velvet mini dress and platform heels through the sweeping veil of many inches of fake lashes.

"I look like a goddamn Bangkok whore," she muttered.

"Alexandra Winters," a voice purred behind her.

She whirled around. *Damn him.* Frank was standing behind her, gleaming in a black suit cut so tight she could see his biceps through the jacket sleeves. His black hair flopped effortlessly back in that way that only he seemed to know how, careless but only slightly affected, hands in his pockets, rocking back on his heels.

"Brennan," she said through clenched teeth. "Before you even start—"

"Winters, you look terrible."

Alex threw the prop handbag down on the ground, exasperated. "Don't stop there, Frank, I—" Her words cut off at the strange sensation of her strapless dress heaving downward suddenly. She looked down and hoisted the top up, then did some not-so-discreet tucking. Then she resumed her rant, snapping at him, "Go ahead and finish. Now that you've started."

He stepped toward her and took his hands from his pockets and straightened his cuffs. Then he knelt in front of her, letting out a low whistle as he traveled down her legs and picked the bag up. He looked up at her and held it out.

She snatched it from him. "Quit clowning and get up," she hissed, "before someone sees you."

He shuffled on his knees closer to her. "But I have to finish." He put one hand on the side of her calf and slid it up to her thigh, his eyes never leaving hers. "Alex Winters, you look terrible."

"You said that already. I know, all right? Seth gave me all this shit about how I had to go to the damn premiere because the reviews are through the roof—that's your fault, by the way—and I've no idea what to wear to this sort of thing, so Mary Li said she'd get me squared away, but I mean, my God. Look at me, Frank. I . . ."

"I am." Frank smiled up at her, then stood up, taking her hand and raising it to his lips.

"You look terrible when you're not in my bed." He kissed her hand. "You look terrible when you're not naked in my trailer." He twisted her hand to kiss her wrist. "You look terrible when I'm not eating pizza off your belly." He pulled her to him. His lips were at her throat now. "You look terrible when I'm not peeling you off the ceiling."

She slid her lips against his jaw and let out a long sigh as he kissed her collarbone, his hands on her ass now, pulling her against him.

"Frank," she said softly.

He kissed the tiny tattoo behind her ear.

"Babe."

"I want to write that down. That shit is gold."

He smacked her ass and bit her neck. "Smart ass. Let's get a move on." He threaded his fingers through hers. "That is, if you'll be my date. I hate to go to the movies alone."

"Frank Brennan, after all this time, after all the borderline-hostile, carb-laden, shame-filled sex you've been having with me, are you asking me out on a *date*?"

"That depends. Can we keep doing all that other stuff?"

"You bet your ass."

"Then yes."

"I really hate this dress, Frank."

"That's okay. You won't be wearing it for long."

AFTERWORD

...

Frank went on to star in Meg's dad's movie and was nominated for an Academy Award for his portrayal of a veteran with PTSD trying to rejoin society. When he won, he spent so much time kissing his wife, Alex, that he didn't even get to make a speech. Which was fortunate, because he'd refused to let Alex write him one, afraid of jinxing things, and the best he would have been able to manage was a terse "thanks." Alex made enough money off the critically acclaimed *Ranging Alone* to start her own production company and was making a name for herself in the indie film world by adapting all her books to film.

Frank's boxing club is always closed on Thursdays, and has a standing order for pizza deliveries.

When asked if they would ever consider making another movie together, Frank said, "No, you have no idea how difficult she is to work with."

Alex agreed with that assessment and added, "No one would be interested in that story. It doesn't wash."

Brennan's Lament

Chapter One

*F*ather Francis Brennan glanced up at the dusty cuckoo clock on the rectory wall. 4:25 p.m. He rolled his eyes and groaned. Confession started in five minutes—an hour of listening to the lusts and imagined sins of every old bat in this godforsaken town. At least it wasn't Mass. Mass took forever, and he wasn't absolutely sure he was doing it right. He jerked the desk drawer open and rummaged around until he found his collar and rosary jumbled in with packets of protein bars and airline vodka. After tucking the clerical collar around his neck with a grimace, he wrapped the heavy black rosary around his fist like brass knuckles. Then he slipped his shoulder harness from the back of the ancient—and uncomfortable as fuck—chair and slid his muscular arms into it, checking to make sure his .45 caliber MK23 was locked and loaded.

This priest business is bullshit. Why can't I just shoot someone already? Frank sighed, frustrated, and turned to the palm-sized mirror that hung on the wall, his considerable height forcing him to duck down to make sure his collar was on straight. How short was Father Morgan, anyway? He tried to recall something about the man he'd shot in the head, jammed in the trunk, and driven to the docks in Portland, but all he could come up with was that he was: fat as fuck, looked weirdly astonished to be dead, and must have had some sort of rock in his breast pocket that dug in and left a fist-sized bruise when Frank had heaved his dead, fat ass over his shoulder.

Shit. He'd spent the afternoon, when he was supposed to be in silent prayer, cleaning his guns, and now there was a smear of machine oil on his clerical collar. He slid the whole contraption to one side and shrugged. Crooked. *Appropriate.* Frank scratched his grizzled jaw. He needed a shave, but there was no time. He reached into the closet and pulled a voluminous robe over his head. Once he'd checked to make sure his holster was concealed, he slipped a knife into his boot.

He arranged his ruggedly handsome face into a semblance of piety and walked out the office door, almost running into the church secretary and altar guild high priestess, Mrs. Blake. *Old polyester slacks, likes to confess to reading smut novels about pirates, has invited me to dinner twice, smells like vinegar and baby powder, notices everything.*

"My child," Frank said in a low voice. *Good. That sounds good.*

"Father Brennan!" she exclaimed, clutching the brooch at her throat as if he'd flashed her. "You're wearing green vestments!"

He glanced down. "And?"

"It's not ordinary time at all! It's Lent, Father!"

He stepped back into his office, slammed the door in her astonished face, and looked down at his green robes. *Shit.* He opened the door again. Mrs. Blake was still standing there, mouth agape.

"So, *not* green?"

"Certainly not green, Father. Purple! Surely by your age you'd know the colors of the liturgical year. What are they *teaching* in that seminary, I'd like to know?"

Frank flashed her what he hoped was a humble smile, grinding his teeth inside his mouth. *At his age. Goddamn it.* Not only was he getting too old to be an assassin—all the flashy jobs going to the young recruits—he was apparently now too old to be a fucking priest. *This is bullshit. I'm barely forty. I'm not that old.* His hand clutching the rosary twitched. He wished it held his throwing knife instead.

"Forgive me, my child. I'm observing a strict fast in this blessed season, and I fear my focus on the divine has made me turn away from earthly concerns."

That seemed to mollify her. She dropped her hand from her brooch. "Well then. Best hurry up, Father. They're already lining up for you. Never saw so many women trotting into confession, nor so regular, with Father Morgan."

She looked him up and down. His vestments did little to disguise his broad chest and lean, muscular build.

"When did you say Father Morgan was coming back? He's never taken a fishing vacation before." She eyed him, nose wrinkled with suspicion.

First person I shoot is you, you nosy old hag.

"That's in the good Lord's hands, I fear." *Or the hands of the guy I paid to dump his dead body in the Atlantic.* He started to shut the door, pausing for a moment. "Purple?"

"Purple!" she snapped, clasping the brooch again and scurrying away, her polyester slacks making judgmental shushing sounds as she did.

Frank Brennan slammed the door again. In one smooth motion, he wrenched the green robe off and threw it across the room, then dipped down to one knee with military precision. His hand flashed as he plucked the knife from his boot and threw it with deadly accuracy into two inches of the thick, paneled wall.

"Motherfucking *purple*," he growled.

He wrenched the knife from the wall and swore again. The purple wasn't even the worst. Or the fact that the stubble on his jaw had shifted from black to salt and pepper. The worst was *her.*

Frank jammed the knife back into his boot. In his kind of work, there was always a girl. Usually a sexy attaché or a kind-hearted prostitute, someone to pass the time with and use for information. Not dangerous, unless they double-crossed you.

No, the dangerous kind was of a different variety altogether. They had big, sad eyes and sweet voices, and were totally oblivious to what a murderous piece of shit you were. The girl next door you never had a shot with, the one that got away, someone you wanted to protect from the big bad world. The kind of girl that made you swear this was the last job, who made you wonder if there was a life outside of all this.

Frank thought of them as landmines. Once you stepped on one, it was just a matter of time before you were a dead man. Twenty years he'd been working special ops, and he knew at his age, he was one job away from a fatal mistake or being disavowed by his employers. He'd already heard grumblings in the intelligence community. There was no retirement plan for guys like him.

He was slipping, and he knew it. That was bad enough. But *she* made it worse. The Widow Winters, his personal landmine. And he'd discovered her in fucking Lament, New Hampshire, of all the goddamn places.

He jerked the purple robe over his head, replaced the knife in his tactical boot, and strode out the door, casting a wrathful glance at the long line of pious citizens lining up for penance.

"Motherfucking purple," he muttered under his breath, and slammed the door to the confessional.

Chapter Two

" *I* took the Lord's name in vain twice this morning, Father, because my Thomas left his dirty plates in the sink and his wet towel on the floor. I had impure thoughts about a man I saw on the TV, and I took shameful pride in my baked beans at the church dinner. My beans are better than Louisa Potterdamm's beans, but it was wrong to be smug about it."

Frank rolled his eyes and scrambled in his pants pocket for the penance cheat sheet he'd printed off the Internet. He scanned it for a minute, scratching his stubbly jaw and trying to decide if multiple blasphemies demanded an equal number of Our Fathers. *Fuck it. Wet towels? That's a dick move, Tom.*

"Okay, let's call it one Our Father for the wet towels and blasphemy, and three Hail Marys for the smug beans. Sound good?" he growled.

"Well, Father Brennan, I don't know. You've left out the lust. Father Murphy would usually add a rosary and an act of contrition."

"Fine. Do that, um, my child."

"Father Brennan?"

He glared down at the crumpled paper again, trying to guess what he'd missed.

"Oh, right. I absolve you of all your sins, in the name of the Father . . ." *Blah, blah, blah,* he thought. *Get out. Next.*

After an hour of listening to the adorable sins of his stolen parish, Frank slipped from the confessional, eager to shed his suffocating robes, slip into his special ops gear, and begin searching the woods again for Schwartz. He closed the door to the confessional, remembered to turn the light off—he hadn't last week, and poor ancient Mr. McDowell had sat there for hours confessing over and over again to no one—and even stopped to genuflect at the altar in case anyone was watching.

He knelt reverently and may have actually been praying as he recited his own catechism.

I will find this motherfucker Schwartz and his gal Friday. I will find them and bring them in and then I am out. I am done with this shit. Sooner or later, someone is going to slip up. The whole town is in and out of this church every goddamn—He glanced up at the crucifix—*Sorry . . . day and one of them knows something. And, if not, a couple more days searching the woods, I might find their fugitive asses myself. I won't stop until I find them and hand them over. And then I am done. I'll disappear, find a beach somewhere and get drunk for the next three years and try to forget about the last twenty.* He glanced back up at the crucified Christ. *Brother, I know how you feel.*

He rose and bowed again, crossing himself for added measure, and then turned to the sacristy to grab a bottle of wine for later that night. But he was right. He wasn't alone. She was there. Kneeling in the back pew, elegant head of rich chestnut hair falling in a veil over her angel face, the widow Alexandra Winters was praying, too. Her lips fluttered in the darkness, flashes of rosebuds, her white hands clasped under her chin like the Blessed Mother herself. *The Widow Winters*, he thought to himself. *How on earth can these backwoods idiots call this gorgeous creature that?* The facts he knew about her were few—young, widowed, kindergarten teacher at the parish school. However, what he felt when he saw her was a Psalm in and of itself. *Beautiful. Gentle. Sweet. Kind. Clever. Funny. Never once enters the confessional, which is probably a good thing because I would definitely violate sanctity. I'd violate that all day long.*

Alexandra Winters raised her eyes then and saw him, granting him one of her enigmatic smiles. Frank felt his heart turn over in his mercenary chest like a junior high kid as he walked down the aisle to her. *Goddamn it. You worthless piece of crap. Stop walking. Turn around. Go back to your office and get hammered. Do not talk to her. Oh shit, too late.*

"Father Brennan."

"Mrs. Winters," he replied, nodding at her.

"Oh, please call me Alexandra, Father."

"Alexandra," he said, trying to keep his voice from rising like a prepubescent kid with a crush.

"Are you settling in well, Father? How long will you be here?" she asked, her face upturned to him like a goddamn doe in the woods.

Frank cleared his throat. "Fairly well. Everyone has been very kind," he answered, purposefully glossing over her second question. His words sounded stilted and forced, even to him. *You sorry ass—think. How did you get that Swedish attaché in your bed in less than an hour? Think, damn it. You've banged or killed everything from here to Fiji. This should be a cakewalk.* He furrowed his brow at her purple and turquoise tweed duffle coat, her little kindergarten teacher jumper and tights, those ridiculous lace-up Pilgrim shoes that looked so deliciously wholesome. Somehow he doubted he could use the same lines on this vision that he did on the Swede. In a panic, he heard himself sputter something unrehearsed, unscripted, the first thing that popped into his head.

"Can I walk you to your front door, Alexandra? It's dark out, and there may be hooligans about." *Hooligans? Did I just fucking say hooligans?*

"Hooligans, Father? In Lament, New Hampshire? The last time we had trouble in these parts was when Isaiah Bishop's goat ran amok in the town square," she teased.

"Well, then—errant, willful goats of the night," he insisted. *That's it. Put a bullet in your head. That is the worst pickup line ever. Errant, willful goats. Great, Frank, you're a real wordsmith.*

Alexandra flushed and looked down at her Pilgrim shoes.

"Thank you, Father. I'd like that."

Holy shit. It worked.

As he walked her across the town square to the little farmhouse where she lived, the feeling in his chest alternated from elation to agony with every tilt of her head. The walk was short—too short. They didn't talk about a single thing of importance—the day Bishop's goats stormed the playground, Mrs. Blake's brooch collection—but every single word seemed tinged with a universe of meaning. Each word she uttered, each glance was a clue into who she really was. Alexandra grasped his hand when they reached her porch steps, then slipped silently inside on noiseless feet, like a cat, casting him one last sad smile before shutting the door between them.

Frank returned to the church in a daze. All his plans for stalking the woods dissolved the moment she'd given him that Mona Lisa smile of hers.

Schwartz can wait a day or so. He's not going anywhere, he thought to himself. He grabbed two bottles of communion wine from the sacristy and polished them off while sharpening his knives. Hours later, he passed out on his desk, dreaming of Pilgrim shoes and long chestnut hair.

Chapter Three

The following night, angry with himself for mooning drunkenly over a backwoods widow, Frank spent the entire evening from dusk till dawn scouring the hunting cabins in the White Mountain National Forest. Invisible in his black-out tactical gear, he stalked Schwartz, the missing Russian mob accountant who had vanished into the woods, but he turned up nothing. A few drunken hillbillies, but no sign of Schwartz or his girlfriend anywhere. Still, in the two weeks since he'd come, he'd managed to methodically eliminate a significant portion of the woods as potential hiding places. And there was always the chance someone would say something in confession. *These clannish motherfuckers. Someone's gonna spill.*

He had just laid his head down on a wadded-up pile of green vestments on his desk after morning duties when a sharp rap at the door sent him bolt upright, knife in hand, before he remembered where he was.

He slid the knife under the desk as the door swung open.

"Yes?"

Mrs. Blake flashed the crumpled green vestments a disgusted look.

"They need you at the school, Father."

"At the school?" he asked, running a hand through his disheveled hair to straighten it. He slid his hand up to his neck. *Where is my collar thing?*

"Yes, Mary Margaret Finley has had another and cannot monitor the playground. Father Morgan always filled in for her."

"Playground duty? You're kidding," he said, locating his collar on the floor by his feet and slipping it on.

"Sure I'm not. Better hurry, Father. Once those kindergartners are out of control, there's no getting them back.

The widow. Kindergarten teacher. Landmines. Don't do it, Brennan. Focus on Schwartz. Finish the job and bolt.

Frank rose from his desk and hurriedly shrugged into his coat. *Shut up, Brennan. It's just recess. It's not like you're going to bang the widow on the rocket slide.* He slipped past Mrs. Blake in the doorway and paused. *Although, now that I think of it . . .*

"She had another what?" he asked Mrs. Blake abruptly.

"Another *child*, bless me, Father. That's number eight."

"Jesus Christ," he mumbled.

"Father Brennan!" she gasped, clutching her brooch again.

". . . has blessed them, indeed." With that, he turned and hurried from the church and sprinted the three blocks to the parish school.

Alexandra Winters was leaning against an oak tree, bundled up against the cold in her speckled duffle coat, the oversized yellow fisherman's boots on her feet making her look less like a teacher and more like one of her kindergartners. Her face lit up when she saw him.

"You're late," she said, wagging her finger in his face, eyes twinkling. "Father Morgan was never late."

"I'm sorry," he gasped, out of breath from his sprint. *Oh, my God. She looks happy to see me. No one is ever happy to see me. That's because you usually snap their necks, Frank. She likes seeing Father Frank, not you, you sorry piece of shit.* "I was just . . ." *Words, Frank. Words. Find some and stop stammering like you're at your first dance.*

She laughed at him. "I was kidding, Father Francis. Father Morgan was always late. Sometimes he would just flat-out refuse to come. Can you blame him? Look at this nightmare."

She waved a hand in the direction of the playground. A churning sea of screaming children surged around them. There was screaming, crying, throwing rocks, jumping off things onto children below, more screaming. The rocket slide he'd been fantasizing about on his sprint over was indeed present, but it was covered with the squealing bodies of half a dozen snot-nosed brats. *So much for experimental slide sex with the hot schoolteacher.*

Frank let out a sigh. "Well, suffer the little children, right?" *Jesus, all that Mass is rubbing off on me. What the fuck did I just say?*

Alexandra laughed, the sound like fireworks in his ears, as she thumped him on his shoulder. "That's the spirit, Father. Well, I'm off. The lunch monitor will collect them from you in an hour. Until then, you're on your own." She turned and headed off toward the woods.

"Where are you off to, Alexandra? Those are some serious boots."

"Oh, I prefer to take my free period in the woods. I like to hike. And I like the quiet." Then she winked at him, and he clutched his collar tightly as she sashayed off toward the woods.

He admired her departure until she disappeared into the tree line, then turned back to face the discordant horde. *Nightmare is right. It's like a prison yard full of munchkins. Fewer shivs, more snot.* Frank shook his head in disgust. *We'll soon see about this.* A small hand tugged on his sleeve, causing him to jump. He looked down into the weepy eyes of a small girl with pigtails.

"Father Francis, Evan pushed me off the swing and I skinned my knee and now he won't do sharing."

"What do you want me to do about it?" he barked at her.

She shrugged her tiny shoulders. "Make him do sharing?"

He turned to glare at the swing set, trying to discern who this punk Evan was.

"Right. Is Evan the squat boy with the green hat, or the petulant boy in the red sweatpants?"

"I don't know what 'squat' means, Father. Or that other word. He's the big, mean one."

"Father Francis?" Frank turned to see a small boy with glasses tugging at his coattail.

"What do you want?" he growled.

"Father, Sissy and Mary held me down and made me kiss a slug they found by the monkey bars. Now my mouth tastes like dirt and slugs. Can I go get a drink of water?"

"They made you kiss a slug?"

The little boy nodded, sniffling and pushing his glasses up as he did. "They said I have to kiss two more if I want to have the soccer ball."

"Right. Let's just sort this all out, shall we?"

He strode to the center of the playground, the two sniffling children still clutching his coat, all the while chaotic kindergartners bounced off his long legs like pinballs. He placed two fingers in his mouth and whistled, an earsplitting train whistle technique he'd learned in grade school. Every one of the ankle biters froze and turned to gape at him.

"Do I have your attention?" Twenty pairs of eyes were riveted on him.

"Right. Mrs. Finley has had another, and Father Morgan is at sea. That means you are stuck with me. And under my playground rules, you vicious little rug rats, there will be no shoving, no fighting, no crying, and in the name of all that is holy, no forced slug kissing. DO I MAKE MYSELF CLEAR, CHILDREN?" he bellowed.

Silence.

"I can't hear you. Sound off with a 'Sir, yes sir' if you understand me!" he barked.

A vague mumble of "sirs" and "yes's" floated around him.

"Unacceptable. SIR, YES SIR! Like you mean it!"

"SIR, YES SIR!" they screamed back at him.

"Outstanding." Frank grinned at the raggedy pack. He shrugged his coat off and threw it on the monkey bars. "Now let's give you all something productive to do. Who here has heard of Krav Maga?" Silence again. "Fantastic. Fresh meat."

It took him the better part of a half-hour to line them up and keep their squirmy little bodies in line. Then he removed his jacket and collar and tossed them on top of the coat. Rolling up his sleeves, he strode through their tiny ranks.

"Eyes forward. Don't look at me. You look where your opponent would be. Which is in front of you, and after a groin kick, on the ground at your feet screaming in agony. Krav Maga, you little whippersnappers, is the Israeli art of self-defense, a hybrid fighting style that blends karate—EYES FORWARD, SOPHIE—boxing, aikido, judo, and weaponry. Today, we will focus—DROP THAT PIGTAIL, EVAN, OR YOU'RE DOING SIT-UPS—on punching and groin kicks. I want you to make two fists, like so." He dropped his fists to either side of his hips. "Well done, children, and then kick sharply up with one foot. Again. Now we are going to alternate like this. Eyes on me now."

Twenty pairs of delighted eyes swung to look at him.

Frank rolled his broad shoulders and dropped his fists to his side, his dark eyes scanning the playground to make sure he had each and every child's attention. Satisfied, he launched off a volley of lightning-fast punches and kicks, punctuating each one with a guttural cry, his showmanship interrupted by a small voice directly in front of him.

"But why are we kravving, Father?" The little round girl with the pigtails again. Skinned-knee girl. She was trying to keep up with his demonstration, her arms pinwheeling as she tried to kick and punch at the same time.

"Gwennie, kick, then punch. Atta girl. Why are we kravving? Because you are the only kindergartners in this school. No one else understands your struggle, your goals, your darkest fears, like each other. You should be a tightly knit squad, united against the older kids, and instead you are a brawling, slug-kissing disaster. You are only as strong as your weakest link, which right now appears to be Lucas. Lucas, why are you lying in the dirt daydreaming? Evan, get Lucas on his feet."

Evan, the swing non-sharer and knee-skinner, hauled Lucas to his feet.

"Good. Now, everyone, repeat after me. You can do this, Lucas!" Frank bellowed.

Twenty voices screamed, "You can do this, Lucas!" The sight of Lucas screaming it, too, very nearly brought tears to Frank's dead shark eyes.

"Groin kick! Punch! Outstanding! Again!" Frank strode down the lines, stopping to correct form, give encouragement, and tie shoes.

"You will kick and punch until I see a cohesive team emerge. A team of non-criers. Non-swing stealers. Non-slug kissers. Do I make myself clear?"

"Sir, yes sir!" twenty voices screamed at him.

"That's more like it. Now, let's sound off. One verse of the Our Father for each properly executed groin kick. Go."

The Our Father has never sounded so sweet, he thought, as the children punched and kicked their way through it a half-dozen times. *My sympathies to anyone who gives that girl Gwennie a hard time. Wicked footwork, that one.*

"Wow. I'm going to have to add a nap time to their schedule, Father."

Alexandra's voice startled him from his concentration. Frank looked down at her, noticed her boots were covered with mud. She had a little smear of mud on her forehead and a few twigs in her hair. *Nope. Not the rocket slide. More like a feather bed in front of a cozy fire, snow softly falling outside . . . Pull yourself together, Brennan.*

"Lunchtime already?" he stammered.

"Nope." Her eyes flashed mischievously up at him, causing the corners of his mouth to turn up as well. "The lunch monitor was too scared to come out here with you teaching them mixed martial arts. You went right past lunch, Father. What are they teaching in the seminary these days?" She turned her back to him and waved her mittened hands over her head.

"Come along, my little doves. You can eat your lunches on the big rug for story time, then we'll have a nap. Say thank you to Father Brennan."

"Sir, yes sir!"

She spun around back to him, her elfish face twisted up in a cheeky grin. "Wow. Where have you been all my life?"

He flushed and scratched the back of his head, looking over to the rocket slide for something to say. It stared back at him. *Some help you are. Is she flirting with me? Don't be stupid, Frank. She's a widow. Widows don't flirt. And anyway, you're certainly giving her nothing to flirt at. You're stammering and yammering. She's just being nice to the awkward, middle-aged priest.* "It's not mixed martial arts. It's . . . it's . . ." He scrambled trying to find something innocuous. "Tai chi?" He glared at the rocket slide. *Fucking useless contraption.*

"Tai chi, huh? And the Our Father?"

"I, uh . . . thought maybe it would calm them down," he stammered. "You know. Help teach them the catechism."

She eyed him, unconvinced. "Right. Well, see you tomorrow, Father."

"Yes, Widow Winters. I mean Alexandra. Same time tomorrow." *Widow Winters? Jesus, I gotta get out of here. I'm starting to sound like Mrs. Blake.*

Frank watched as the sea of children surged around her, watched her hands as she caressed their heads and listened to their excited chatter. Watched her boots sloshing through the early spring sludge on the ground and then disappear into the parish schoolhouse.

I would kill the entire population of Lament to see those boots up over my shoulders, either on the rocket slide or in a log cabin. He shook himself, trying to banish the sentimental voice in his head. *Shit. Maybe it is time to get out of this job. I'm getting soft. I have to be out of my mind to be panting after a widowed kindergarten teacher in fucking Nowhere, USA.*

He stormed back to the rectory, shoving his arms into his jacket and coat and wrestling the collar back around his neck. *Must be this stupid papist noose,* he thought. *It's cutting off the circulation to my brain. Fuck this job. I've got to stay away from her, she's a landmine. I'll find someone else to play recess monitor, and from now on I'll keep my focus on finding Schwartz and off the widow with the sad eyes.*

Frank slammed the door to his office and paced, swearing and throwing things until he calmed down. Then he gave himself a long look in the miniscule mirror, changed into his blackout gear, and slipped out the window to spend the afternoon looking for Schwartz, his mind going blissfully blank while he searched cabin after cabin and slogged miles through the marsh-like woods. Hours later, he slumped to the ground, exhausted, bedraggled, and done. The small, insistent voice in his head finally broke through his professional focus.

She's exactly the person I should have met years ago, before all this. I should have left the Marines after my first tour, found her, and crawled on my hands and knees until she agreed to marry my worthless ass. Should have gotten a job as a vinyl siding salesman, kept her pregnant for the next twenty years, two weeks every year in the Outer Banks, minivan full of rugrats, and spent every Saturday night fucking that sad look out of her eyes while I got paunchy and grew old with her. But none of that is ever going to happen. There's no happily ever after for people like me. All I bring to the table is death and misery and this empty husk of a human I am now.

Chapter Four

*F*rank spent the next four days avoiding Alexandra Winters. When he saw her in the church—kneeling, lighting candles that reflected in her upturned eyes, helping the altar guild with dusting, kerchief tied around her long hair, marching the little children through town like some sort of diminutive, elfish pied piper—he abruptly changed course, trying very, very hard to be wherever she wasn't. He kept mostly to the confessional—*Father, bless me I swore at Bishop's goat again and served my husband burnt toast on purpose*—and the rectory, slipping out for a few hours during the day and all night searching for Schwartz. The forest in spring was like an endless swamp, miles and miles of moss and mud and streams dotted with hunting lodges that ranged from little more than duck blinds to log cabins. But no sign of Schwartz or his gal Friday. No tracks in the deep mud other than his own. But he pushed himself past his endurance every night, knowing full well the price of failure at his age in his profession.

He thought he spied Alexandra in the woods one twilit evening, thought he saw the flash of yellow boots, but it was doubtful she saw him, dressed as he was in black tactical gear and face paint. Between the map in his pocket and the GPS on his sat phone, he'd eliminated miles and miles of national forest and dozens of hunting lodges. *He's here. He has nowhere else to go. I'll find you, you thieving son of a bitch. At least, you better hope I do. My people want your ass alive. The Russians want you on a kebab, pal.*

But despite all of Frank's careful plans, Alexandra Winters found him anyway. He ran into the Quick Shop on the square to grab some supplies for another long night of trudging through the forest, throwing fistfuls of protein bars and an armful of energy drinks into his cart. He considered for a moment before adding a packet of dried apricots and a fifth of vodka.

"We've missed you at recess, Father Francis."

Frank jumped at the sound of her voice. *How did she sneak up on me like that? She moves like a damn cat.* She reached down with one hand into his cart and plucked out a protein bar, amused. "This is the worst bachelor meal I have ever seen. You don't eat like this every day, do you?" she laughed.

He took two awkward steps backwards, jerking the cart and bumping her as he did. "Sorry. I'm um . . . fasting."

Alexandra raised one eyebrow at him, and then glanced down to the vodka. *Shit.*

She reached down and pulled his white knuckles from the cart handles. Her hands were soft and smooth, but surprisingly strong. "I cannot allow this. Leave this horrible cart and come to dinner. Everyone in town thinks you are too high and mighty to take them up on their dinner invitations. Father Morgan made the rounds, you know. I don't think that man ever cooked for himself.

He certainly did make the rounds, Frank thought, remembering heaving his fat ass into the trunk of his own car, and reached up to rub the rock-shaped bruise on his shoulder.

"I don't know, I . . ." he started feebly.

"And Mrs. Blake is outraged, and Mrs. Potts is telling everyone it's because you think her beans are mealy," she continued like she didn't hear him. "You'll start a war. Come to my house for dinner tonight. I'll go easy on you."

"I'd love to, but you see, I . . ." he heard himself saying. *No. No, stupid. You're not having dinner with the widow tonight. You are scouring sector five again by the river. Be firm. Landmine. Do not jump headlong onto this landmine, you ass.*

"Come at seven," she said, pushing him out the door of the store. "And no more horrible carts, Father."

Frank walked, bewildered, back to the rectory. How had she done that? He was avoiding her, he was focusing, he was buying protein and booze, and next thing he knew, he'd agreed to dinner at her house. He wasn't quite sure he'd actually said yes. *Goddamn it, Frank. You're a dead man.*

He took a hasty shower in his room and shaved, wondering if the ancient Aqua Velva Father Morgan had left behind could be considered retro chic or if it was just dank, then scanned the dismal closet and its limited choices. *What passes for priest casual in this shit berg?* he mused, flicking through the hangers. He finally settled on a black sweater, his collar, and a pair of black pants. *I look pretty good,* he thought, trying to look at himself in the microscopic mirror. *Or at least, four square inches of me looks good at a time.* He shrugged and slid his sidearm and knives deep in the back of the closet. He wouldn't need them tonight. He ran his hands through his hair and eyed himself one last time in the mirror for a pep talk.

The only way to deal with this, Frank, is to bang the shit out of the fetching widow and get it out of your system. Then you can ditch this priest bullshit and just focus on the forest. Eat dinner, charm her out of her little corduroy jumper, get between those delicious little thighs, and disappear into the forest at dawn. Find Schwartz, and be rid of this town and her once and for all.

Except he did none of those things. The entire evening went nothing like that. She bewitched him from the moment he entered her little farmhouse. He sat, transfixed, in her cramped kitchen while she plied him with fried chicken, mashed potatoes, baby peas, wine, more wine, cheese, a brambleberry tart, vanilla ice cream, and coffee. She dipped and spun about the Spartan kitchen like a dancer, cooking and serving, putting the finishing touches on things, peppering him with funny stories about her class and the more eccentric inhabitants of the small town. The conversation was easy and non-threatening, charming and warm. Finally, full to bursting, he pushed back from the table and groaned.

"Good grief, how do you eat like this and stay so small?"

Alexandra thought for a moment, and then replied, "My daily walks? And chasing twenty five-year-olds around all day helps."

Frank gave her a crooked smile. "Maybe you have a tapeworm."

She shrugged. "Maybe."

"So, tell me, Alexandra. Have you always lived here in Lament?"

She shook her head. "No, I grew up in Detroit. As far away as you can imagine from New Hampshire."

"How did you end up here?"

"Oh, it's not a very interesting story, Father." She busied herself with her napkin, wiping up an invisible spot on the table.

"I'd still like to hear it."

She pushed her own chair back and propped her feet up on the rungs under his chair. Crossing her arms over her chest, she stared at him so long, he wondered if he'd upset her.

"Well, my father died when I was nineteen. Suddenly. And one thing led to another, a series of very unfortunate events, and I left town because of my job. And now I'm here."

"Why here?" *Why? Why on earth is such a magical crea-ture hiding herself away in this backwoods dump?*

Alexandra flushed and looked down at her feet. "Oh, the oldest reason in the world. A man."

Her husband. Poor bastard. Imagine landing this and then kicking it. She was twisting and wringing her hands in her lap, so he reached over and placed his hand over hers, holding them until they stilled under his firm pressure.

Alexandra let out a long sigh and looked up at the ceiling, shaking her head. "And now I'm a teacher. It's a good job and not a bad life, all around. And I must say, Father Francis," she said, her winsome grin returning, "you made quite the impression on my little ones the other day. They're like a different bunch of kids. Little Gwennie, especially. Evan better watch his back."

Frank flushed and shifted in his seat, carefully because he didn't want her to move her hands or feet. "It was nothing. And you can call me Frank. Father Frank. Only my mother calls me Francis."

Her eyes shone at him. "Well, *Father Frank*, it wasn't *nothing*. It's a big, mean world out there. They need all the confidence they can get. There's no nobility in being trusting and weak. More coffee?" she asked, rising suddenly and slipping her hands from his, leaving Frank acutely aware of their absence. *How long was I holding her hands? What were we even talking about? Oh, right. Kindergarten.*

"So, did you always want to be a teacher?" he asked, hoping to draw her back.

"Oh, I don't know. Sort of fell into it, I suppose." She sat back down, placing the coffee pot in the center of the table. She did not replace her feet on the rungs of Frank's chair, and he realized he was more consumed with getting her feet back where they had been or wrapping her hands in his than getting her into bed. *She's a witch. A goddamn north woods witch. I want to hold her hand and take her to a carnival. I want to kiss her on the cheek and tug on her hair. If she let me make love to her, I think it would kill me. I cannot think of a single solitary way this ends well.*

"I thought about being a lot of things, like a writer or a barista," she laughed, oblivious to his misery, "or a Skeeball wizard. But then my father died, and next thing I knew, I had no choice but to support myself."

"As a teacher. In Lament, New Hampshire." *Ridiculous. Random. Wrong. There was something wrong about this whole story, something . . . .*

Alexandra nodded, her eyes downcast. "Anyway, enough of my tale of woe. Tell me about you. How does one become a—what did Mrs. Blake call you the other day? An amateur priest?"

Frank laughed. "Is that what the old battle axe is calling me?"

Her eyes widened at his slip, then she immediately looked down to her lap. Frank groaned inwardly. *Shit. Too much wine, you're getting sloppy.* Alexandra continued to study her hands, but he caught the tinge of red on her cheeks and knew she was biting back her own laughter.

"This was after you skipped the Gospel at the noon Mass." She squinted up at him, clearly delighted. *That face. Right there. How do I keep that expression on her face forever?*

"Well, I guess she's not far off. It's a long story."

"Cognac?" she offered, eyes twinkling.

"I really shouldn't." *Just one. One can't hurt.*

"Oh, I think you should."

––––––––

By the time Frank finished his cognac, Alexandra had teased out of him a white-washed version of his past— heavily edited, of course, but far too close to the truth than was safe. He felt the words flowing out of him effortlessly under her sparkling gaze. It was all a game of nouns, really. For every lie, you make sure there's a kernel of truth.

So the military became the seminary, a tiny white lie here, a glossing over there, and he realized he'd told her the closest thing to the truth about his past that he had ever told anyone. Before he knew it, she'd wrestled a promise out of him to return to kindergarten duty, and somehow he found himself offering to do the dishes for her while she graded some papers the next day. And he hadn't even banged her. Well, he almost banged her. But then something horrible, something unspeakable, something never before in his entire life happened while he was washing the dishes.

He was elbows-deep in soapy water, grimly scrubbing the frying pan, when Alexandra slid up silently next to him and began drying the plates. He didn't look over to her, but instead shut his eyes and felt her closeness, smelled her perfume, something Asian that made him think of Thai food and sex with just the edge of machine oil—*that's probably coming off you, you murderous scum*—the sound of the plates clinking softly together while she stacked them. Her voice, when it came, startled him out of his reverie.

"It's so nice having someone here. You know, at the end of the day. It gets lonely. This life." She continued drying, but he heard the edge of a tremble in her voice that sent a tremor through his knees.

Frank turned the water off and took the towel from her hands. With one hand he tipped her face up to his and used the towel to dry her tears. Before he knew it, he'd kissed her, was kissing her, her lips sweet like cookie dough, clutching her like a dying man. Her small, lithe body was pliant in his hands, and in a delicious, terrifying moment, he knew she trusted him, somehow. That she felt safe with him, him of all people, a cold-blooded murderer, a heartless assassin. Fast on the heels of this revelation came a smothering cloud of sickening guilt over what he was doing.

Was he really such a piece of shit that he'd try to bang a widowed kindergarten teacher—this luminous sweet, kind creature—knowing he was just using her? *Never mind she thinks you're a priest. God. You are a monster, Frank. You need to get out of this line of work. You have lost all conscience.*

And so Frank did something unprecedented, unspeakable, something entirely out of character for him. He pulled back. He gently untangled himself from her arms, kissed her forehead one more time, and left in silence, her sad eyes following him all the way back to the rectory.

That was the noblest thing I have ever done. Not my finest hour, he thought miserably the next day. *I should just put a bullet in my own head. This. This is how it all ends. My illustrious, shady career. It ends at the hands of a nymph in rain boots.*

Chapter Five

*F*rank was sitting at his desk the next day, trying to look busy, pious, and not like a lovesick school-boy, while Mrs. Blake dusted around him. Horrified, he heard himself blurt out, "How did the Widow Winters' husband die?" *Oh, my God. Listen to me. I sound like a seventh-grade girl.*

Mrs. Blake clutched her brooch at his sudden outburst and exclaimed, "Bless me! I don't know, Father. It's none of my business." She eyed him suspiciously again. "Why ever would you ask me that?"

Frank's eyes narrowed. *Wait. What does she mean, she doesn't know?* "What do you mean, you don't know?" he barked, sending Mrs. Blake into paroxysms of brooch clutching. "How can you not know literally everything about her? Alexandra Winters has lived here for a while, right? I've been here three weeks, and I know how many of Isaiah Bishop's goats go mad in the square every year!"

Mrs. Blake let out a snort, released her brooch and resumed dusting. "That one? She showed up here a few weeks before you did. And it's none of my never mind what happened to her husband." She paused to give him another disapproving sniff and then sailed out of the room. *No doubt to take her high road straight to the other guild members and tell them how Father Frank was asking after the fair widow.*

He stormed to the door and slammed it shut behind her, ripping his collar off as he did. While he changed into his gear, an explosive volley of obscenities echoed in the small office.

Fucking idiot. Stupid. He jerked his black face mask on. *Old. Sloppy.* He was a stupid ass. It was her. The girl. He'd been looking for Schwartz, but had found—and made out with—Schwartz's gal Friday, the secretary. Alexandra Winters. *Oh, she was good.* Frank jammed his knife in his boot, slid his holster over his shoulders, then slipped into his tactical vest. *Think, moron. Last night.* He replayed the evening in his mind. She'd told him almost nothing about herself. *No more than you told her. And where was Schwartz?* He shut his eyes and mentally scanned each room in the farmhouse. Bare. They were all bare of anything personal. No pictures, no clutter, nothing on the fridge. *Shit. I've lost my edge. I should have seen her coming a mile away. I was too busy trying to smell her perfume.*

Perfume. Wait just one fucking minute. That smell in the air. It was machine oil—he'd bet his soul on it. And it hadn't been coming off him. Someone else had beaten him there, which would explain the machine oil smell in the kitchen. Probably one of the fucking Russians, casing the joint, lying in wait for her. *Oh shit. Fuck Schwartz, where was Alexandra right now?* He had to find her, and fast. How on earth had a creature like her ended up with a nasty old toady like Schwartz? It didn't add up. Didn't wash. She was heaven, and Schwartz was . . . Schwartz was a chemical toilet.

He was missing something here. Something big. Something was off. And he'd been too busy trying to get laid to zero in on it. He glanced at the clock. Recess time. The woods. *I have to get to her before they do.*

———

Frank spied Alexandra's yellow boots about two miles in, downriver. She was heading toward the abandoned mill-house, oblivious that he had stalked her for the last half-mile. He waited until she disappeared through the old wooden door, then followed her, feeling sicker inside than he had the night before.

She was standing near the old mill wheel, gazing down into the slushy water, and didn't hear him slip inside. Her yellow boots had been cast to one side, and she now wore thin, black knee boots. Frank slipped his face mask off and let it fall to the ground, a sinking feeling in his chest at the sight of her.

"Alexandra," he said in a low voice.

"Father Frank!" she cried, startled. "What are you . . . what are you . . . dressed up for?" she finished, her face at first confused as she took in his black ops tactical gear, eyes widening when she saw the gun in his hand.

"Shh . . . shh, Alexandra. I won't hurt you. Don't be afraid."

"Why did you follow me?" she asked, stepping away from the opening in the floor and walking backwards away from him. "What's happening?"

"Alexandra, I haven't been honest with you." *That's the understatement of the century, Frank. Hey, I'm not a priest, more like an international covert ops assassin type, no biggie. Let's make out. I might have to kill you.* He crossed the room to her, hands held up but still gripping the gun.

"No, Father," she said, shaking her head and looking up at him tearfully. "I haven't been completely honest with you."

He reached down and tentatively took one of her small hands in his, dropping his gun to his side.

"You haven't been here more than a couple weeks, have you?"

Eyes downcast, she shook her head.

"You're Schwartz's girlfriend."

"How do you know that name?" Her voice trembled, and he felt sick to his stomach.

"Listen, Alexandra, you are in terrible danger. I'm not a priest. I'm a bad man. I do bad things. And other people—bad people, Alexandra—are looking for you. If I found my way here, someone else will, too. The Israelis, or God help you, the Russians. And they're not all as nice as I am." He clutched her hands. They were so small. "They'll hurt you, Alexandra, in ways I can't bear to think about, to get to him. Let me help you."

"There's no way to help me. You know there's no way out for someone like me," she whispered.

"Please, you have to listen to me. I know it sounds crazy, but I care about you, Alexandra. I've never felt this way before. It's a horrible feeling, like someone is taking a hatchet to my ribcage every time I look at you. You're everything I said I never wanted, but I'd walk away from it all, all of it, for you. Please, Alexandra. Let me help you."

She pulled her hands from his and turned away, but before she did, he caught a flash in her eyes, a glistening at the corners. She stumbled away from him, shoulders hunched as if she were crying again. He crossed the room to her, dropping his gun to the floor as he did, the cold steel shell around his heart cracking as well.

"Alexandra, I can keep you safe. I promise. I have a unique set of skills. I can make you disappear. Just tell me everything you know, and I'll get you out of here." He ran his hand down the back of her hair. "Together. We can leave all this together. Fuck my job, fuck this case. It's not worth it anymore. Maybe it never was."

Her shoulders jerked upright then, and he could have sworn he heard her make a sound suspiciously like a snort.

The next thing he knew, she whirled around on him, striking his neck like a cobra with the side of her hand, and pistol-whipping him with the other. *Jesus, is that a 9mm Makarov?* he thought as he dropped like a bag of sand at her feet, just before she kicked him in the jaw with what he, too late, remembered was an Israeli tactical boot. *You can tell by the soles—the rubber is thinner than the Italian model. Huh.*

"I'll keep myself safe, thank you very much." He heard her laugh as everything went black.

Chapter Six

The snake of pain in Frank's head told him not to open his eyes. He did anyway, not so much to see where he was—freezing on the floor of the old mill-house—but to see if he could figure out what his legs were bound with—Hojo Cord—and what was stuffed in his mouth gagging him. It tasted like sweat and wool. His hands were bound behind his back but he could just move his fingers to feel the binding. *That's interesting.* He crossed his eyes and saw she'd gagged him with his own ski mask. *Nice. Shit. I'm a fucking cock-blind idiot.*

He looked up and saw Alexandra standing over him, grinning like a cat. He tried to smile back through his gag as his head spun with a tumult of feelings. *Murderous rage. Self-loathing. Grudging admiration.*

"Mmnoof urfgh ommmgh," he mumbled winningly. *Well, winningly for someone who just got his ass handed to him.*

"Good morning, sunshine," Alexandra beamed down at him. "Now let's try this again." She yanked the ski mask from his mouth. "You tell me everything."

Frank spat a mouthful of lint out before replying. "You're good."

"Only compared to some." She squatted down in front of him, just out of his reach, a fixed blade knife in her hand. *Not that I could reach her, trussed up like this.*

He wiggled his shoulders again to take a better inventory of his situation. *Nice.*

"*Ushiro Takatekote?*" he asked, jerking his chin down at his arms.

She nodded.

"Where did you learn traditional Japanese bondage? Kinky."

"Flattery will get you a shrimp tie. Actually, I considered doing that last night. But I wasn't sure torture was necessary. You're such a cupcake, Francis." She reached over and pinched his cheek.

"Wait. You *tried* to get me to bang you. What the hell? Whatever happened to honor among thieves and all that?"

"Um, I think you tried to bang me first. I just went along. Always kinda wanted to tap a priest. Hot."

"How did you make me?" He found the first knot with one finger.

"I made you right away, pretty boy. New priest who just happens to be cut like a brick shit house and likes to teach the elementary school kids hand-to-hand combat?" She snickered at him. "Which agency are you with?"

Frank grinned at her and tried to get his fingers threaded through the knot. *Shit. She is really good at this. Just loose enough to give me hope. She is worse than a landmine. She's a goddamn aircraft carrier full of daisy cutters.* He leaned back against the wall and gave up on the rope. "Well, if you are who I think you are, you know there's all kinds of agencies, Alexandra. Three-letter agencies, two-letter agencies. Hell, there's even a one-letter agency, although in all honesty, those guys are major douches. And then there are the agencies with no acronym. I'm the latter."

"Am I supposed to be impressed?"

He tried to shrug, fairly certain it looked like a small seizure. "Most people are. But then I'm not usually the one bound and gagged when they figure that out."

"Poor Francis. It's a drag getting old. How old are you anyway? Don't they put guys your age out to pasture?" Alexandra rocked back on her heels when he kicked his feet at her and missed.

His lips curled up as he spat, "None of your goddamn business, sweetheart. How old are you?" *And how in the name of God did someone your age get the drop on me? Me!*

"Twenty-eight. Ouch, that must smart. What are you, about fifty, Frank?"

"I am not *fifty*! Jesus, I'm barely forty! That's not even middle-aged!"

She made a tutting sound with her teeth, eyes gleaming at his sputtering outrage. "Just keep telling yourself that. Anyway, I rolled into town weeks before you and tracked Schwartz down. So much for your lack of acronym, Grandpa."

"But how did you get the whole town in on your cover?"

"Oh, I breezed in all cuteness and light. Introduced myself as a widow." She began digging into the splintered wood floor with the knife. "Widowed schoolteacher tests through the roof. Can't believe you didn't guess. Whole town took three days to fall in love with me and form a shield around the delicate Widow Alex and her big, sad eyes."

"So what happened to Schwartz?"

Alexandra gestured over to the opening in the floor around the base of the watermill. "He's chilling."

"As in?"

"As in I killed him on day one after I joined the altar guild and shoved his body down in the water under the mill. I caught him coming out of the confessional. I figure I have until spring to find the diamond. If my people give me that long. And then with a little luck, I am out. Out of this whole shit show." An anxious expression played across the planes of her downturned face.

"You killed Schwartz," he said, the blood draining from his face.

"You're not going to faint, are you? Did I tie those too tight?" she said, peering at him.

"No, they're perfect, actually. It's almost a pleasure to be tied up by you. It's just . . . my job was to bring him in. Alive."

"Awkward," she said, squatting on her heels.

"Well, there's always the girlfriend."

She pointed the tip of her knife at him.

"What girlfriend?"

Frank grinned but didn't reply.

"I said, what girlfriend?" She held the knife up to his neck, sliding the tip down until it rested in the hollow of his throat.

"What are you going to do? Kill me like you killed Schwartz?"

Alexandra swore and threw the knife across the room, where it stuck in the wall, quivering. Then she rose, gave his leg a savage kick, and began pacing.

"Listen, I don't know what no-letter agency you work for, but the people I work for don't accept failure very well. At all." She wrenched the knife from the wall and whirled back to him.

"That's not really my problem," Frank spat.

"Where is the girlfriend, Father Francis?"

"Why?"

"I need her."

"I need her more."

"Do you think she has the diamond?"

"What diamond?"

Alexandra sank to the floor in front of him and crossed her legs. She ignored him in silence but threw him the occasional glance while she continued to carve into the wood. He waited and watched until she'd finished most of a crude hangman, and then he broke.

"Fine. I represent an organization that wants Schwartz and his gal Friday strictly for information to nail the people you probably work for. Why are you here?"

"I want the diamond Schwartz was carrying when he ran off."

She groaned at the blank look on his face.

"Imagine the Hope Diamond, pretty boy, but uncut. And bigger. He took it and ran, and my employers want it back. They give a shit about Schwartz and his bimbo. And that diamond is my ticket out of this whole mess."

"Listen, if you work for the people I think you work for, there is no out. You know that."

She flashed him a frigid glare. "That's not really your problem, either. Where is the girlfriend?"

He grinned at her again but remained silent.

"Well, goddamn it, Frank." She crawled over to him, straddled his lap, and held the knife to his face. *Oh God. Do I want to kill her? Let her kill me? Let her bang me then kill me? All of the above. I'll go with all of the above.*

"Cross me once, and I'll show you the other things I learned to do in Japan. Understand me, Francis?" She kissed him on the nose, then reached behind him and slashed through his ropes. He pushed her off him and stood, stretching the soreness from his muscles.

"You really killed Schwartz?"

She sneered at him and scrambled to her feet. "See for yourself."

Frank stared at the opening in the mill floor and gazed into the frigid water. Deep at the bottom of the near-freezing lake under the mill, he could just make out the bloated corpse of Eustace Schwartz, accountant. He squinted through the slush. *Garrote. Nice. Up close and personal. Interesting.*

He turned around to face her, pushing down the marry-fuck-kill lottery going on in his head. *Enough. Do your fucking job before she garrotes you, too, dumbass.*

"Outstanding. Now let's get looking."

"Together?" she asked, surprised.

"Why not? Honor among thieves and all that, right?"

He bent as if to tie his boot, but instead fumbled with his laces and checked to see she hadn't taken his knife. His fingers brushed the knife handle in his boot. *Nice. She'd missed it. Amateur hour was over.* He looked up at her and smiled. *This actually simplifies things. No more wide-eyed doe.* He felt more like his old self again.

"And stop calling me Francis, Alexandra."

"And you can stop it with that Alexandra shit. My name is Alex."

He crossed the room and held his hand out. She returned her knife to the sheath on the small of her back.

"Pleasure to meet you, Alex. I'm Frank. Frank Brennan."

She held her hand out warily. "The pleasure is all—" Her words cut off as he swept his leg behind her, knocking her on her ass, and then raised his foot to stomp her chest. *Sorry, sweetheart. It's just business.*

But she was too fast for him. She rolled even as she hit the mill floor, vaulted up into a handstand that he would have whistled at if she hadn't kicked him square in his ear and flipped back to her feet.

He clutched his ringing ear and advanced on her again. "Nimble," he accused.

"Lucky for me," Alex spat at him, along with a mouthful of blood, and backed away.

Frank bent and pulled his knife out. It felt strangely light in his hand. *Adrenalin. And some sort of weird, one-sided sexual tension. Finish this and throw her under the mill with Schwartz.* "You're really cute, Alex, but you're way out of your league with me. I'll make this quick and painless. Mostly because that fried chicken was delicious."

She backed into the wall, hands scrambling behind her to grasp an old shovel handle that was leaning there. "What are you gonna do? Throw that at me?" she purred, crouching and brandishing the stick.

Frank looked down. *Son of a bitch. She'd broken the blade off his knife and slipped it back in his boot.* "Maybe," he shrugged, then launched the heavy composite handle at her forehead, barely nicking her as she spun away. She cartwheeled the stick as she did, a triumphant "ha" escaping her lips. But he spun with her, kicking her in the back, knocking her to her knees, the "ha" evaporating into a grunt of frustration. He reached out to grab her, but she drove the stick up into his groin and circled away, still on her knees. Then she rolled backwards across the room with the stick, leaving him clutching himself in agony where he'd fallen.

Alex stood panting across the room, stick raised as high as her sardonic eyebrow. "On your feet, Frankie boy."

Biting back the bile in his throat—she's favoring that shoulder—he vaulted back to his feet.

"Huh. Stick fighting. Never did get around to learning that." He grinned, then ran at her, her stick barely connecting with him as he spun into a volley of roundhouse kicks, each blow hitting her left shoulder, the last finally catching her in the jaw. She staggered back as he sent one more vicious kick at her chest, his boot snapping the shovel handle in two. She spat another mouthful of blood, this time at the floor, and grinned at him between her bloody teeth. "Thanks, now I have two."

Frank ran at her again, aiming for her weakened left shoulder with a sharp downward chop. Her arm collapsed, and the stick fell from her spasming fingers, giving him just enough opportunity to ram her into the wall, pinning her. She kicked and spat at him like a Siamese. He was pretty sure she'd have clawed his eyes out, too, if he hadn't been able to capture first one hand, then the other, and wrench them up over her head.

He pulled her up the wall until her eyes were level with his. His were calm and cold, hers were feral. She kicked at him, so he pulled her up higher and pushed the length of his body against hers. *Holy mother of God, who are you, Alexandra Winters?*

She spat something sharp at his face and grinned, blood dribbling down her chin. "Your boys must not be hurting too bad." She ground her pelvis into his, against the hardness that grew there. "You seem to be enjoying yourself."

He shook whatever she'd spat off his face. "What was that? Tooth?" he whispered in her ear, blood racing.

"Filling. You caught me good with that last kick." She sighed, her breath on his neck.

"What do you think, Alex? We even now?" Frank slid his jaw across hers and kissed the spot just behind her ear. She smelled like Play-Doh and machine oil. *Son of a bitch. She's the attaché, the prostitute and the kindergarten teacher all rolled up in one. The kind of girl you can bang on the rocket slide or the feather bed, depending on the day of the week. Shit.*

"Yeah, we're good. Enough foreplay. I'll show you mine if you show me yours," Alex whispered, slipping her tongue in his ear. He rammed her against the wall again as she wrapped her legs around his waist. *Worse. This was so much worse than the angelic schoolteacher.*

"Maps?" he said, releasing her hands and letting her drop to the ground.

"Of course maps. What did you think I meant?"

Alex stood and stepped toward him, sliding one hand behind her back until a fierce scowl replaced the smirk on her face.

"Looking for this?" Frank tossed her knife up in the air and caught it by the blade.

She swore.

"You're a sneaky little minx, aren't you?" He laughed, then threw it at the opposite wall, about twelve feet up. "Enough recess, Widow Winters. Let's find that bimbo and the rock."

Chapter Seven

The old mill shuddered, the bracing wind of the driving, freezing rain shaking it to its foundation. Alex smoothed her map out on the floor next to Frank's, her hangman carving on the floor between them.

"How about that? We were working in almost concentric circles to each other. How did I not see you?" she murmured, as her fingers slid across the damp, wrinkled map, tapping each crossed-off site.

Frank frowned and began crossing her sites off on his map with a black marker. "How did I not at least see your footprints?" he said, scratching his head. "Well, I did see those boots of yours once." He jerked his chin across the room at the yellow boots. "Hard to miss. But it was dark and I was in my blackout gear, so I doubt you saw me."

"Oh, right. The boots." She looked up across the map, eyes flashing. "Not very covert. But I needed them."

He threw the marker down and sat back. "Why?"

She unfolded her legs and stretched them out across the maps, her legs spread wide as she bent in half to touch her toes. "I had to keep my climbing boots dry and clean."

He tilted his head at her. "Climbing boots?"

"Thin, grippy soles. I was working the treetops between each cabin. I figured he hid the diamond in one of them. I would have."

"No footprints." His face lit up. "Clever girl."

She leaned forward even more. "Want to know a secret?"

Frank leaned into her and tapped the toes of her boots with his fingertips. "Oh, I want to know all your secrets."

"Those are Schwartz's boots."

"Why do I find it weirdly attractive that you stole a dead man's boots and wore them to teach kindergarten?" he whispered back. *Jesus, she's like a puzzle box.*

Alex reached out and ran a hand through his hair, smoothing it back off his face, the scowl returning briefly as a stubborn hank of his hair fell back over his eyes.

"Everyone has their kink, I guess." *Look. Mine's sitting across from me sporting a fat lip I gave her,* Frank thought wryly. *I guess all that 'God works in mysterious ways' crap was spot on.*

He untangled her hand from his hair and fanned her fingers out across his palm. "And there I was thinking you had the smallest, softest hands I'd ever seen."

Alex grabbed his wrist, turned his arm over, and slipped her hand over his arm and inside his shirt. "I'm not even going to tell you what I thought about your arms, Frank. I mean, fair play, you did make a hell of an impression in that priest collar." She raised that one brow at him. "I almost threw you down on the playground and had you on the monkey bars. Would have scarred those kids for life."

"Rocket slide," he whispered.

"What?" she asked. "I didn't catch that." She leaned closer to him, her ear a fraction of an inch from his lips.

"Nothing," he said, breathing in her scent again. *Sugar and spice and everything nice, with a wicked edge of machine oil. That's better than Thai food and sex.* "I'm not keen to go out in this bullshit weather. You?"

She drew away from him, pulling her knees to her chest, and shook her head. "Fuck that. I say we wait it out. Blow cover tomorrow. I can't do one more day in that school, and you are the worst priest ever, Father Brennan. Tomorrow morning, we hit here," she stabbed her finger into his map, "here and here."

Frank nodded and then stretched out, sprawling on his side, and looked at her for a while. She met his gaze without wavering, her expression unreadable.

"So, how did you get recruited?" he asked finally.

She shook her head and snorted. "Is this where we share our war stories, pretty boy? Forget it."

"I'm not trying to distract you with my verbal sleight of hand. I'm just passing the time, Alex. It's not often two people like us meet and don't kill each other."

Alex glared at him. "What would be the point? I mean, technically, we're both nothing more than accomplished liars. And even if we told each other the truth, wouldn't we just use it to ultimately betray one another? Or do they not teach you that at your acronym-less agency?"

"Fine," he groaned. "I'll go first. What I told you last night was mostly true." He glanced over at her in time to see her roll her eyes. "I'm ex-military. Special forces. Wasn't all that keen on rejoining society. The whole assassin gig is a slippery slope. First, they have you taking out compounds, then you blink and next thing you know you're capping military dictators in their hot tubs. Did a couple jobs in the Middle East, couple more in South East Asia. Next thing you know, I don't have a name anymore, and if I die, I won't even get a star on the wall like those NSA bastards. I'll spend my life in service and die alone. It's not that far off from the priesthood. You know the old liar's adage; 'A kernel of truth in every lie'." Frank yawned. "You?"

She stretched out on her stomach and perched her chin on her fists.

"My father. I mean, that much was true." Her eyes dimmed. "He made a deal with them. Stupid, wonderful, sweet old man, thought he could deal with those Russian monsters once and walk, right?" She wiped her eyes. "Anyway, deal goes south, job goes belly up, daddy dearest fucks it all up, and they give his one and only a chance to do the job for him and save his life." She shook her head. "So I did the job. That was that. Here we are."

"But you saved your father's life. That's noble. What I do isn't noble."

"No, Frank. I did the job, then they sent me his head in a box and gave me another job. There's a word for that, and it ain't noble, sunshine."

"Jesus, Alex. But how did you . . . ?" His voice trailed off while his mind filled with images of the years of intensive training he'd gone through to become the perfect weapon.

She looked back up at him, his eyes fathomless again. "I figured it out on my own. On-the-job training." She looked back to the dark, rain-splattered window. "I guess you could say I'm adaptable."

I'll bet you are, he thought. *No training and you nearly kicked my ass.*

She sat up abruptly and crossed her legs. "And now every day is one last job. Isn't that what we tell ourselves, Frank? Isn't that the catechism of people like us? Except there is no last job, right?"

Frank nodded slowly. "Too many loose ends." He sat up and swung his legs around, crossing his own knees so they were almost touching hers. "So what went wrong with your dad?"

She sighed and started scratching into the floor of the mill with her thumbnail. "It was stupid. Dumb. He was just a mule, right? He delivers a package, gets a package, takes it to the Russians, walks away with enough money to square his debts. It should have been easy money. But while he was waiting for the meet . . ." She shook her head. "It's so random. And stupid."

"What happened?" he asked, voice thick with concern.

"I went to high school with this douchebag named Mark. I barely knew the guy, outside of the fact that I have firsthand knowledge that he sees sex as payment for pizza and Skee-ball." She shook her head and held both hands up. "Not telling that story, so don't ask. Anyway, Mark happens by. He recognizes my dad and calls out to him. 'Hey, Mr. Winters. Tell Alex I said hi.' Except the guys he was meeting thought he said 'Alexei' and freaked."

"I've heard of Alexei. I'd freak, too. He's a butcher. That Tokyo job." He shivered. "Gruesome even for him."

"Yeah. The whole deal went south, and next thing I know, the top half of dad gets FedExed to me and I'm indentured to a bunch of Eurotrash. Thanks, Mark."

Alex looked back over at him, her eyes luminous in the dim light. "This is boring. Want to practice knots? I can teach you that arm tie." She reached down into a pocket of her cargo pants and pulled out another bundle of rope. "Can you do a good rope cuff? Mine sucks."

Frank took the rope from her as she held her wrists out. "Allow me, my lady."

His fingers moved fast, creating a simple slipknot around each of her wrists, pulled it tight, then began winding it.

"See? It's a quick twist with the thumb. Need me to do it again?" he asked.

She shook her head.

"Fine. Then get out of it, tough stuff." He laughed, tying off the ends.

She grinned at him and began working her fingers in the rope, her eyes never leaving his.

"What?" she mumbled, her teeth biting into the Hojo Cord.

"What do you mean 'what'? And no teeth. That's cheating."

She stuck her tongue out at him. "Why are you looking at me like that?"

"I'm trying to imagine you in high school."

She flushed. "Not much to imagine. I was underwhelming."

"I doubt that. What did you like to do back then? Before all this."

She wrinkled her nose. "Skee-ball," she said, embarrassed. "I played a lot of Skee-ball."

"You like Skee-ball," he repeated.

"Yeah. A lot. It's relaxing. You like Skee-ball?" she asked, tilting her head like one of the kindergartners.

"I don't know how to play Skee-ball," he said, distracted. "You'll never get out that way." His forehead pleated in frustration while he studied her hands. "You're going about it all backwards."

She screwed her nose up at him, thoughts playing across her face, then shifted her efforts, biting her lip in concentration.

"Now you've got it," he said admiringly. "Well, what did you do before all of this?"

"Oh, there barely was a 'before this.' I never made it past my first year of college."

"And that's when . . ." he said, squinting at her.

"Dad's head. Box." She shrugged.

"What were you going to do, Alex?"

"Doesn't matter."

"Sure it matters."

"I don't know. I never got a chance to think about it. Teacher. Barista. Skee-ball champ." She laughed and dropped her bound hands into her lap. "Writer? Or maybe I was meant to be a mercenary. Who knows?"

"Writer? You?" he repeated, his voice skeptical.

"Sure, why not?"

"Give up?" he said, tugging on her hair where it fell across her chest.

"Never. But you see, Frank, it doesn't matter. It's like," she sat up on her knees, her hands writhing and twisting in the rope. "Something happens to you, and it's game over. It's like pinball. You're sailing along and then bam. You hit the flapper and get sent off in a totally different trajectory. So everything you could have been doesn't exist anymore. You're just this new thing, and all of that dies."

"I don't think that's true at all. All of this, this job, this life. It doesn't change who you are in here." He tapped her forehead. "Deep down, you're still the same person inside. All that potential. All that goodness. It's all still in there. It's just . . ."

She held her hands up. "Tied up?"

"Yeah, you just have to find that loose end." Frank stared into her eyes for a long moment, and he knew that somehow the fragile little schoolteacher was in there.

Hell, maybe the barista was, too. A million different variations of her and every one of them was his personal poison.

Alex put her bound hands on his calves and leaned in. He heard her take a deep breath and then she kissed him soft on his lips, so soft he could barely feel it. Her hands tightened on his calves as she let her breath out.

"Are you kissing me or the priest?"

"Both, I think."

"You're right," he said, kissing her back. He slipped his hands around her wrists.

"I'm right about what?" she purred, biting his lip.

"That *is* enough foreplay," he said, pushing her over on her back. He caught her head before it hit the ground, then yanked her hands up over her head, pinning them. Reaching back into his boot, he pulled another knife out and slipped it between his teeth.

"Hey, no fair. What happened to *détente*? And how many knives do you have in those boots, anyway?" She stretched her legs out and rubbed one of her shins between his legs, the other wrapped around him. He ignored her teasing and held her arms up over her head with one hand, while he drove the knife into the center of her rope cuffs, pinning her.

Frank kissed each of her bound wrists, and then her eyelids, and finally her lips.

"There. Now hold still. You're too squirmy."

She raised an eyebrow at him. "I think I need a safety word, Father Francis."

He kissed her again, his lips sliding down to her neck. "Hey, what about me?"

"Are you really worried I'll hurt you?" she whispered, glancing up at her hands.

He fixed her with his eyes, his brow furrowed. "I'm fairly certain you're going to."

She craned her neck up, and her lips found a spot on his neck just below his ear. "How about 'please'?"

"That's a problematic safety word, Alex."

"Tough," she purred.

"That one's worse," he growled.

He braced himself above her, his knees straddling her hips, and kissed one side of her neck, slowly working his way to the other. He took her earlobe between his teeth, then pulled her shirt to one side, his lips and tongue tracing the line of her collarbone. Threading his fingers through her hair, he settled himself on top of her and kissed her lips again, his tongue gently parting them, kissing her deeper as he trailed his hands down her shirt and her cargo pants, gripping her hips and pulling her up against him. She arched her back and let out a grunt of frustration when she tried to pull her hands free.

"Stop squirming," he whispered.

"But I want to—"

He put a finger over her lips. "Tough."

Alex let her head fall back, her eyes closed tight. He watched her for a moment. She was holding her breath.

Frank pushed her arched back down to the floor and spread her legs with his, grinding his pelvis into her slowly, forcefully. He grazed her neckline down to her breast, his thumb and forefinger rolling her hardened nipple between them while he bit her lower lip. A soft moan fell from between her lips into his, and he grabbed her waist, tracing a long line down her center until he found another spot with his thumb that made her thrash under him.

"Jesus, Frank," she gasped.

He clamped his mouth down over hers and pulled her hips against him, her legs wrapped around him, and he pushed against her hard—harder—trying to stay just ahead of her frantic pants until she broke free of the ropes and wrapped her arms around him. He let out a cry, she whispered his name, then he collapsed on top of her, breathless and incredulous. *It's like junior high all over again.* After a moment he rolled off her and unwound the rest of the ropes off her wrist, looking a little shamefaced.

"Where did you learn *that*, Father Brennan?" Alex turned his face to her, her voice catching.

"When I was fifteen in the back of Susie Masterson's dad's car." He could feel his face flushing.

"Wow. Where were you when I was fifteen? All I got was Skee-ball and a slice of pizza off my dates."

"I just didn't want to take advantage."

She ran one hand across his jaw and pulled him back down to her.

"I mean, you're alone out here with me. We've already tried to kill each other tonight. I don't want you to think you have to have sex with me to survive the night. I'm not that guy." *Wait, I am that guy. I'm totally that guy. But not with you. So I just dry humped you because I had no idea what else to do.*

"You know what, Father Brennan?" Her lips were against his ear.

"What's that, Widow Winters?"

"I think you might be a really nice guy. You know, aside from the assassin business. Deep down in there. That's a dangerous combination, mister." She tapped his forehead. "What were you going to be before all this?"

"Not a priest, that's for damn sure." Frank rolled off her and pulled her back against his side. "Now go to sleep, tough stuff. We have a long day tomorrow. And please don't kill me in my sleep. You damn near wore me out the last few days."

She wrapped one arm around his chest and drew her knee up over his stomach. "I'll try."

"Please," he asked, his voice an inexplicable mix of exasperated and elated.

He could feel Alex's silent laughter against his chest in the dark millhouse, and thought he heard her say, "Tough" before the gentle lapping of the lake underneath lulled him to sleep.

Chapter Eight

They left before dawn the next morning. The woods around the old millhouse were laced with thick fog, the ground a soggy swamp from the night's rains. They trudged in silence through the agreed-upon route, professional masks firmly in place after an alarming amount of early morning tenderness and awkwardness. They made their way along the river, searching for tracks, sweeping every shuttered hunting lodge and shack. But no trace of Schwartz's girlfriend.

"Does this girlfriend have a name?" Alex asked, breaking the silence.

Frank rolled his eyes. "Does it matter?"

She shrugged. "Point taken." Then she stopped abruptly and squatted.

He knelt beside her. "Well, that's bad," he said shortly. *Russians.*

She nodded and picked up the *Sobranie* Black Russian cigarette butt.

"You're not kidding. You could start a forest fire this way." She looked up at him, the careful mask gone, her eyes now wide and terrified.

"Why are they here, Alex?" he whispered.

She looked down at the cigarette butt as she shredded it between her fingers. "You know as well as I do. They've lost faith in me. They've abandoned my finesse approach and have decided to bring the sledgehammer. They will level this town and every single adorable old lady and kindergartner in it to find what they want. And I'm a dead woman."

She stood and brushed her hands off on her black pants. "The smart thing for you to do would be to get out of town. Now. I'll go find them and stall them. Shouldn't be too hard. Alexei probably sent his usual goon squad." She stopped talking while she slipped a hair band from her wrist into her mouth, then used both hands to work her hair up into a tight bun. "Twenty or so ex-Soviet military. Clumsy but vicious."

Frank reached over and stayed her hands. "Alexei?"

She flushed and looked down. "Of course. Who else would be sick enough to mail a head? Just go. Don't try to be a knight in shining armor, Frank."

"Alex, I . . ." He stopped, sniffing the air suddenly. He pushed her out of his way and walked a few feet north, then east, whipping around to the west.

"What is it?" she whispered.

"Smoke. Wood smoke." He pointed across the river. "That way." He grinned at her. "Better shimmy up that tree. I think we found us a bimbo. And with a little luck, she's got that rock."

Eyes gleaming, Alex hoisted herself up into the nearest soaring oak, kicking the yellow boots off as she did.

Her nimble feet found purchase where he saw none, and her fingers scrambled in the bark like a free climber. She kept climbing until Frank began to worry about the way the slender limbs bent and swayed, and then she disappeared from sight entirely.

Three long minutes, and then she reappeared, sliding down the trunk like a monkey. She landed with a flourish in front of him and pointed behind him. "That way. Two miles, give or take."

"You're amazing. Sure it's not the Russians?" he asked.

She shook her head. "Not unless the Russians started hanging Lycra and spandex out to dry. In the rain. In the woods. Like a dumbass. If that's not a city bimbo, I don't know what is. Let's go, Frank."

She sprinted off, her thin, light boots barely sinking in the muddy earth, her own black gear making her look like a black arrow flying toward a target. Frank took a deep breath and gave himself a few seconds to admire her departure, and then raced after her.

Chapter Nine

"This is a hell of a lot farther than two miles, Winters." Frank wiped a hand across his eyes, streaking more mud when he did.

It was a downpour. They were drenched, mud-spattered, and shivering in the middle of the White Mountains National Forest. While they could smell the smoke, they didn't appear to be getting any closer to it.

"Shit," she spat, wiping more mud on her already muck-slick pants. "It's this fucking topography. Mountains, river, hills, forest. It screws with my line of sight. Maybe another mile?" She glared down at her mud-caked boots in disgust.

"Alex, we've come at least four miles. And this downpour is getting worse." He wiped the rivers of rain from his face again and scanned the woods. "If I remember correctly, there's another lodge about five hundred yards that way. Let's hole up until this torrent slows. No way the Russians are out in this shit, lazy bastards. Then we'll find the bimbo." He chucked her under the chin. "Come on, kid, buck up. This place is a maze. You and I have been stumbling around in here for the better part of a month. An hour, tops, to dry off and regroup. Okay?"

Alex squinted up at him, eyelashes dotted with rain-drops, rivers of rainwater dripping off the tip of her nose. "Did that no-letter agency teach you how to start a fire, Mr. Commando? I'm freezing." She ran her tongue over her lips and gave him a look he felt in the pit of his stomach.

Frank squatted for a moment, his breathing heavy, and wiped more mud from his face before he squinted at her. Then in one explosive burst, he rammed his shoulder into her pelvis, grabbed her legs, and heaved her over his shoulder.

"Smart ass. I'll show you how to start a fire." She went limp over his shoulder, but he could feel her silent laughter against the back of his chest.

———

"Well, it's dry at least," Alex said, turning to take in the run-down hunting shack. Frank squatted by the fireplace and started stacking kindling, his hands moving methodically as he, too, scanned the room. An old kitchen cabinet—empty, two folding chairs—rusted and liable to snap, and a cot covered in old army blankets. He struck his knife against a flint, sparks flying, while Alex grabbed the top blanket and shook it out. She grimaced when three dead mice fell at her feet, then threw the blanket back down on the cot and walked around it.

Frank leaned against the stone mantel, bedraggled, mud-slicked, his face camouflaged with moss stains and dirt, the fire cracking wildly behind him.

"You're a fucking mess, Frank." She bit her lip and stared back at him, her eyes a black mirror image of his own.

"So now what, junior agent?" he asked her, trying to keep his voice low and level.

She shrugged out of her heavy wet coat and let it fall to the floor. Then she sank down to the cot and began unlacing her boots from the knee down, glancing back at him to make sure he hadn't moved, taking her time. First one boot, then the other. She stripped her socks off and wiggled her toes.

"That's better." She glanced back over at him and stood up again, her hands smoothing her pants down awkwardly, then fluttering up to her collar. She unbuttoned one button, then another. She tilted her head at him, an endearing flash of uncertainty on her face. He swallowed so hard he wondered if she could hear him across the room.

"I'll show you mine if you show me yours. We never did play that game the other night, did we?"

Frank unzipped his tactical vest and tossed it onto one of the folding chairs, then bent to pull his own boots off. With one hand, he pulled his shirt over his head, the firelight behind him illuminating his broad chest and arms and the myriad scars that covered them, his twenty-year career written across his body.

"Your turn," he whispered.

She shrugged one arm, then another, out of her shirt, then pulled it off.

He gasped across the room.

"Good God, Alex."

She unhooked her bra and let it fall as well, then raised her arms and spun in a slow circle. "Oh, the front's nothing. You should see the back."

He crossed the floor on bare feet, his fingertips tracing the scars on her back.

"Knife?" His lips found one and kissed the jagged scar.

She nodded. "On-the-job training. I learn the hard way."

He grabbed her wrists and raised her arms, rotating them out so the light would catch them.

"Those are burns. Set fire to a chemical dump for cover. Wasn't as fast as I thought I was," she said before he could ask.

He turned her around, his hands finding the bullet wound low on her abdomen. He then noticed its twin on her left shoulder.

"I shouldn't have kicked you so hard there." He pictured her arm crumpling when he kicked her in the millhouse, her hand twitching. His lips landed like rain on her collarbone.

"You didn't know."

Frank ran his hand down her shoulder, barely skimming her nipple, and stopped at the tattoo that nestled between her small, pink breasts.

He gazed up at her, a question in his dark eyes.

"This looks familiar somehow." His hand left her chest, and he ran it through her hair, pulling a lock to his lips. She tasted like sugar. "I feel like I've seen it before." He looked back up into her eyes, but she was staring behind him into the fire.

"It's an evil eye. I got this to remind myself that everything I care about dies."

"I thought the eye was to ward off evil, Alex."

Alex reached out to caress the large crosshatch scars on his ribcage. "Same thing," she whispered. "What are these?"

"Eurotrash with an axe. I wasn't exaggerating when I said looking at you felt like an axe in my chest." He dipped his head down and kissed her nipple, then the wound on her shoulder again. "I actually know what it feels like."

She reached down and unbuttoned his pants, stepping back to remove her own. He kicked his aside and stood frozen, uncertain exactly of what to do. *Terrified. I think that's what this feeling is. Blind terror. Panic.*

She knelt in front of him and ran her hands down his muscular legs, her hands soft and gentle. Her kisses plotted points from each bullet wound, every piece of shrapnel, every burn. She leaned her head against him, and the crackling of the fire seemed to pause just long enough for him to hear her sigh, and that small sound dragged Frank to his knees. He pushed her backwards, catching her head again, and kissed his way down past her breasts, stopping to outline her tattoo with his tongue.

"So this is for protection?"

"Mm-hmm," she murmured.

"Then we have a real problem, Alex."

He felt her stiffen, and he closed his eyes to hide from her expression. "Why?" he heard her ask.

"I think I'm falling in love with you." He let his head fall to her stomach as he kissed her hipbone. *Yep. There it is. Right there. I give up.*

Alex reached down, her hands damp and salty, and pulled him up on top of her, letting him slide into her so slowly it ached. She threaded her fingers through his and arched her back, pulling him in deeper.

"Please," she whispered. "Please, please, please."

Chapter Ten

*W*hen the rain let up, they dressed in silence. Frank was unable to meet her eyes, mortified at his juvenile confession. Alex kept hers downcast, as if she was unwilling to risk looking at him at all.

She'd been right—the trek to the smoke was just a bit less than a mile. They stopped, crouched in the scrub a short distance off, and surveyed the area. It was a cabin in a small clearing, with a four-wheeler parked to one side, an outhouse to the other. On a small, sagging line across the porch, like fairy lights in the gloom, was a strand of cheap, brightly colored bras and underwear, spandex pants, and halter tops.

"It's laundry day for the bimbo," Alex said, finally meeting his eyes.

Frank's shoulders slumped in relief. "How the hell did she get all the way out here? We're miles from Lament." *This is worse than the axe. I'll take an axe to the ribs any day compared to wondering what is going on in that head.*

Alex stood and pulled the 9mm Makarov from her jacket. "One way to find out," she said shortly.

She strode up onto the porch and knocked with one hand, gun concealed behind her back in the other. *Shave and a haircut. Two bits.* Frank trailed behind her, cutting back and forth across the clearing, gun drawn, looking for a trap or any tracks other than their own.

The front door flew open, and he whirled around, dropping his sidearm when he saw the washed-out, nightie-clad woman who stood there, looking about as threatening as a nail technician.

"Oh, thank God you're here. I was about to go mad out here in the middle of nowhere. Come in! Come in! Who's your friend? And what on earth are you two dressed up for?"

Alex turned to glance back at Frank, a bewildered expression on her face, as Schwartz's gal Friday pulled her inside, clucking about mud.

Casting one last glance down the narrow track deeper into the woods made by the four-wheeler, Frank followed, his senses on high alert. *This feels like a trap. We need to get out of here as soon as possible, no time for finesse.* Fortunately, Alex was already interrogating her. Frank shut the door, then jerked the curtains closed. That four-wheeler track going the other way. There were too many footprints beside it to come from one person. He scanned the room, located the back door, and planted himself at a right angle to it.

"Who exactly do you think I am?" Alex was saying, even as she backed the woman into the corner.

The woman's hot-pink lips quivered. "Hey, put that gun away. I won't cause no trouble."

Alex narrowed her eyes and cast a look over at Frank, then slipped her gun back into her pocket. He kept his at his side.

"Let's try this again. Who are you?"

The woman looked back and forth between them. "I'm Delores. You mean Schwartzy didn't send you?" She turned away to rummage about in a leopard-patterned purse. "Where's my smokes? Shit, I hope you brought more. All this rain, stuck inside. Nothing to do but smoke, right?"

Alex turned to mouth *Schwartzy* at Frank, then winked at him. A crooked smile bloomed across her face, the smile he'd wanted to see before they left the shack, that singular combination of sweet and wry. He felt his ears turn red and his heart start pounding in his chest. *Not now. Don't go all schoolboy now. We need to get Delores to talk and then get the fuck out.* He shook his head tightly at Alex, his lips a grim line. The flirtatious grin fell from her face as she turned back to Delores.

"Of course Schwarzty sent us. To check on you. How are you holding up?" she said, her voice dripping with schoolteacher concern. *More flies with honey. Good job, cubbie. Fastest way out of here is to cozy up to her. Wait. That's what she did to me,* he thought with a grin.

"How do you think I'm holding up?" Delores stood and flounced across the cabin. She grabbed a pack of cigarettes off the counter, placed one between her shellacked lips, and lit it. Through the ring of smoke, she began bitching. "He drags my ass out of New York, middle of the night, says he got this big score, got the jump finally on those filthy Russians, will I come with him. I said, 'Schwartzy, you're drunk. I'm not going anywhere with you.' Then he shows me that rock." She paused to take a drink out of a nearby wine bottle. "I changed my tune right quick, let me tell you. That baby was 250 carats if it was one. Next thing I know, I'm on the back of a four-wheeler with my boss, hauling ass through New Hampshire. He left me here, said he was going to hide the rock, but he'd send someone to check in on me. That was six weeks ago! Look at me, I have a full inch of regrowth, I look like trailer trash," she finished, flicking her ash into a nearby bowl. "So who are you two?" she asked them. "And did you bring smokes?"

Frank's heart sank as Alex collapsed on the nearby couch, shoulders heaving, a dry hiccupping sound coming from her chest.

"What's her problem?" Delores demanded.

Frank crossed the room and put a hand on Alex's shoulder.

"Keep it together, Alex." *Oh, shit. But you've got to keep it together. Because I just barely am. If you lose it, I'll lose it.*

He jumped back when Alex burst out, "*Keep it together?* You and I just spent the last month hunting for something we're never going to find! He's dead, she's useless, the Russians are waiting for my ass, and the diamond is who-knows-where. He could have hidden it anywhere. And now we'll never know." She slumped back, tears streaming down her face, laughing. "I give up. Put a bullet in her head and then put one in mine, Frank. I tap out. I'm done." She continued laughing, a brittle high-pitched keen, her eyes wild and unnaturally bright.

The sight of it filled Frank with a blind rage. He charged at Delores, grabbing her by the arms and shaking her. "Where did he say he was hiding it, Delores? No more fucking around. Where is the diamond?"

"Schwartzy's dead?" she sputtered, lips trembling. "My Schwartzy?"

Another sound exploded out of Alex, something between a sob and a snort.

Frank shook Delores again, harder, spurred on by Alex's hysteria. "And you'll be dead, too, if you don't tell us where that diamond is. The Russians are here. In the woods. You tell me where the diamond is, and I swear to God I'll do whatever it takes to get you out of here. If you don't, I'll leave you for dead, you get me, Delores?" He shook her again once for good measure, then released her. He crossed his arms over his chest and planted his legs wide, blocking the line of sight to Alex's breakdown, and stared her down. *Don't give up, Alex. Don't you dare.*

Delores raised one shaking hand to her mouth, tears streaming down her face.

"But–but–Schwartz took it with him. Said he was giving it to his old high school friend, Father Morgan. Said no one would ever think to search a priest. I swear I don't know any more than that." She slumped to the floor, head clutched in her hands. "My Schwartzy."

Frank went cold. He turned slowly back to Alex. She'd fallen silent and was staring at him, wide-eyed.

"Fuck," she whispered.

He threw himself down on the couch next to her and dropped his head into his hands. *And here's where I lose it.*

"Fuck," she repeated, louder. She elbowed him gently.

Frank threw his head back, something between a laugh and a choking sound escaping him.

"Fuck is right. I guess that wasn't a rock in his pocket." He turned and winked at her, rolling his still tender shoulder, the one she'd peppered with kisses only an hour ago.

"This isn't funny at all," she said, shaking her head and grinning.

Frank burst out laughing, her sparkling laugh like fireworks punctuating his deep baritone.

"No, it isn't funny." Delores said from the floor. "Why are you two laughing?"

Frank reached out and pulled Alex toward him and held her tight, helpless with laughter.

"What did you do with Father Morgan?" she whispered in his ear.

Frank whispered back, "I shot him in the head, stuffed him in the trunk of his own car, and hired a buddy to dump him in the Atlantic. I thought it was a fucking rock in his pocket that gave me that big bruise on my shoulder."

Alex looked into his dark eyes and kissed him, then burst out laughing again.

"Oh, my God, Frank. We're fucked."

He pulled her face to his, kissing her. "We are. We are so fucked."

Delores stood up, adjusted her nightie, and gave the two hysterical people on the couch a disgusted look. "There is nothing funny about this. At all. My boss and boyfriend is dead, and there are Russians in the woods. You two really are fucked. You're fucked in the head if you think any of this is funny. I'm going to the powder room to compose myself." With that, she flounced out the front door, slamming it behind her.

Chapter Eleven

*F*rank released Alex and slumped back on the couch, rubbing a hand over his eyes.

"I am so sorry, Alex. This is all my fault. I knew better. I know better. I really am too old for this gig."

"Don't blame yourself. If I hadn't killed Delores's Schwartzy, he might have told us where it was, and then it wouldn't have ended up at the bottom of the ocean in a priest's pocket."

He stood suddenly, his giddy expression disappearing under the weight of a darker one as he began pacing.

"Frank, what's wrong?" she said. "I mean, other than," she waved her hand in the air, "this whole business."

He jammed his hand in his pockets and leaned against the mantle. "I'm sorry for what I said today. About," he turned red and gestured between them, "about this." He shook his head, furious with himself. "I've been following you around like a love-sick, angry puppy, and I'm sorry for that. I didn't mean to put you on the spot like that. It's just, from the first time I saw you, all I could think was 'This is the girl. The one I should have met years ago.' I meant what I said last night in the millhouse. Before we uh . . ." He shook his head. "I meant every word. But look at me, Alex. I'm a piece of shit. I lied to you and manipulated you, beat the crap out of you and messed with your head. And now, on top of it all, I've fucked this all up for you."

"To be fair, Frank, I did the same things to you. And I was just getting my second wind." She searched his eyes, her uncertain smile trying to coax one from him.

He shook his head again, his lips arranging themselves into that grim line. "This is exactly what I was worried about. This," he gestured between them again, "is a landmine. We're both standing right on it. No way this ends without an explosion. No way we both get out alive."

She rose and crossed the room, stopping in front of him, that sad, hurt look on her face again. "What do you mean, landmine? How am I a landmine?"

"Goddamn it, Alex, what I'm saying is that you're *it*. You're the exact perfect thing I have never deserved, ever. And because I am a monster, I will destroy you. It's inevitable."

Her face fell. "There's no way you feel any of that for me *now*. I mean, maybe then. Maybe when I was her. She was wonderful. Everything I can't ever be. Not full-time, anyway. But not me. You can't feel that way about me."

"It's worse than that. Because you're her. And you're you, Alex. You are perfect. Perfect to me. I couldn't have one without the other."

"Frank, I—" A scream and the sound of gunfire cut off her words.

They both dropped to the floor and rolled to cover.

"Russians?" he whispered.

"Or your people. Hang on." She rolled across the room and peered out a window, ducking when a bullet shattered the glass.

She shook the glass from her hair and looked back at him. "Russians," she said grimly.

"How many?" he said, scrambling for his sidearm and checking the magazine.

She grimaced and slid her gun into her pants. "All of them." She crawled across the room to the door and grasped the handle. "Looks like Delores went to join her Schwartzy."

"What the fuck are you doing?" Frank hissed.

She ignored him as she stood and opened the door. "Stay down. Whatever you hear, do not leave this cabin, Frank. Please."

The door slammed behind her. Frank's mind shifted into gear while he mentally scrambled for scenarios that got them out of the Russian-infested woods alive. Impossible. They were both as good as dead. *Unless.*

He heard her voice through the door, followed by the coarse voice of one of the Russians.

"Greetings, Igor. Comrades. What brings you to the great north woods? Not just to visit little old me, I hope," she quipped.

He could just barely hear her voice tremble. *Which means they can, too. Blood in the water. This is my fault.*

"Alexei feels you are taking too much of his precious time about diamond business. Better firm hand than feminine touch," the coarse voice replied.

"Aww, it's sweet of you boys to worry, but I've got this well in hand. Tell Alexei I'll have his rock for him in another day. Tops."

Her wavering bravado was like a gut punch. Frank slid on his belly toward the back door of the cabin and peeked out. Nothing. The coast was clear. *Fucking dumbass Russians. They were butchers, but they were also idiots.*

"Is no good, Alexandra. Alexei feels you are, how you say it, washed up? Dead weight? Tell us where diamond is, little angel, and I promise you bullet in back of head and nice shallow grave in these beautiful woods. No boxes for your pretty head. Come now, be reasonable. You know you cannot outrun us."

Frank slipped out the back door and rolled his shoulders, digging deep inside for the worst he'd ever been. He clawed around until he'd dredged up the ruthless asshole he'd pretended to be for the last twenty years, shoving down the man Alex had coaxed out. *You can wait, pal. I only get one shot at this and I need the old Frank. We aren't getting out of this alive . . . unless.* Unless they thought one of them already was. Dead, that is. *She wasn't going to like this. Not at all. Hell, she might kill him herself.*

Moving fast, his feet silent on the wraparound porch, he raced up behind her. The moment when he grabbed her from behind and the moment the Russians aimed their guns at him was seamless.

"Howdy, boys." He jerked her against him, hard, and grabbed a fistful of her hair, pulling it.

Alex let out a startled cry and tried to look back at him, but he held her firm. *I'm sorry, Alex. There's just no other way.* She sputtered his name, so he pushed her down to the porch floor, spinning her around, and backhanded her across her mouth, trying not to catch her too hard. She fell back, senseless, gasping.

"Who are you?" the big ugly Russian demanded. *That must be Igor.*

Alex was scrambling to her feet, so Frank kicked her in the chest, sending her down again, harder this time. *Stay down, Alex, for the love of God.*

"I'm the guy with the diamond." He scanned the Russian-filled woods when every gun cocked almost in unison. "Of course, I'm not dumb enough to have it on me."

"Tell us where diamond is," Igor demanded.

"Do I get a head shot and a shallow grave, too?"

"No. Kind offer was for small angel. We go way back. You, I would toy with for some time. I know who you are, Frank Brennan."

"Then you know what I bring to the table." He reached down and yanked Alex up again. "Alexei is getting soft, sending in amateurs like her. All it took was a little sweet talk, a little shoptalk, and this pretty birdie sang for me. She told me everything." He sneered into Alex's devastated eyes, struggling to keep his dead and empty. "Pathetic. And not even a good lay."

A chorus of raucous Russian laughter filled the woods. He felt her go limp in his arms.

"What are you suggesting, G-man?" Igor asked.

"I'm suggesting I bring you the diamond and defect from this government shit show. I've had enough running around, doing pissant jobs for noble causes and no money. I want in. I'll bring the diamond tonight to the old millhouse. You talk to Alexei. Tell him I took out his top trollop," he said, yanking Alex's head back, "and I want out of my agency and into his. I'll pay my way in by ridding him of her and bringing him the diamond Schwartz stole."

Alex finally found her voice. She twisted in his arms and began hitting him in his chest. "You lying son of a bitch. I should have known. All along. You monster, you—" Her voice cut off. She whispered, low so only he could hear, "How could you, Frank? I thought you . . ."

Frank shook her hard to stop her from finishing her sentence and then kissed her, brutally forcing his tongue into her mouth for the benefit of their audience, hating himself more than he ever had. She bit him, and he dropped her with a laugh, then turned to leer at the Russians as he wiped the blood from his mouth. "You guys can have her when I'm done with her. This dumb bitch has been eating out of my hands for days. Tonight. Old millhouse. Midnight. Double-cross me, assholes, and you'll never find that diamond. If you like, I'll bring Alexei her head. I know how he likes a matched set of souvenirs. He can put her on a shelf with her dad."

Igor eyed him, his lips curled up. *Shit, he's not buying it.* Frank grabbed Alex's right arm and jerked her toward him as gently as he could risk. She looked down at her left shoulder, confused, then up to him, her face suddenly blank and unreadable. *This is going to be unpleasant.* She wrenched her right arm out of his hand.

"He's lying," Alex screamed. "I know where the diamond is, and you'll never find it. Don't listen to him, he's lying. Don't leave me here with him. He's an animal. Please, Igor, not like this. I can get you the diamond, I swear it."

Igor studied her for a moment, his eyes swinging between Frank and Alex, then he laughed. "I think is you that is lying, princess, to save your pretty little head. Is shame, but is the way she goes."

Alex spun around to Frank, blocking his view of Igor's smug expression with her anguished face.

"Frank," she whispered. "*Please.*" The devastated look vanished from her face. Replacing it was the most glorious mixture of the shy wide-eyed widow and the nimble assassin. *She figured it out. She knew what he was doing. Thank God.* She raised one eyebrow and took his breath away.

Frank winked at her and drew his fist back, raising his voice so all the Russians could hear him reply. "Tough."

He decked her square in the face and watched her crumple at his feet.

"Tonight, boys," he called out as he threw Alex over his shoulder and kicked open the door to the cabin. "I need a few hours with this one, conscious or unconscious."

He slammed the door behind him and raced out the back door of the cabin, listening for the sound of the Russians making their way back to the mill in the other direction. Alex hung limp and unconscious over his shoulder, her nose bleeding, but he had no time to do anything about it. *Holy shit, can she take a punch.* He crouched, wrapped her around his shoulders and ran like hell for town. With luck, he'd get there before dark.

Chapter Twelve

*F*rank could just see the lights of the square and the church steeple when Alex started groaning and struggling in earnest. He held her firmly and soldiered on, ignoring her protests.

"Jesus, Frank, put me down already. Why do you have to be so rough? All this jostling is making my head hurt worse," she complained. He stopped, unable to keep the relieved grin from his face, and set her down, bracing her with one hand.

"Steady now, kid. Take a minute."

Alex opened one bruised eye and looked around. Forest canopy. Muddy ground. Her hands. She reached up and touched her face.

"Ouch."

"I hit you really hard. Goddamn it, I think I broke your nose, honey." He peered down at her woozy face and hazarded a quick kiss on her forehead. "But it had to look real. Here." He rummaged inside his pockets, scrambling for anything to clean her up with. All he found was a bundle of receipts from the Quick Shop. "Shit. I don't have anything but a bunch of receipts for protein bars and vodka. Here, hold still." She tilted her face up to him in the twilight as he wiped, as gently as he could, the blood and dirt from her face.

"Better?" she asked.

Frank winced. "Not much. I can't tell what's mud and what's bruise."

"All right, all right, enough fussing." She smacked his hands away from her, her eyes flashing open. "I can't believe what you did. What you said."

"I did and said exactly what I had to make sure they told Alexei you were dead. I told them whatever it took to make you disappear. Don't you see? You're out. For real. They think I killed you. I'll go to the millhouse tonight and make sure they think that."

She reached up and felt her nose again.

"Frank?"

"Alex?"

Her arm drew back faster than he could block, and she drilled him right in the jaw. He reeled back, vision blinded by stars.

"There. That's better," she said, leaping on him and wrapping her arms around his neck. She clung to him like a monkey while he carried her out of the woods, rubbing his jaw.

"I deserved that."

"No, you deserve this."

She turned his face to hers and kissed him. He stopped walking and pushed her up against a tree, feeling her against every inch of him.

"Thank you, Frank," she whispered.

"For punching you?"

"For what you did back there. But now they know you're here. Frank, Alexei won't stop until he finds you."

"That's not your concern."

"I'm making it my concern, Francis." She grabbed his chin and made him look at her. "You save me, I save you. That's how this is going to work. Or it won't work at all."

Frank shook his head. "No. I'll go to the millhouse tonight and finish this. My people will pull me in. I'll disappear, a year, tops. And this all goes away. The heat is off you. Then I'll find you."

"But it's on you then."

"Let me do this for you."

"Not for me."

"Fine. Then just let me do this. Never mind why. I have my own scores to settle."

Alex was quiet for a moment and then nodded. "I get that. But I'm coming with you tonight."

"Alex, no, I . . ."

"Frank. I'm coming with you. One last time."

He hugged her close to him. "One last job, huh?"

"Something like that. Guns blazing."

Chapter Thirteen

"We still have a couple of hours." Frank shifted uncomfortably as he scanned Alex's porch. It was all clear, but he felt unsettled, like he was forgetting to anticipate something, worse than the feeling he'd had in Delores's cabin. "They're expecting me at midnight, so we'll roll in there at ten. There's no reason they'd come here, no point in searching a dead woman's house. Go, get some sleep." He scratched his head and smoothed his hair back. "I'll head back to the rectory and get all my gear, meet you back here at nine. Then we'll head out into the woods together. I'm sure they'll try to double-cross us, but likely it'll be in the woods. Not here. Too many witnesses."

Alex nodded and turned the lock on the front door.

"Would you come inside for a minute just the same?" That tremble again in her voice, just like that night at the sink. *It gets lonely,* her voice repeated in his head, *this life. I know,* he thought. *I had no idea how lonely until I met you.*

He stepped inside behind her, casting one more glance up and down the street, just to be sure. But the entire town seemed deserted. Not even Bishop's goats were out tonight. Fucking Russians were probably in the woods digging tiger pits and setting trip wires.

She shut the door firmly behind him, then took his hand and led him to the staircase. He followed her without question while she led him upstairs and stopped outside a closed door. She released his hand and leaned against it.

"I wondered . . ."

"What?" he asked, sliding his hand up the door and leaning into her. He bent down and whispered in her ear, his lips fluttering against her lobe. "What were you wondering, Alex?"

"I wondered . . . everything is always so complicated. So intense. You know, for people like us. So much performance goes into it all. I mean, look at us, Frank." He ran his hand over her blood-crusted nose even as she placed a gentle hand on his bruised face. "Isn't it exhausting?"

Frank slid his lips from her ear to her temple and placed a kiss there where a purple bruise bloomed. "What's exhausting?"

"Sex. I mean, it's all ropes and scars and witty banter and who can out-weird the other, you know? I mean, when was the last time you had sex like a normal person?"

He burrowed his face into her hair and whispered in her ear, "Alexandra Winters, after all the borderline-humiliating, manipulative, violent sex you've been having on me, are you asking me to make love to you?"

"I mean, if it's even possible. We could try, right?" She flushed and looked at her feet while she reached behind her. He heard a click when she opened the door to her bedroom and felt her bury her face in his chest as she did.

He looked up from her hair and into her room. Old concert t-shirts and cargo pants littered the floor, a half-eaten box of donuts, three open gun cases, a bed piled with old quilts and mismatched pillows, a raggedy old stuffed dog. Over her bed was a tattered print of the Detroit skyline.

"Is this part of your cover, too?" he whispered, running his hand through her hair.

Alex shook her head against his chest.

"Well, then."

Frank bent down and put his arm under her knees, plucking her from her feet, and carried her over the threshold into her bedroom. He laid her down on the bed and bent to kiss her lips once, softly. He undressed her methodically, his hands barely skimming her naked body as he did. He unbuttoned her shirt with deft fingers, and slid her pants down slow, letting just the tip of his fingers follow the curve of her hips. She sat up while he unhooked her bra and waited as he folded each article of clothing and placed them in a bundle on her dresser. Then he picked up the dog and set him in a chair near her bed. He slid her legs under the quilts, pausing to kiss her lips once more, longer this time. Then he turned off the lights and shut the door, locking them both inside.

Chapter Fourteen

Frank sat up, groggy, and reached across the tangled sheets, but she wasn't there. He jumped out of bed, instantly awake. *I must have fallen asleep. She was just so ... Damn.* He looked down at his watch. 10:55 p.m. He scanned the room again. The gun cases were gone. The puppy was holding a note. *No. Oh God, Alex, no.*

> *I couldn't let you go. I couldn't bear it if one of those butchers killed someone else I love. I'll handle it. And if I can't, then at least the heat is off you. Goodbye, Frank.*

He dressed in a flash, cursing the whole time, images of her alone in the woods with those fucking Russians sparking in his frantic mind. He flew down the stairs and sprinted across the deserted square back to the rectory, shouldering the locked door open. He walked out the back door ten minutes later, armed to the teeth, duffle of ammo over his shoulder, and hurried on silent feet into the dark woods.

He smelled it before he saw it. Smoke. Thick, black, choking smoke. A few hundred yards more, and embers writhed all over the ground around him. The flames had long since died down, leaving only scorched remnants of the millhouse behind. It was gone, all of it—the entire structure had been consumed. A few fallen and charred cross beams were all that remained. Frank threw his duffle bag of ammo on the bank of the frigid lake and, abandoning all stealth, ran into the smoke-filled field.

"Alex!" he screamed. "Alex!"

No answer came, just the sparks of fire crackling and the crunch of beams collapsing. He ran a circuit around the entire crater, stopping and gagging when he found the pile of bodies. A hideous tangled mass, charred and smoldering, impossible to distinguish one from the other.

All of them, he heard her say. *All of them.*

He tried to get closer, to see if one of them wasn't a giant ugly Russian corpse. To see if one was small and nimble and wearing black climbing boots. But it was impossible. The corpses were hot and heavy, and he burned his hands trying to shift them.

Alex. He sank to his knees in the muck at the lakeside and sobbed. *Alex, goddamn it. You goddamn fool. Why didn't you wait for me? We could have done this together. Or at least gone out together. You and me. Guns blazing.* He lay there in the mud, a broken man, until he heard the sound of forest rangers and fire trucks approaching. *You're too late. Show's over. She's gone.* He ran off through the woods back to Lament and sought shelter in the sanctuary of the church.

Frank fell to his knees at the candlelit altar, eyes bleary and red from the smoke, his head buried in his hands. *I'm not even sure if I believe in you, but if you are there and you can let me know she's okay, that Alexei didn't grab her, that she's alive and safe, I'll do anything you ask. I'll stop killing people and everything. I'll go straight. Please let her be alive and not dead under a pile of ugly Russians.*

He opened his eyes and looked up to the crucifix, rage building in him at the silence. *What did I expect? A miracle? There are no miracles. Except for her. She was a miracle. She was my miracle.*

And that's when the candlelight caught it. A folded piece of paper nailed to the bottom of the crucifix with a six-inch stainless-steel blade, Marine-issue. His hand dropped to his boot. *She took my knife again.*

How on earth did Russians get such a badass rep? Those duraky weren't that badass after all. But just to be safe, I bolted. You should, too. Three of those guys I barbequed were NSA. Looks like someone got disavowed, Francis. I've got a bit of a head start, but that shouldn't stop someone from an acronym-less agency.

P.S. Bring the rope. Please.

Frank leapt to his feet and ran out of the church into the cold night air. *She's alive. That sneaky minx is alive. And she barbequed twenty Russians.*

He stopped and turned around in a slow circle, taking in the town square of Lament. The lights were off in her little farmhouse. He knew she was gone. That the inner room with the poster of the Detroit skyline, the concert t-shirts, and the stuffed dog was gone, too. He laughed and ran back into the church.

"Hey, God? All that stuff I said about not killing people anymore? I'd like to amend that to scaling back. I'm going to wean myself off after I deal with the bastards that double-crossed me. Then I'm going to find Alex."

Afterword

Frank pulled up his rented Jeep in front of a rundown Detroit arcade. The parking lot was full of rusted cars and broken beer bottles. The façade was a spider web of gangland tags and concert fliers. It was hot out and muggy, and the pavement was sticky under his boots and smelled like fried chicken and pickles, like exhaust and asphalt.

He walked slowly through the front doors, eyes passing over old men at video lotto machines, young men playing loud Japanese arcade games, young women giggling in karaoke booths. He could hear the echo of wood against wood, of balls hitting targets and alarms going off, the sound of winning tickets being discharged like gunfire. He rounded the corner and found the bank of Skee-ball games, and the girl in the old faded concert t-shirt and cargo pants. Alex stopped mid-throw and froze, caught like a deer under his gaze. She dropped the ball.

"You came," she whispered.

Frank walked across the grimy linoleum and knelt. He picked the ball up and handed it back to her.

"It got lonely."

She pulled him to his feet and wrapped her arms around his neck, climbing him and wrapping her legs around his waist. She kissed him long and hard, and he tasted salt on her lips.

"It took you long enough."

Nose to nose, he squinted into her eyes. He crossed his eyes to see her lips. She was smiling.

"Had to tie up some loose ends."

She cocked her head at him. "Which ones?"

"All of them. Anyone who might decide to go looking for either of us."

Her smile faltered.

"Tell me you didn't do that for me."

"I didn't."

He kissed her forehead where a bruise was still healing. She had a scattering of burns on her cheek that looked like raindrops.

"I did it for us."

Alex kissed him again, her hands winding through his hair.

"I love you, Frank Brennan."

"I thought maybe you did."

"So now what?"

He set her down. "You think you can teach me how to play Skee-ball? You owe me one. I taught you how to tie that wrist cuff." He chucked her gently on the chin.

Alex nodded and bit her lip. "And then?" She cocked her head up at him and flashed him that heart-stopping smile she'd given him just before he punched her.

Frank reached out and took one of her small hands in his. "Oh, I don't know, Winters. Maybe you and I could teach each other how to be normal people? Think you're up for that, tough stuff?"

"You bet your ass I am, Brennan. Remember, I'm adaptable."

BANGKOK VENGEANCE

PROLOGUE

Frank Brennan sat in his Jeep and watched Alexandra Winters order a donut and coffee. Following her Thursday routine, she clutched one in each hand, notebook under her arm, and navigated the small dining area toward her usual rickety table.

Her old haunt. Tim Hortons. One old-fashioned, rationed out in sections that she nibbled on for the quarter hour. One large coffee, black. Endlessly writing in that little notebook of hers, pausing every so often to look up, eyes closed, biting her lips, thinking.

He gritted his teeth, squeezed his eyes shut and punched the dash. *Just do it, already. March in there and get it over with. Stop stalking her, you coward.*

Five years had passed since the first time he'd seen her. Alexandra Winters had been nineteen, sitting alone in a cut-rate funeral chapel with eyes bigger and sadder than he would have thought possible. All he had felt when he'd looked at her then was guilt.

Peering through his grimy windshield, he squinted against the summer sun that rippled the air between them and tried to ignore this new feeling. A feeling that had done nothing but grow in the weeks since he'd found her again in Detroit. He shoved whatever it was down, hard.

Just take it like a man. Go in there, apologize for ruining her life, and leave. She'll probably smack you. Or punch you. Whatever she does, he thought as he strode through the door of the coffee shop, *it won't be a fraction of what you deserve, you piece of shit.*

His normally confident stride pitched, then capsized. The first moment he was caught in her direct gaze was like a riptide yanking his feet out from under him. His breath left him when her expression shifted from confused to something strangely inviting—one eyebrow arched, lips twisted in a sardonic Mona Lisa smile. Frank jammed his hands into the pockets of his jeans and found himself giving her a nervous schoolboy smile instead of a penitent one.

Tell her, you asshole. You've been practicing this speech for the last five years. Spit it out and go.

He opened his mouth, but instead of a terse apology, his words rearranged themselves into a terrible pick-up line.

"I'm new in town. What does one order at a Tim Hortons in this part of Michigan?"

A quizzical tilt to her head, but the grin stayed. In fact, it widened.

"This time of day, the only thing that's not stale is an old-fashioned. I think they have more lard than the other ones." She used her foot to push out the chair across from her, inviting him to sit.

His eyes traveled down from her concert t-shirt—REO Speedwagon—to her baggy cargo pants, cuffs rolled up unevenly, ankles a graceful curve above a pair of cheap flip-flops. He swallowed hard. *I did not notice the ankles when I was doing surveillance. Son of a bitch. Do not sit down. Do. Not. Sit.*

Frank sat down, grabbed a quarter of her donut and popped it in his mouth, watching as her expression shifted from surprise to annoyance.

"Outstanding." *What the fuck are you doing, Frank?*

"Hey, get your own," she protested.

Her voice. He hadn't expected her to have a voice like lemon meringue pie. Sweet and tart tones he wanted to bury his face in. He studied her to see what reaction came after surprised and annoyed. *Amused. Oh God, how do I keep that look on her face? Think, Frank, think. No, don't think. Get out of here. Get up and walk out. She's a goddamn witch.*

"Can I get a dozen old-fashioneds? And a large coffee, black," Frank called out across the dining room. When he looked back, amusement was still in her eyes, but there was something new around the edges.

"Who are you?" She leaned forward, her stage whisper egging him on.

"Frank Brennan."

Incredibly, she reached over and took his hand in hers. *Holy Christ.*

"Alexandra Winters. But everyone calls me Alex."

He turned her hand over in his and ran his fingertips across the inside of her wrist.

"Alex."

"What *is* this?" she asked, her whisper equal parts astonished and bewildered as she gestured between the two of them with her left hand.

Frank was still holding her right. Or was she holding his? *Drop her hand, you sick fuck, and leave. Get out before you do any more damage.* He hazarded a glance up from her wrist to meet her liquid brown eyes and told his inner monologue to take a hike.

"Two lonely people sharing a donut and coffee. What do you say, Princess Lexie?"

At that, she slid her hand from his and cast him a withering look. "First of all, don't you ever call me that again, *Francis.*"

He flinched and groaned. *Oh God. She's perfect.*

"My apologies, Miss Winters. Won't happen again." He smiled broadly at her now, the penitent, chastened look he should have worn only apparent at the corners of his eyes.

"Princess Lexie sounds like a cat's name," she whispered, slipping her hand back in his, her fingernails tapping his wrist.

"I like a cat with claws."

"Francis, huh?"

He colored and laughed. "Francis Xavier Brennan. Named after a Catholic priest. A missionary."

She turned his hand over in hers and ran her finger down a scar that stretched from his elbow down his forearm to the knuckle of his ring finger.

"And are you a priest?"

He shook his head and felt the inside of her wrist where her pulse throbbed under the thin white skin.

"No, ma'am. Marine, two tours. And I would not include missionary on my list of skills."

This time she colored and lowered her eyes to the table. The new expression was raw and singular, and Frank could not name it to save his life.

"Alexandra. Pretty name. What does it mean?"

"Oh . . . well—" Her voice cut off, and her forehead pleated in uncertainty. Then she scowled, an enchanting blend of mortification and frustration.

I should never have come back. I'm a dead man.

"What, Alex Winters? Tell me."

She cleared her throat and looked up into his eyes. The scowl vanished, and in its place was a shy smile. "It means defender of warriors." *That* look again.

Frank laced his fingers through hers. The expression on his own face, raw and singular, was mirrored in her eyes, and he felt the moments between them sync.

"Aren't we a pair?" he whispered.

She nodded and laughed, and he was done.

———

Before Frank knew it, a dozen donuts turned into a long walk turned into a short drive to his motel room. By the time he'd buried his head between her legs, intoxicated and enchanted, he'd convinced himself that there was more than one way to say 'I'm sorry.' That maybe, just maybe, he could spend the rest of his life telling Alex

Winters he was sorry by worshipping her every day as long as she let him.

They stayed holed up in his room for two days. When he woke up, shouting, terrified, drenched in sweat, she smoothed his hair back and held him until his pulse stopped racing. Then she read to him from her little notebook of short, funny stories that were just like her in written form—sharp, sweet, tough, delightful.

"Every one of your stories could be a movie, Alex," he said, kissing her bare shoulder, amazed at how she healed him.

She pushed him back on the bed and straddled his waist, pinning his arms over his head.

"You speak Russian when you're dreaming," she murmured.

"I do?" he whispered, alarmed.

"Sexy," she purred.

I should never have come back. The mistake I made was expecting the kid, the girl crying over her father's casket. I never anticipated the woman. This woman.

Weeks passed. Then months. He got calls about a few jobs. Consulting. Security. Intel. He did them, and when she asked, he said he found a job as a vinyl siding salesman. She laughed and told him she loved him. He told her the same and made sure she never saw the extra satellite phone he kept for work. She asked him to move in with her. He said no. When her face fell, he fell with it to one knee and asked her to marry him instead. Then her face lit up, something more brilliant than the sunrise and Christmas morning all rolled into one.

He drove her to Niagara Falls because it made her laugh to do something so absurd. Instead of rings, she insisted on tattoos, matching ones on their wrists of the evil eye.

"You're my talisman, Frank Brennan," she said when they exchanged vows, "against every evil in the world. And I'm yours. Forever."

With those words, she unknowingly wiped away years of self-loathing and regret, burying the man Frank had been and forging the husband and father he'd become.

Well now you've done it, idiot, Frank thought when she told him he was going to be a father. *You better pray to God she never finds out. You better pray you covered all your tracks, covered them so deep and so well that your past never comes back and rips apart this whole world you are making with her, her of all people. You should never have come back. Every day with her is borrowed time, buddy. Borrowed fucking time.*

CHAPTER ONE

lex Winters Brennan ran a hand across her husband's expansive chest, unable to resist placing a small kiss on his grizzled jaw. The once coal-black hair scattered over Frank's muscular torso had turned to salt and pepper, as had a mere inch of hair just above each ear. She smoothed his hair back, delighted as ever as the one lock that refused to stay put tumbled back across his face.

Dawn was breaking, and the light through the window cast interesting shadows across his rugged good looks while he slumbered on, unaware of the inventory she was taking. Broad shoulders, muscular hands, a myriad of jagged scars and burns he'd dismissed as souvenirs from two tours in the Marines, and finally the small tattoo of the evil eye on his wrist. Alex traced it with her fingertip out of habit.

Frank's jaw was a little softer than when they'd met, and he had the beginnings of a paunch that grieved him during his waking hours. But his arms were still just as powerful as ever; the same arms that had swept her off her feet ten years ago in a Tim Hortons. No matter how much time had passed, she still privately believed he was handsome enough to be a movie star. Not a pensive, dramatic type. *More like one of those off-the-cuff action heroes in tactical gear, oozing swagger and smolder. Not that I'd ever tell him that. He'd just roll his eyes and growl, "I don't need to pretend to be an action hero, princess. I was a Marine."*

"You are far, far too good for me, Frank Brennan," she whispered.

And there it was—the only blot on her happy life. A wicked snarl, a deep bruise that never seemed to heal, no matter how long they were together. He was unreal, her husband. Larger than life, quick-witted, big-hearted, sexy as hell. He could have chosen literally any woman alive. And yet he chose her. An orphaned ex-kindergarten teacher who spent her time scribbling stupid stories, laughed too loud, swore too much, and ate too much grease.

No, he settled for me. Nothing else makes any sense. And I can never ask him why, because I love him more than life itself, and if I did . . . if I asked . . . and he gave me one of those blank, distant looks of his, I think it would kill me.

So she locked her fears back up tight and placed a small kiss on his wrist. Then she slid between his legs and carefully maneuvered the waistband of his boxers toward his ankles, pulled the blankets up over her head, and stifled a giggle from her otherwise engaged mouth. Frank woke with a start, grasping her hair under the sheets.

"Goddamn, Alex." His growl rumbled in her ears, even under the weight of the blanket.

She stopped her early morning ministrations long enough to peek up at him from underneath the covers.

"Happy first day of vacation, Frank," she purred.

He squinted down at her, a cocky smile spanning his sleepy face.

"Don't let me interrupt you, princess, I was just—" His words cut off when the bedroom door burst open. He yanked the covers back over Alex's grinning face like a flash of lightning.

"Frank Junior!" he exclaimed. "What did Mommy and Daddy tell you about knocking?"

A long, silent pause followed, broken by three small, sticky raps on the open bedroom door. Alex stifled a giggle.

"About knocking *before* you come in our bedroom, champ?"

"That I'm supposed to?" was the confused rely.

Above Alex, Frank sighed. "What is that all over you, buddy? What are you two doing down there?"

"Gwennie made me breakfast, but now it's a mess. She said to go get help."

Rolling her eyes at the antics of her headstrong daughter, Alex resumed her below-covers activities.

"JesusMaryandJoseph." Frank's hands grasped her head beneath the sheets. "I mean, Frankie, go tell your big sister to stop whatever it is she is doing. Daddy will be down in a few minutes, and I'll clean you all up. Then we'll go on our big trip in the airplane. Okay, buddy?"

"'K, Daddy. How many few minutes?"

Alex reached around behind him and cupped his ass, pulling him deeper into her mouth.

"Like, fifteen. Maybe twenty. Shut the door behind you, buddy."

The door slammed shut, and Frank ripped the covers off Alex. In one fluid movement—*God, how does this man still move like that?*—he pulled her up over him and flipped them both, pinning her beneath him.

"I should take you on vacation more often, Mrs. Brennan." He kissed her, stifling her laughter, then slid down her body and under her nightgown.

"Yes, you should," she gasped.

From beneath her nightgown came a muffled reply. "Nag, nag, nag."

Alex wrapped her legs around her husband's head and turned to look at the nightstand and the pile of passports scattered there.

"Frank?"

"What?" he growled, sliding back up her chest. He reached up to grasp the headboard to keep it from banging into the wall.

"You're going to destroy your rotator cuff doing that. Honestly, we should just put the bed in the middle of the room," Alex said, locking her ankles behind his back as she arched to kiss his neck.

"Yeah, I'll get right on that, babe."

"The Outer Banks would have been fine. I mean, everyone else goes there." She tugged on his earlobe with her teeth and raked her nails down his back. The head-board slid out of his hands and banged into the wall. "And besides, I've been busting my ass with Gwennie at mother-daughter kickboxing. If we'd gone *there*, the other mothers could look at my high, tight ass and suck it. *Bitches.* I hate the suburbs, Frank."

Frank groaned as he sank deep into his wife, his teeth on her neck, his hands gripping her hips. "The Outer Banks is for douchebags, princess. And besides, I wanted to take you someplace different. See the world a bit. Show you where I was stationed. Stop your bitching."

"Could we at least talk about moving when we get back?" she implored.

He squinted down at her. "Look, are we doing this or what?"

Grinning, Alex pushed him off of her. "Oh, we're doing this."

With a maneuver slightly less elegant than his, she rolled him over with a grunt and settled herself on top of him. Once she was comfortable and he seemed adequately engaged, she flashed him a mischievous smirk. "Poor Frank. Your better half is so *squirmy.*"

"Jesus, hold still, Alex." He gripped her waist with his firm, iron hands. "Stop squirming. Unless you want that twenty minutes to drop to sixty seconds."

Still grinning at him, she raised her hands up over her head and rocked her hips against his like a belly dancer, whispering his name in a singsong.

"Fraaancis."

"Goddamn it, Alex."

———

Moments later, she whispered in his ear, breathless. "But Southeast Asia? Who takes their family to *Bangkok* on vacation?"

His face shuttered with an unreadable look. As quickly as it appeared, the blank look was gone, replaced by that familiar cocky smile. He winked and kissed the tip of her nose. *Oh, Frank. Where do you go? And why can't I follow?*

"This guy does. Get moving, princess," he said, smacking her ass affectionately as he vaulted from the bed. He retrieved his boxers from the ceiling fan and slid them on, then tugged one of his old Marine Corps t-shirts over his head. "I'll go deal with Miss Gwennie. Get your skates on, Princess Lexie. Thailand awaits."

Alex threw a pillow at his head, but he dodged it, his laughter a charming rumble.

"Do not call me that, Frank. I hate it when you call me that."

He darted in to plant one more kiss on her rueful face, the door shutting behind him a second later. Alex listened to the thundering of footsteps while he jogged down the stairs, followed by a beat, snorting with laughter when his bellow echoed up the stairwell of their suburban home.

"Gwendolyn Winters Brennan, you are not allowed to make oatmeal ever again. Bathtub. Right now. Both of you. You don't want to miss our plane do you? Don't you want Daddy to show you two knuckleheads around Thailand?"

Alex rolled over and stretched, lazy and content as a cat, and fanned the plane tickets and passports across her jumbled nightstand. *He loves you. You know this. I mean, look around you, stupid, he's given you everything you ever wanted. Everything except whatever he keeps locked up tight inside him. Everything except that.* She sighed and shook the thought from her mind while she studied the plane tickets. Four tickets to Bangkok, Thailand. Brennan, family of four. She ran her hand over her stomach and smiled. *I have secrets too, Frank.*

No matter, she thought, jumping out of bed and heading for the shower. Her husband might be a vinyl siding salesman, she might be a housewife stuck in the Detroit 'burbs, they might both be inching into middle age, but there was no denying it—Frank Brennan sure as hell knew how to show a lady a good time.

———

Frank Brennan knelt in the bathroom, surrounded by a landscape of wet towels and oatmeal shrapnel, unable to keep the stupid grin off his face. *Sure, maybe other dads would be livid, but not this guy. There is literally nothing else I'd rather be doing than cleaning up after our two monkeys.* He sat back for a minute and closed his eyes, listening to the sounds of his family. Gwennie and Junior were in the next room, freshly scrubbed and dressed, speaking in their strange code language while they copied down the latest moves in their ongoing chess game.

"Duck pez head to queen's die four, Frankie. I'm watching. No cheating. I'll have you in three moves once we're on the plane."

"Awww, Gwennie, you will not. I won this game one move in, you just haven't realized it yet."

Frank had no idea what they were talking about. Crazy little munchkins with their incomprehensible games and rules. He adored them so much it hurt, like an axe in the chest. Gwennie—pig tails, perpetually scraped knees, sturdy like a boxer, freckled face that alternated between scowls and a crooked smile, minus front teeth. Frank Jr.—small, slender, asthmatic, nearsighted, with his dimpled, bespectacled face always set in intense concentration bordering on concern whenever he tried to teach his thick old man how to play chess. Frank suspected he let him win.

Junior was a lot like his mother in that respect—he held all the cards but he was too tender-hearted to use that to his advantage. Gwennie was a four-foot-tall version of her old man. *God help me,* Frank thought, his contemplative smile widening impossibly when he heard his wife call the kids downstairs, her lemon sugar voice distracted and excited about the trip.

"Frank? Frank? Did you call for the cab?"

"Yeah, babe," he called down. "They'll be here in forty-five minutes. Keep your panties on." He sat back in the sea of oatmeal on the tile floor, grinning and waiting.

"Frank?"

"What?" he bellowed down the stairs, his smirk belying his tone.

"Do you have Junior's inhaler?"

Frank patted the pockets on his cargo shorts.

"Got it!"

"Frank?"

"Jesus, woman, what now?"

"Can you check the gutter by the back door before we leave? It's full of leaves, and if it rains while we're gone, the basement will flood. *Again.*"

Frank laughed to himself, delighted as ever at her barrage of checklists, then barked back, "Sure, I'll get right on that, princess."

Downstairs, he heard Alex swear, a distinct melodic, "Fucking hell." *Music to my ears.*

He stood and stretched, dumped the oatmeal into the toilet, and flushed it. Turning to go deal with the gutter, he caught his face in the mirror.

You don't deserve any of them. At all. You are a lucky motherfucker, Frank Brennan.

CHAPTER TWO

"Frank, if you make me look at one more reclining Buddha or muddy river in this heat, I will die of sunstroke, and you'll have to raise your spawn alone."

Alex threw herself under a palm tree in Santiphap Park, sweaty and exhausted. The children ran in circles, chasing birds and no doubt terrifying the Bangkok locals who had also come to this inner-city oxygen park seeking respite from heat and the grime of a Southeast Asian summer.

Respite my ass, she thought. *It's like going from a pizza oven to a steamer. The only difference is instead of being cooked on pavement, I'm being steamed in leaves.*

In a word, Bangkok was overwhelming, a city with a strange blend of progress and stillness. Its identity seemed to shift from street to street. Bustling crowds moved in an elegant, frantic ballet through pathways clogged with random congregations of food vendors demanding attention, then flattening out to cool, sprawling parks filled with statues and ponds.

They'd arrived at dawn the previous day, and Frank had barely given his family time to drop their bags at the hotel before he took off on a manic tour of temples, gardens, and back-alley mystery foods that was literally wiping her out.

Alex scowled up at her husband's grinning face when he sat down next to her and wiped the damp hair from her forehead.

"And to think I used to jog in my full gear here. Wimp."

Frank leaned over and studied her face, his teasing expression vanishing. His hand dropped to her wrist to take her pulse, his face blank, empty. *Where do you go, Frank? And why?* He studied the minute hand on his dive watch, his fingers absentmindedly caressing the evil eye tattoo, the twin of his own, that covered the thin skin of her wrist. The seconds ticked by while he counted her heartbeats, his jaw clenched in concentration. She watched him make the quick calculation in his head, his brow wrinkled. Her pulse was too high, but she didn't need him to tell her that.

"Alex, you don't look so good." Frank leaned down and put his cheek against her forehead. "You're all pale and clammy. Jesus, babe, you look green," he worried.

A brisk rummage in his backpack produced a water bottle. Frank poured some into the palm of his hand and trickled it over her forehead, then rolled the cold bottle across her wrists and neck. She slipped it from his hands and took a sip.

"I'm fine," she insisted, elbowing him away from her.

"You look like shit, princess," he said matter-of-factly.

Alex rolled her eyes. "Such a charmer, Frank. *Maybe* that's because this place is like a twenty-four-hour *schvitz*. I'm a northern girl. This heat is for the birds. I'll be fine. Quit fussing," she insisted, struggling now to get up.

Frank pushed her back down firmly, his giant hands gently forcing her shoulders back to the ground. "Nothing doing. You're done for the day. Heat stroke is nothing to mess with here, Alex." He pulled Frank Jr.'s blankie from his backpack, a worn quilted blanket with army men on it, and fashioned it into a pillow for her.

"For once, I'm glad he's still dragging this rag around. But when we get home, that's it. No more blankie. He's not a baby anymore, princess."

Alex settled herself comfortably on the improvised pillow, breathing in the familiar scent of her youngest. "He's my baby, Frank." Her voice caught against her will. *Goddamn hormones. Oh my God, I'm crying. Why am I crying? Because he won't be my baby anymore.* A sob escaped her lips.

Frank's face softened as he kissed her forehead. "You stay put and watch the babies play. I'll go get you a shaved ice. Grab the kids some lunch."

"Okay," she said. The thought of shaved ice on her roiling stomach sounded like heaven.

"When you're feeling better, we'll take a cab back to the hotel and the babies can play in the pool." Frank darted in for a quick kiss. "Maybe you and I can make out in the cabana. Sound good?"

Alex nodded gratefully up at her husband, wiping her eyes and wondering if now was a good time to tell him the truth. *No. He'll just worry. Better to wait. I hate it when he's worried. That blank face will show up and never leave.*

Alex reached up, grabbed him by his ink black hair, and kissed his lips three times fast. "Hurry back." *When we get home. What's two more weeks? He'll be fine with it. We never talked about more, but it'll be fine.*

"Back before you miss me. There's a boat noodle joint next street over. Best in the city. Doesn't that sound good, babe? Hot pork and beef noodles?"

Alex swallowed a mouth full of vomit and tried not to gag. "Awesome. Sounds great. Don't forget the ice, Frank." *No fucking way can I gag that shit down.*

Alex watched him jog away, pausing to give Junior two puffs of his inhaler. Then he bellowed at both kids to listen to their mother and vanished into the throng of people, motorbikes, and cars that surrounded the park.

So sleepy. I'll just close my eyes for a minute. A second later, she sprawled dead asleep under the smothering blanket of the tropical heat, drooling, sweating, and ten weeks pregnant.

Frank navigated the tight streets of Bangkok like a shark, weaving through the bustling crowds. Something of his old self seemed to fall over him, as if he'd never left, even as he tried to push down the worry about Alex.

That look in her eye. I don't like it. There's something there, something that wasn't there before. He shook his head, dismissing the thought. *She's never been out of*

Detroit, unless you count our honeymoon in Niagara, and I don't. Poor thing just needs a day or two to acclimatize. Then she'll learn to love this town like I do.

Frank Brennan loved Thailand. The heat, like being in a sauna all day, the way his sweat condensed on his skin when he entered their cool hotel room, all conspiring to make his body feel loose and nimble. The smells of street food, flowers, trees, the rivers, and the exhaust that all seemed to merge at the Victory Monument, along with the swells of people and busses and cars that swirled around it. He loved everything about this place despite the events that had led him to leave it ten years ago. Sure, he'd made good friends and bad enemies here, but now that the new government had driven out the latter, he could breathe a sigh of relief not only for himself but for this beautiful city as well. *And besides, all the intel was good. It's clear. This place is safer than the States, now.*

Frank's pace slowed when he spied a hat stand opposite the boat noodle vendor, a grin lighting up his face. Pointing one meaty finger at the biggest hat they had, one so bedecked with flowers it looked like a float in the Thanksgiving Day parade, he began haggling good-naturedly with the vendor in fluent Thai. A few minutes later, he strolled away, smug about paying five baht less than he'd been willing to, imagining the look on Alex's face when he made her wear it. But Frank's smug grin vanished when a hand gripped his shoulder and a hauntingly familiar voice stopped him in his tracks. *No. This is not happening. It can't be.*

"*Bozhe moi,* can it be? Frank Brennan, my old friend, is you?"

Frank swallowed hard, the flowered hat so tight in his hands he nearly shredded it. *Alexei.* He'd know that Slavic bastard's voice anywhere. The idling engine of his Formula One mind sputtered, turned over, then punched through all eight gears and landed on mercenary. In a flash, his easy-going grin vanished, replaced with the grim mask he'd cultivated years ago when he was still in the brotherhood. He shoved the hat into the startled hands of a Bangkok businessman who immediately dropped the overwrought confection. Frank spun around to face his old archnemesis Alexei Morozov.

"Alexei," he stated as if no time had passed since the day ten years ago that the Russian mobster had tried to kill him and failed. "How's tricks?" He swallowed his revulsion when the lanky, silver-blonde mobster clutched him in a bear hug and slapped his back soundly.

"But how is it you are *alive*, old friend? The warehouse was leveled. There were no survivors. I mourned you like brother, Franchesko. "

Since you had four of your own brothers and one sister put to death, I'm flattered, asshole.

"I managed to get out just before it blew. The Red Lotus crowd wasn't so lucky," he growled. *Come on, Frank. Stay frosty. You can do this. Just like riding a bike.* Unfortunately, instead of conjuring the old Frank, the word "bike," conjured an image of Junior wobbling on his two-wheeler after Frank took the training wheels off. *Shit. Wake up, old Frank.*

"Nimble, Franchesko. So very *nimble*."

"Lucky for me, old friend." Frank locked his expression at two parts sneer, one part calculating. *There we go. I got this.* "Let's take a walk. This place is crawling with ears."

He steered Alexei in the direction opposite the park where his wife and children waited, counting the minutes, praying she didn't rally enough to come looking for him. *Shit. Fuck. Goddamn it. I should have risked the East Coast. I'm going to kill the source that told me Asia was clear. This fuck-up might have just gotten my whole family killed, never mind me.*

Alexei tugged on Frank's flowered bowling shirt, the one Alex had given him the year his team went to regionals. "What is with fucking tourist wear, my old friend? Is cruise wear or retirement home wear?" Alexei wiped one elegant hand off on his own pristine, bespoken suit as if he'd been sullied.

"I'm doing a job. It's cover." *Keep him moving, keep him talking.*

"You look like, what do they call it in your country? *Douchebag?*"

Frank laughed and clapped Alexei overly hard on his slender back, gratified as the smaller man coughed and winced.

"I had forgotten, Franchesko, how strong you are. Like bear. Is shame you are not Russian. You would make excellent son of Mother Russia."

I'm actually going to kill you this time, Frank thought, forcing to keep a grin on his face. *This is my favorite shirt, you Russian sleaze. I bowled a perfect game with the Pin You Downs in this shirt. Okay, think Frank. Five minutes since you bought the hat. Ten minutes to shake him, fifteen back to grab Alex and the babies. Fuck.* How the hell could he pull off the miracle of getting them out of the country before Alexei discovered their existence? He ground his teeth together. He'd have to call D'eng. He hated to bring his old friend into this, but there was no other way. No matter what, every second he spent talking to Alexei was one step closer to disaster. *I should never have come back.*

"Well, nice seeing you, Alexei. Like I said, I'm on a job, so no time for chitchat. Give my best to your goon squad," he growled, smirking at his nickname for the twenty-odd Russian guards the mobster took with him everywhere. He held his hand out to shake Alexei's hand, but Alexei's ice-blue eyes froze him in place as he gripped Frank's shoulder.

"Don't be so hasty, old friend. We must catch up. We have much to discuss." He drew out the "s" in "discuss", a singular affectation and inflection the Russian snake was known for the world over. *In addition to his penchant for mailing heads in boxes.*

Frank felt the ground under his feet start to give as the situation tumbled from chain reaction to critical mass. *No way out.*

"Fine. I gotta do a thing right now. I'll meet you at the club. Tonight. Nine o'clock."

"Excellent, Franchesko. I knew you would see reason. We can discuss, among other things, your debts. All three hundred million of them. And I haven't forgotten our deal."

"What deal is that, old pal?" Frank spat.

"The girl. You remember. Your life for hers? Your soul in exchange for her freedom?"

And there it was. The fly in the ointment, the hook, the gut punch, the thinly veiled threat that meant Alexei knew. But how much? How much did he know, and how much did he suspect?

Alexei turned and strolled away, his white linen suit a still, cool point in the Bangkok heat, the innocent souls that thronged around him unaware that they were brushing elbows with the most lethal, bloodthirsty Russian mobster of the century. And Frank's old boss. The man he'd tried to double-cross. Frank's blood ran cold as Alexei stopped and picked up the flowered hat the businessman had dropped. Turning on one heel, he waved it in the air at Frank, winked, and kept walking. *Alex. Gwennie. Frank Jr. Oh God, what have I done?*

CHAPTER THREE

\\

Alex was dreaming she was a donut frying in oil. Hot, sticky, bubbling oil. *I am a donut,* she thought. *A big, fat old-fashioned donut.* There seemed to be a heavy weight on her stomach, and in her dream state, she decided it must be either jelly filling or Boston cream.

She moaned out loud, "I don't want to be a jelly donut." The titters of her children made her eyes fly open. *Where the hell am I? Okay. Sky. Tree.* She turned her head. *Judgmental Thai family staring at the sweaty, deranged housewife.* She looked the other way. *Pond. Buddha.* She looked down to her jelly filling.

"What on earth are you two doing?" she hissed at Gwennie and Frank Jr.

What she had dreamed was donut filling was actually Frank Jr.'s chess set, the one he'd built himself out of an old lunch box and a variety of junk he'd found around the house. Pez heads for the king and queens, army men for rooks, tiny plastic saints for bishops, each knight a red or black six-sided die.

Frank Jr. shrugged and pushed his glasses up.

Gwennie cast her brother a withering look and explained, "We got bored of waiting, and Daddy said not to let you get fussed, so Frankie and I decided that we needed to be as close to you as possible to stop any fussing. We were playing chess while you had your nap. Why are you so sweaty?"

Alex ignored her precocious daughter and struggled to sit up, the legions of improvised chessmen spilling off her lap as she did. She squinted up. The sun seemed lower in the sky.

"Where's Daddy? What time is it?"

Both kids shrugged at her in unison.

"I'm hungry," Frank Jr. said. "Daddy said he was bringing me noodles off a boat."

"Boat noodles, you half-wit," Gwennie corrected.

"Gwendolyn, do not talk to your brother like that," Alex chastised absentmindedly. She glanced at her watch. Two o'clock. She shook her watch. *Two o'clock?* But she'd lain down at noon, she was sure of it. She'd seen the time on Frank's dive watch when he took her pulse.

She stood a bit shakily and held up a hand to shield her eyes, scanning the park. *Where the fuck was Frank?*

Across the city, Frank dug into the pocket of his cargo shorts and pulled out his sat phone, the one he kept ready at all times in case of, well, *exactly* this. He grimaced as he dialed the number, furious with himself. *I should have given Alex a phone. Hell, I should have given her the truth. Too late for all that now. Come on, D'eng, answer already.* A click followed by a loud stream of near incomprehensible joyful Thai exploded in his ear, forcing him to jerk the phone away from his head.

"Jesus, D'eng, calm down," Frank barked, still scanning the street. *Shit. Where are you, you ugly Russian bastards? Show yourselves.* "Yeah," he said into the phone. "Yeah, same old Frank. No shit, Sherlock. I know that *now.* No."

He was walking fast, trying to keep moving away from the park. Alexei's goons had to be about somewhere. He scanned the crowd while D'eng yammered about bad intel, Alexei's sudden appearance in Thailand, and something about a government snitch, but he couldn't make a single one of Alexei's goon squad.

"No, I know you have a life, D'eng but this is *life and death.*" He stopped walking and spun in a slow circle, slicking his sweat-damp hair back from his face. "Whose? *My family's.*" He took a small measure of smug pleasure out of the stunned silence on the other end of the line.

"Good. Bring the van. And my bag. You know exactly what bag I mean. Tough shit. I need my clothes and my gun. Of course they'll still fit. Maybe *you've* put on a few. I have not." Frank sucked in his stomach and winced. *I gotta stop eating pasta.* "Fine. Victory Monument, south side, one hour. You still driving that shitty white panel van?" He laughed. "Jesus, D'eng. Okay, hurry." Frank paused and then said something he knew would shock D'eng even more than the revelation that Frank Brennan had a family.

"Please," he whispered into the sat phone, his voice broken and strained. "Please hurry."

Back at Santiphap Park, Alex studied her children with alarm. They were sunburnt and bleary eyed. The Southeast Asian heat was transforming her pale, northern babies into limp, sweaty ragdolls. Gwennie's freckles stood out more than usual, and Junior's tubby little stomach was panting like a chubby puppy. A slight wheeze rattled in his chest. *Shit, Frank has his inhaler.* Squatting, she pulled another water bottle out of the bag.

"Here, scoot together, you two," she urged and arranged Frank Jr.'s blankie over their heads. "Get your heads out of this sun." She ran a hand over Junior's back. "Easy now, buddy. Daddy will be back soon." He squinted up at her, his glasses slipping from the sweat beads on his tiny nose, and nodded. She handed Gwennie the water bottle. "Share this with your brother, baby girl."

Heads bent together, her two offspring passed the bottle back and forth as they wrote down their chess moves from the interrupted match in the notebook Junior kept. It was a tattered composition book filled with cryptic runes like Duck to Infantry 1 or Lion to Red Die 9. It was all gibberish to her. The current match between her two quick-witted children had lasted two months. The record was five.

She scanned the direction in which Frank had disappeared. *Something about a noodle stand one street over?* She started in that direction and then stopped. First of all, she doubted he would be there two hours later. And second, she didn't see how she could drag two kids on a wild Frank chase. A flash of Frank's random vacant expressions shot across her mind, and she shook her head to clear it.

You're imagining things, Alex. There could be any number of reasons he vanished. For two hours. In Bangkok. Leaving her under a tree with no money, two kids, and pregnant. Shit. Alex tried to remember where the hotel was. *Think, Alex. It was a fat white building by a tall skinny building,* she thought. *That's no help. I wasn't paying attention. I was too busy not barfing. Goddamn it all. Fucking pregnancy brain.*

Cursing under her breath, Alex sank to her knees next to her tented children. *He's probably off having a fine time while we wither like worms in the sun.*

"I'm sure Daddy will be back soon. He's probably just—" Alex's head jerked up, her consoling sentence evaporating in midstream.

Screams. A rolling cascade of screams spread throughout Santiphap Park as an old white panel van jumped the curb on the other side of the park, sending drowsy tourists running. *What the hell?* It seemed to be flooring it straight toward . . .

Toward . . .

She fell backwards, arms pinwheeling to catch herself.

She heard her children gasp at the same time she did.

Straight toward them.

CHAPTER FOUR

’eng Nabeet, you son of a bitch," Frank growled, lifting the smaller man off the ground in a bear hug. "Missed you, man."

"Put me down, American motherfucker. You break my ribs with your ridiculous entitled muscles, G-man." D’eng grinned up into Frank’s face good-naturedly. He reached back into his panel van and tossed a duffle bag at Frank’s feet with a grimace.

"Here’s your bag. You sure about this?"

"I don’t have a choice, D’eng. I got pulled back in. I gotta square my debts, deal with Alexei."

"No, I mean you sure you gonna fit in your old clothes, fatty?" He reached out and poked Frank in the gut. "You got a spare tire, Frankie."

Frank glared at his former driver and sucked in his gut. "It’s like ten pounds, man, lay off."

After picking Frank up in the organized chaos that was Victory Monument, D’eng located a back alley so Frank could change and apprise him of the situation.

Frank rummaged through the bag he'd left behind ten years ago before the explosion, talking as he pulled clothes out.

"So here's the deal," he said, casting an eye around and pulling his shirt off. "We got three targets in the park. I need them taken in safely and quickly, but I need it to look like a kidnapping. One adult female, two children." He pulled on a white tank top, then dropped his trousers, kicking them off with his sandals.

D'eng was nodding. "Yes, yes. Three targets. Hey, more like twenty pounds, Frank."

Frank glared at him and pulled out a pair of black track pants. Slipping them on, he continued, "Santiphap Park, across from the fountain. Youngest target has asthma, so try to keep things calm. Middle target bites, so stay in the van unless it's necessary for you to get out. Adult female bites, too. And kicks," he muttered, running his fingers inside the waistband of his track pants. *These feel way tighter than they used to.* Rummaging in his discarded shorts, he grabbed Junior's inhaler and jammed it in his track pants pocket. He pulled out a matching black zip-up jacket and a gold chain. He slipped his arms into the jacket, zipped it half-way, wound the chain around his neck, then reached for his tactical boots. They slid on like a glove. *Damn, I look cool. This was a cool look. Tracksuits and guns. I look badass.*

"You look like an asshole. No one dress like that anymore," D'eng laughed, shaking his head at Frank's getup. "Hey, what's this got to do with your family, Frank?"

Frank finished lacing up his boots and tucked them inside his track pants. *I've still got it. Feels good, I can do this. Little rusty, but I got this.* He reached into the bag for one final item, his P-96 pistol. He inspected it to make sure D'eng had kept it cleaned and oiled, then checked that it was loaded.

"They *are* my family, D'eng." He ripped the passenger door open, ignoring the look of shock on D'eng's face. "Let's hit it, man."

Jumping into the passenger seat, his adrenaline slowed just enough for him to register the stink coming from the back of the panel van. "D'eng, what the fuck is that smell?"

"Delivery at the docks. Didn't have time to clean before you called. Frank say urgent, D'eng come right away. No time to hose out. Tough shit, old pal."

"It smells like the deck of a whaling ship."

"Close." Flooring it out of the back alley, D'eng merged with the cacophony of frantic Bangkok traffic, laughing.

Shit, Frank thought, reaching across to grab a pack of cigarettes off the dash. He put one between his lips, lit it, and coughed as the nicotine from his first cigarette in ten years burnt his lungs.

Alex wasn't going to like this. Not at all.

———

As the van careened toward them, Alex scrambled to her feet, hauling the kids up by their spindly arms. The white van slid sideways to a halt twenty feet away, turf churning under its tires.

"No, wait, come back!" she begged the judgmental Thai family when they sprinted away to safety, leaving her alone and cornered between the runaway van and the tree.

A grinning Thai man in the driver's seat waved at her even as the van's panel door slid open.

Mouth agape, she stood speechless as Frank, her husband, ex-Marine, vinyl siding consultant, and Detroit regional bowling champion (four years running) leapt out. His flowered bowling shirt was gone, and in its place was a too-tight tracksuit more suited to an '80s mobster, a gun holstered on his bad shoulder, and his familiar face entirely blank and void of emotion. She stumbled backwards, the children slipping from her grasp as this new Frank crossed the distance between them. He grabbed Frank Jr. and Gwennie, tucking one child under each arm, barely looked at her, then strode back to the van, the children a mass of squirming arms and legs. She found her voice and feebly called out, "Frank?" He turned, and she thought she saw the mask flicker once, but instead of replying, he threw Frank Jr. and Gwennie into the back of the van. He froze there, hands clenched in fists at his side. She could see he was breathing heavily.

"Frank," she said again, her voice thin and clipped.

"Get in the van, Alex." His voice rumbled low, she could barely hear him. "*Please.*"

She heard the transmission slip into gear, park to drive. The wheels began to turn. Stunned, Alex scrambled to her feet and sprinted toward the van. She shoved

Frank to one side, then threw herself inside, legs scrambling for purchase as the van started to roll away. She felt Frank grab her legs and push her the rest of the way in. Her face landed in a puddle of something foul—*Is that a fish head?*—so she tucked her body and rolled, her children's legs stopping her before she hit the back of the van. Struggling to right herself while the driver accelerated, she locked eyes with her husband when he slammed the door shut. *I'm going to fucking kill him.*

———————

Frank had smoked two cigarettes in the ten-minute drive to the park. When he jumped out of the panel van, he couldn't meet Alex's eyes. Worse, he couldn't even speak to her for fear he'd start apologizing under the weight of those big brown eyes and blow their whole kidnapping cover. Instead, he grabbed one child under each arm, tickling them so they wouldn't be afraid, and threw them into the van, knowing she'd follow. He reached into his pocket and underhanded the inhaler to Junior, winking at him as he did. Then he stood clenching his fists in front of the open panel door, waiting. She shoved him sideways, and he barely felt it. The sight of her trying to throw herself in the van nearly broke his manufactured cool, but the look Alex gave him when he slammed the panel door shut said it all.

Alexei, his Russian goons, his wife. No matter how you cut it, I am a dead man.

She's *going to fucking kill me.*

Alex clutched the children to her in the dark recesses of the panel van while it bumped and sped along. Her eyes were riveted on her husband. Frank sat in the passenger seat, occasionally casting blank glances back at his family, his dead shark eyes sliding past hers, but not lingering. The only sound was the wet, sloshing noise of the fish gut swill they were sitting in.

"What are we covered in, Mommy?" Gwennie whispered.

"Why is Daddy dressed like that?" Frank Jr. whispered. He took a puff of his inhaler.

She clutched her children tighter and shushed them.

"Francis Xavier Brennan, why in the name of *God* did you kidnap your family at gunpoint and why the *fuck* am I in a van covered in fish guts?"

She saw Frank gulp, the first real Frank expression since he'd tossed them all inside this fetid van. Relief washed over her.

Frank turned then and crept into the back, throwing a dark glare at the driver. "Keep driving, D'eng. Lap the entire city before you even think about heading there. Back door. We can't arrive until after dark. And turn up the radio. You're too fucking nosy." The driver turned up the radio, the sounds of K-pop harmonizing with the sloshing sound.

Frank crept closer to them, but Alex pointedly scooted away. Frank's face fell and suddenly it was *him* again. His voice rumbled low so only she and the kids could hear.

"One more puff, buddy," he said to Junior, tapping his nose.

Junior nodded and obliged, then handed the inhaler back to his father.

"Atta boy." Frank took a deep breath and looked Alex in the eyes. "I was in the Marines. That much is true. Then things happened. I was kind of a double agent. Look, all you need to know is that a Russian mobster named Alexei wants me dead, and he cannot know about you and the babies. At all. Ever."

Alex met his eyes unwavering, astonished to see that behind the blank look, hiding all along, had been fear. *He's terrified. What the hell could terrify Frank?*

"Ten years of marriage, two kids, and you ditch me in the middle of a Bangkok schvitz, and all the explanation you can manage is some horseshit about a Russian? Try again, asshole, or I'll kill you myself," Alex spat.

The driver yelled back, "I like your wife, Frank. She has a real way with words."

"D'eng Nabeet! Shut your goddamn hole and drive!" Frank bellowed.

"Dagnabbit?" Alex hissed. "Is this a *joke*?"

Frank groaned. "No, Alex, not 'dagnabbit'. His name is D'eng Nabeet. One of my oldest friends. Used to be my driver back in the day. Don't be casually racist, princess."

"Let me ask you this, Frank. Who's on first? Let me guess. Yosemite Sam?"

The children giggled, and Alex shushed them.

"Listen. I can't explain things now." Gritting his teeth, he let his breath out in a hiss. "I'm not even sure where to start."

"Why don't you start with the whole, 'I was kind of a double agent'?"

Frank's head sank into his hands. "Please. I can't even deal with all that until I get you three somewhere safe. Somewhere I can leave you and go take care of this. Can you please wait until I get you to the safe house? Then I'll tell you everything. I promise."

Alex gripped the children tighter and scooted farther away from him, enjoying the hurt look on his face.

"Where exactly is this safe house, Frank?"

From the front of the van, D'eng's laughter rang out. "She's not gonna like this, Frank Brennan. You better pray Alexei get you before angry American wife does."

"Dagnabbit," Frank cursed and crawled back to the driver's seat.

"Where the hell are you taking us, Frank?" Alex hissed.

"Somewhere . . . safe," Frank mumbled. His head slumped against the passenger window, and he said no more.

CHAPTER FIVE

They drove around Bangkok in the stinking van for hours. Alex and the children fell asleep, covered in fish juice and sweat, lulled by the bumping of the van as the sun set over Bangkok.

Alex no longer dreamed she was a donut—she now dreamed she was on a small boat with Robert Shaw, chumming for great whites. "We're gonna need a bigger boat," she moaned, waking with a start when the van stopped suddenly.

Both D'eng and Frank wordlessly exited the vehicle, slamming the doors behind them. Ten minutes passed, and then the panel slid open, letting in a much-needed wave of fresh night air. Frank stuck in his head, and Alex resisted the urge to kick him in his perfect teeth.

"Hurry. Please," he said tersely.

Alex pushed the sleepy children toward him. He gathered them up in his arms, the children instantly awake and scrambling like monkeys over their father's broad chest. They gripped his neck with their arms and his waist with their legs, leaving his hands free to pull Alex from the van. Alex flung him off once she was out, then stood rocking on uneasy legs.

"Oh God, babe. You're a fucking mess," Frank mumbled.

Alex looked down at herself. Grass clippings were stuck all over her bare legs, held in place by some sort of sticky slimy fish-smelling veneer that covered the rest of her. She raised her arm and sniffed, then gagged. *Oh God, I'm not chumming for sharks. I am chum. I'm going to be sick.*

Before she could say a single word on her list—*specifically words like vomit, fucking bastard, murder, divorce, chum, shower, help*—Frank grabbed her by her hand and dragged her down a dark alley cluttered with trash and pallets, and through a dark doorway. She trailed behind him, jogging to keep up, a giggling child bouncing on each side of him.

From the dark van, to the dark alley, to the dark doorway, Alex could not make heads or tails of where they were. Suddenly, the door opened, and a wash of cool air surrounded them like a cloud. Marble floors. *Air-conditioning,* Alex thought. *Oh thank God.*

A long hallway stretched to both her left and right, and soft Asian music played, something heavy on the zither, punctuated with cascading flutes. Giant planters spilled over with ferns and palms under a soaring vaulted ceiling. Thin, gold silk curtains swayed in an invisible breeze.

The door closed behind them while Frank let the kids slide off him down to the floor. Gwennie and Frank Jr., unfazed, prowled about, leaving fish gut footprints on the pristine floor of the oasis as they did.

Alex had just opened her mouth to offer Frank one of the words from the list she'd made when a door opened down the hall. A woman, clad only in a bra, panties, and garter belt stepped out. She tilted her head quizzically at the motley crew. D'eng called out something incomprehensible in Thai, which caused an instant uproar in the deserted hall. Alex thought she heard Frank's name in the gibberish and very distinctly heard the name Madam Li.

One after another, doors flew open and more girls, dozens of small lovely women in underwear and men in robes poked their heads out. Giggles and Thai whispers filled the marble hall. *What is this place?* Alex thought. *And why is everyone in their underwear?*

Just then, a heavy blanket of silence fell, every voice cut off in unison. A woman appeared beneath the vaulted arch at the far end of the hallway. A vision in ivory and gold that seemed to float just above the marble floors, she drifted toward them like a specter, her lovely porcelain face set in a disapproving mask. She stopped in front of Frank and stared at him in silence for a long moment.

Frank bowed and took the woman's hand. "Madam Li."

The woman let him kiss her fingertips, then she threw her arms wide and embraced him. Frank returned the hug, patting her tiny ribcage and laughing, relief apparent in the set of his shoulders.

With a snort, the woman pushed Frank away to circle Alex and the children, her nose wrinkling in distaste. After the beautiful, ageless woman finished her circuit and arranged herself next to Frank, Alex grabbed the children and retreated, leaning against the exit door. She tried the handle, her mind swirling around a horrifying possibility but unwilling to land on it. Locked. *Shit.*

"Frank Brennan. I never thought I'd see you again. Not after what happened."

"Trixie, listen. This is my wife, Alex, and my kids. Alexei knows I'm alive."

"Unfortunate," Madam Li clucked.

"That's an understatement, Trix."

The woman's porcelain brow furrowed. "I did not know he was here. I swear it, Frank. He left here years ago. This puts us all in danger. What will you do?"

"I'm going back in. I'll take care of this. I need you to keep my family safe until I'm finished." Frank cast a glance back to Alex and the kids, his cold mask once again firmly in place.

"Of course. I have plenty of rooms. I cannot think of a safer place for your beloved family then in my establishment. Although I am not sure you have fully considered the repercussions of this . . . indiscretion."

"Fuck the indiscretion, Trix. I am out of options. Just keep your clients away from them, okay?"

Establishment. Alex's spinning head sent that word to the top of her list. The men with giggling girls who had emerged from all those rooms. *Clients.* Everyone wearing underwear and robes. *Indiscretion.* Alex cleared her throat, her low, even voice cutting through the commotion. "Frank."

Every head in the hallway turned. *That's right. The show is right here. Step right up and get your tickets to see the fishwife.* Every head except Frank's. He stared at his ridiculous boots.

"Frank, is this a *whorehouse*? Did you bring your *children* to a Bangkok whorehouse?"

He turned and looked at her, his face ashen. *"Honey…"* he trailed off, then gritted his teeth.

A strange look crossed Madam Li's ethereal face. She clapped her hands together twice and leveled the crowd with a withering stare. Instantly, the assembled girls and businessmen scattered, leaving only Frank, Alex, D'eng, the children, and herself. Frank looked up from his boots to flash her a look of gratitude.

"Thanks, Trix. Can you give us a minute?"

"Certainly. Come along with me, children. We will get you cleaned up. D'eng, I am astonished at you. Careless way to treat honored guests."

The children, for once, listened without arguing, both of them clearly under the thrall of the diminutive madam. They slipped from Alex's clutching hands and skipped off with the tiny goddess.

Oh God, Alex thought, *she's so . . . and she's . . . and he . . .* Her hurt gaze flew from the draped vision gracefully exiting the room with her children back to Frank's wary face. He looked like himself again, all scruffy and chastened, as if he'd forgotten to take the trash out. The familiarity, the *casualness* of his posture enraged her. *How dare he look like my Frank? He is not my Frank.*

"Alex, babe, listen to me—" he started.

Alex cut him off. "Don't you 'babe' me. What the fuck is all this, Frank?" Alex flew across the room at him. "And *Trix? Trix?* You son of a bitch."

Frank threw his arms up to deflect the punches she rained on him. "Babe, stop. It's not what you think. Ow, damn it, Alex, that's my bad shoulder."

"Tough shit, Frank." She whirled around and kicked him square in his bad shoulder, then dropped into a wobbly crouch.

Frank clutched his shoulder and muttered, "Fucking mother-daughter kickboxing." Then louder, "Baby, please. Why do you have to be so rough?"

"What the fuck is going on, asshole?" she hissed, her fist darting out in a vicious jab.

Frank caught her hand and stopped her easily, dragging her to him and pinning her against his chest. "Princess, listen to me," he whispered, then roared when she bit him.

"Don't you 'princess' me, Frank Brennan. Don't you dare!"

"You right, Frankie. Adult female target *does* bite!"

Frank and Alex's heads whipped around at D'eng. Alex took the moment to wrench her wrists out of Frank's grip.

"You no tell your wife you an arms dealer assassin, Frank? You stupider than I remember."

"D'eng, wait in the car, goddamn it. Let me talk to my wife."

Alex sneered as the giggling man slipped out the back door. "Are you kidding me? Russian mobsters, a whorehouse, and a driver named D'eng Nabeet, Frank? Is this some kind of sick joke?"

Frank didn't answer her. He glared at her darkly, clutching his chest where she'd bitten him and breathing heavily.

Alex went cold. She'd never seen that look on her husband's face, ever. Whatever this was, it was worse than angry. Worse than scared. Worse than a stranger. She took two steps away from him, shaking.

"Did you sleep with her?" she whispered hoarsely.

Frank slumped into a nearby chair, his head sinking into his hands. "I mean, not recently," she heard him mumble.

Alex's legs went out from underneath her. She fell to the floor as if he'd punched her.

Frank's eyes were hollow. "Listen, you have to understand. This whole nation was a powder keg. She was sympathetic to the revolution. And it's not what you think. At all."

"I bet she was sympathetic," Alex spat.

"Alex, I have been faithful to you and only you since we met. Do not hold my past against me. I have never held it against you that you went out with that douchebag pinball wizard."

"How is that the same thing as dating a Bangkok madam in a whorehouse during your assassin years, Frank? And for the last time, he was a skee ball wizard. You know how much I love skee ball! My head was turned! I didn't even know you yet!"

"I thought when we got married, we agreed to let the past go," Frank pleaded.

"You mean your free-wheeling, assassin-ing, arms-dealing, whore-whoring past? Is your name even Frank? Who are you, you son of a bitch?"

"Yes! Francis Xavier Brennan. I swear to God, babe. You know everything real about me. Except, well . . ."

"The assassin-whore-arms dealer business? Except *that*, Francis?"

"I walked away from all that. All of it. You and the kids are all I want. And I wasn't really an assassin. D'eng is exaggerating. I was an agent."

"Who assassinated people? And dealt arms?"

"Well, I mean . . . from a certain point of view, you could say . . ." He paused. "Honestly, I'd need a map to explain all this." He glanced around the elegant hallway hopefully, as if a Cold War-era spy map was about to materialize.

I should have known. None of this was real. Him. Me. Us. None of it.

"Get out, Frank." Alex's voice was frigid and shaken, but it brooked no debate.

He tried anyway. "Alex, I—"

"Get out, Frank. Get away from me." Alex rubbed the tattoo on her wrist furiously, like it was a hive. *Oh God, all this time. I'm so stupid.* "I can't look at you. You make me sick. Who are you, really?" she asked, her face a mask of bewildered disgust.

"Alex, no, let me explain—"

"I don't want to hear your explanations. I want to go to my children, and I don't want to hear any more of your horseshit. How *could* you, Frank? How could you do this to me? To us? Do we mean anything to you at all?"

The gutted face vanished, erased by that hollow rage she'd seen only moments before. Frank stood, delivering a sharp kick to the chair as he did and flipping it backwards into the wall with a crash. He strode past her from the room, slamming the exit door behind him.

The jarring sounds of the chair falling and the door slamming echoed in the marble room, a shockwave that shattered the dam that had been holding back her tears. *Who was he?* A stranger.

Alex's hands slid down to her stomach while she sobbed, not even registering when Madam Li entered the room on silent feet. She was so exhausted, so terrified, so heartbroken. *So nauseous,* she thought with alarm. *I'm going to barf.* She scanned the hall at ground level for a trash can—anything—and saw only small gold slippers and perfect little ankles. *Oh God, I think I already have pregnancy cankles. Her ankles are the size of Gwennie's wrists.*

Alex's eyes trailed toward the ceiling while she tried to force down the vomit. Gold and ivory robes, long gold nails, tiny white hands, ageless sardonic face. Madam Li. Trixie. Frank's sidepiece. Or whatever she was.

"Come, come, Mrs. Frank Brennan. Frank is very dear to me. I will take good care of you."

Her overly familiar words seemed to trigger the burgeoning nausea. Alex vomited all over the madam's pristine slippers, then passed out cold on the marble floor. The last thing she registered was the look of disgust on Madam Li's lovely face.

Frank wrenched the door open on D'eng's van and vaulted inside, slamming it so hard behind him that the entire vehicle rocked.

"You watch temper with my car, Frank Brennan. Not my car's fault you lie to American wife."

Frank turned in his seat and fixed D'eng with the stare that had convinced a secret government agency to send him up against the Russians as a double agent. It was a silent look that said murder, war, and no remorse. D'eng visibly paled and then started the car.

Once they drove on and were absorbed by traffic, Frank allowed himself to slump in the seat, heedless of the glances D'eng was casting at him.

This is like a nightmare come true. All of it. Everything I worried about and then some. Oh God, the way Alex looked at me.

"You okay, Frank? Where we going?"

"The club," Frank said in a low voice. "Now."

"No, no, no. No club. Frank, listen . . ."

"Shut up and drive, D'eng," he growled.

Frank slumped forward, his head dropping into his hands.

I thought I had it under control. Thought I could keep her safe from all this. But now . . . now that she knows what I am, even after all this time, maybe she won't want me anymore. And she doesn't even know the worst of it yet.

CHAPTER SIX

Frank stepped into Club Euro and surveyed the dining room. Dark velvet walls, low hanging golden chandeliers, a band playing the entire Dean Martin playlist in Thai. *Alex loves The Rat Pack*, he thought, then immediately squashed the recollection. *Not now.* Across the sea of white linen, he spied Alexei at his favorite table in a dark corner, back to the wall. *Assassin's chair*, Frank thought. *Best seat in the house. Can see everything coming.* He walked across the dining room, trying not to look like he was sucking in his gut. His pale blue linen suit, tailored for him ten years ago, was oddly tight around the middle, and Frank made himself a silent promise to lay off pizza. *Maybe I'll look into one of those caveman diets when I get home. If I get home. If I live and Alex lives and if she even lets me come home.*

He paused at the table, painfully aware that Alexei had arranged Frank's seat with his back to the room. *Worst seat in the house. Way to set the tone, pal.*

"Alexei," Frank growled, sliding into the offending chair.

"You look like fucking Don Johnson in Miami Vice rags, Franchesko. Have you not bought proper suit since last we met?" Alexei's laugh was a shard of ice.

Frank nervously smoothed the lapels of his old suit and adjusted the collar of his pink pocket tee underneath. *No I haven't, asshat. I've been living in cargo pants and t-shirts for the last ten years. Fucking lame-ass suits. It's not like I had time to run out and get the latest in mob fashion. Quick. Say something to change the conversation. God, I'm out of practice in the field. Something clever. Something espionage-y.*

"Fuck you, man."

"Ah, that's old Frank I loved. So," Alexei said, motioning for the waiter.

"What about you, asshole? How many times a day do you change your clothes?" Frank asked. Alexei was no longer wearing the white linen suit from earlier. He was now in black linen over a black silk shirt that was a shade blacker, his red tie a vicious crimson stain that reminded Frank uncomfortably of Alexei's favorite pastime. *Fingers.*

Alexei ran a hand over his suit and raised one eyebrow. "Last chess match got little messy. Jorge was . . . *reluctant* to settle his debts. I had to insist."

Alexei Morozov was obsessed with chess. One of the brightest, most ruthless players in all of Russia as a child, he had trained in the rigorous Soviet school of chess and was at one point considered its brightest star—until he was discovered playing back alley chess matches for money and fingers. Alexei was abruptly cut off from the international chess community before he'd reached the status of Grandmaster.

If the fucking Russians had overlooked his finger gambling obsession, he might not have become a mobster. He might have retired to a dacha in the country by now. Morozov was still a voracious player, and no matter where his nefarious business took him, he found willing—and sometimes unwilling—opponents. But while his opponents played chess for glory or money, Alexei still played for fingers.

"Last time I saw Jorge he had two left." Frank motioned to the waiter for a whiskey and water.

"I left him one. Last time I saw *you*, Francis, you were on your way to finish business with Red Lotus for me." Alexei poured himself a glass of vodka with a flourish and handed the bottle to Frank. "Next thing I know, warehouse is crater, Red Lotus is dead, and we feared same for you. I mourned you, brother. Why did you not come to Alexei and tell me you were alive?"

Frank took the bottle and set it next to his whiskey. Crossing his arms over his chest, he fixed Alexei with a steely gaze. "The whole thing felt dirty. Snitch on the inside, I couldn't make who it was. I showed up to the drop, all the players were there, and wonder of wonders, the whole building wired to blow. Now I wonder who on earth would want to take out the entire Red Lotus and yours truly." He clenched his fists, his knuckles audibly cracking.

"Franchesko, I am outraged that you would suggest I would do such a thing to my old friend." Alexei narrowed his eyes, then grinned. "But however did you escape such cunning trap?"

Frank furtively rubbed the tattoo on his wrist under the table. "I figured whoever was responsible had a sniper outside the warehouse. So once I saw which way the wind was blowing, I headed for the subbasement and swam my way out through the sewer. Still caught the blast though. Whoever wired it wanted to make sure no one got out alive." He smiled at Alexei, an expression that stopped short of his eyes. "I made my way to the coast, caught a boat to a plane, and spent a year in rehab in that Swiss clinic covered with burns and shrapnel. Sorry I didn't drop you a postcard, pal."

Alexei downed his vodka and poured another. "You are resilient like Russian bear, Francis. I'll keep that in mind."

"Yeah, do that, Alexei." Frank turned in his chair and looked around the club. "So where's the goon squad?" The goons had been with Alexei for as long as anyone in the industry could remember, but as Frank scanned the room, he did not see even one of their familiar faces. *Odd. I don't like it. I don't like not seeing where the shit is coming from when it hits the fan.*

"Oh, unfortunate business in New Hampshire. Someone barbequed them in national forest. Diamond business gone wrong." He shrugged. "Perhaps was blessing. They were getting old. Now I have their sons and daughters to take their place. Is good, steady work for them. Steady work in Russia does not come easy. I am happy to help them after all their fathers' years of service."

"You're a real humanitarian, Alexei," Frank sneered.

Alexei steepled his hands under his chin, considering Frank's acid face.

"And this little angel and her cherubs I saw you with today?"

Frank went cold. *He'd seen them. But how much?*

Sidestepping the question, he flashed his shark smile at Alexei and shrugged. "I don't like to mix business and . . . other business. Not your concern."

"I saw you push them into the back of a panel van. Something I can help you with, old friend?"

Frank let out an internal sigh of relief. He hadn't seen them together since they landed, not really. Alex and the kids were safe. *For now.*

"Nothing to worry yourself about. Wife and kids of an attaché. I'm here on behalf of someone who wants to make sure the attaché is a good little errand boy. Just a small job I'm doing for a friend."

"I am your friend, too, Franchesko. I could arrange for . . . disposal . . . if need be."

Frank ground his teeth. *I'm going to kill you, you bastard. Slowly.*

"I'll keep it in mind." He gulped half his whiskey and slammed the tumbler on the table. "Well, nice catching up, Alexei. If you don't mind, I—"

Alexei reached over with one iron hand and gripped Frank's forearm.

"Oh, but I do mind. I mind very much."

Frank resisted the urge to swallow hard. "I don't have time for this."

"Oh, but you must make time for Alexei. I know you are man who likes to pay his debts. And you owe me very great one, *friend.*"

Frank sat back in his seat. *Oh, I owe you pal. I owe you a bullet right between the eyes.*

"I'm listening."

"One last job for me, Francis. And then we call it, how you say, square? I never did locate missing three hundred million. I assume you transferred it to Red Lotus before explosion?"

Frank nodded. "I wouldn't cross you, Alexei. I know how that usually turns out. I would imagine it'll sit forever in an offshore account." He shrugged, eyes blank. "Pity."

"Fine. You do this for me, and I will even forget deal you made with me years ago after unfortunate business in Detroit. Then you go back to whatever you have been doing for last eleven years, and I do not feel need to put your head in FedEx box and send to lovely dark-haired women you were seen with at airport."

Shit. Shit, shit, shit. He had *seen them.*

"Dark haired…? Oh, right." Frank rolled his shoulders and sneered. "She's nothing. Just some dumb bitch who wanted into the mile-high club." He grinned at Alexei, even as his stomach twisted at the mention of his wife. "Fine. One last job. No loose ends. What's the situation?"

"I have acquired certain things from freighter bound for Africa. I need to move these things to some interested buyers as soon as possible before certain unpleasant freedom fighters and their machetes realize what has gone astray."

"What's the cargo? Let me guess. Hammers and sickles? Plows and shares?"

"You remember our little code, Francis. I am touched," Alexei said, pressing one hand to his chest, where his heart would be if he had one.

"What do you need from me?"

"These buyers do not know they are dealing with me, and I would prefer to keep it that way. People become very anxious when they see poor Alexei. They do stupid things and complicate my life. I like simple life, Francis."

"Yeah, I can't imagine why they freak when they hear your name, Alexei. That Tokyo job. Gruesome, even for you."

Alexei fluttered his hand in an approximation of a salaam. "You say gruesome, I say inspired. I will never have to ask Japanese twice to be reasonable."

"What do you need me to do with these buyers? Lure them to a building wired to blow?"

"No, no, no, Franchesko! I need you to meet them and make sure deal goes off without hitch. That's all. As my representative. Nothing messy."

"That's all. Just arrange the drop?"

"Not even that! Is arranged! You go, you make sure they are happy with product, you take money, you bring to me, we shake, and never cross paths again."

"When?"

"Two days."

"What am I supposed to do stuck in Bangkok for forty-eight hours?"

"Never fear, I will keep you busy. It will be like old times. I still have number of little Russian dancer, do you remember? She can still do trick with matryoshka doll and clothespins, comrade. Let me arrange for you. As sign of my good faith."

Oh shit. Frank had a flash of what Alex would do if she ever caught wind of him in any scenario that involved a Russian ballerina prostitute and clothespins. *No happy ending there.*

"Kind offer. I'll pass on the dancer. But I will take another drink."

"Excellent, old friend. Here's to new beginnings."

Frank lifted his glass and clinked it against Alexei's.

"New beginnings," Frank repeated, thinking to himself, *Fuck your new beginning, chump. Here's to happy endings.*

CHAPTER SEVEN

Alex woke up wondering why she felt naked. She rubbed her eyes and thought, *I feel naked because I am practically naked*. Silk teddy, no underwear. Tiny, delicate robe that ended at her hips. She raised her arm to admire the fall of thick lace on the sleeve, breathing in a heady rush of perfume as she did.

At least I don't smell like chum anymore. But who the fuck took my clothes off and rubbed me down with lotion? I smell like Thai food and sex. Where the hell are my panties? And whose lingerie am I wearing? An image of the tiny Madam Li floated across her mind, but she dismissed it out of hand. *That woman wears a size three toddler. I'm more of an American eight. Okay, ten.*

She heard a series of whispers at her side. Gwennie and Frank Jr. were coloring on the floor nearby.

"Hey, babies," she said. "I see they got your clothes, too."

Gwennie preened, and Junior shrugged and pushed his glasses up. They were both wearing women's teddies and flip-flops.

"After I'm done killing your father, I'll find your clothes, okay?"

"I like my dress, Mommy. And Chaem Choi said I can keep it!" Gwennie squealed.

Awesome, Alex thought, swinging her legs over the side of the bed. "What are you drawing, baby girl?"

"Fancy ladies. This place is *full* of fancy ladies."

Dear God.

"It's okay, Mommy," Frank Jr. said, standing and putting a small, dimpled hand on her arm. "I don't mind wearing the lady-dress as long as you're okay." He gave her one of his heartbreaking smiles. "Are you better yet, or are you gonna keep yelling about donuts and chum?"

She leaned over and pulled him to her chest, squeezing him. At least Frank Jr. still smelled the same, a mixture of animal crackers and sweat, construction paper, and freshly sharpened pencils.

"I'm better. No more donuts and chum, chief." Content with her answer, he sat back down and continued coloring.

Oh my God. It's a panel van and a gun. My children are drawing whores, panel vans, and handguns.

Alex stood, tugging the teddy down as far as it would go, which wasn't very far at all, and surveyed the room. It was cavernous, dominated by an embarrassingly large lotus-shaped bed draped in red satin. To one side was a clawfoot bathtub for two, and on the other was a small fountain and another reclining Buddha. The children were already jumping up and down on top of the bed since she'd vacated it, their delighted squeals echoing against the room's marble walls. Alex sat down heavily on a gilt chair.

Well, at least someone is enjoying this. Let's see. She slumped back in the chair and clutched the small satin robe around her bare thighs. *Frank is not a Midwest salesman or consultant or whatever he pretended to be doing. He's some sort of arms dealer G-man assassin. He dumped me in a whorehouse. The madam is a close friend, close enough he felt cool about dropping his family off with her in the middle of the night.*

Her eyes narrowed, remembering how they'd hugged each other. *Sure, Frank. Who doesn't have a hooker as a best friend? In Asia. He'd dumped their* children *in a* whorehouse. She cringed when she glanced over at them. They'd abandoned the bed and were throwing thongs and garters up in the air and catching them.

"Gwendolyn! Francis! Put the panties down! Right now!"

And he'd left her. In a Bangkok whorehouse. While some man named Alexei was trying to kill him.

She tallied all this up against her missing underwear, Trixie's tiny ankles, being ten weeks pregnant in a foreign land, her husband running around in a tracksuit and gold chain, and made a decision.

If he doesn't kill you, Frank Brennan, I will.

Alex jumped at the soft rap at the door.

"Missy Frank?" a small sweet voice called out as one of the girls she'd seen in the hall swept in on her tiny bare feet, the bells on her ankles ringing softly.

"Missy Frank, Madam Li wishes to take tea with you. Ah! You are looking so much better than when you arrived covered in fish guts and vomit! Excellent, Missy Frank. If I may, Missy Frank, your new garments suit you better than sensible American cargo shorts and t-shirt of artist known to all of us once as Prince, no?

Tea? With Frank's girlfriend? I don't think so.

"I think he switched back to Prince before he died . . ." She shook her head. *What the hell am I rambling about?* "Anyway, please tell her thanks, but I can't leave the children. I'm sure you understand, I—"

The young girl waved her protests away with an elegant hand. "Missy Frank does not need concern her beautiful self about babies. I shall take the babies to the courtyard fountain. Mr. Frank's babies? You want come with Little Chaem Choi and swim in fountain? Come, come babies. We swim, then I make you mango sticky rice treat for good babies."

Alex felt tears in her eyes at the sound of this young Thai girl using Frank's familiar term of affection for the children. *I will not cry,* she thought, looking down to her waist. *Do you hear me in there, kid? Stop making me cry.*

So, without actually agreeing, Alex found herself trailing Little Chaem Choi down a gilt hall to yet another massive marble room.

"Just in here if you please, Missy Frank. Madam Li will be here soon."

Alex stood awkwardly in the doorway while her children skipped away from her down the hall with the pint-sized prostitute. Then she slipped inside and surveyed the room. Larger than hers, this room was dominated by a brilliant white satin lotus bed with gold throw pillows, an oversized desk with a laptop on it, and a small gilt table already set for tea. The entire room was a stunning palette of white and gold, from the elegant paintings on the wall to the flowers that seemed to grace every surface, but her eyes were drawn back to the bed. She swallowed hard, imagining Frank's hairy arm hanging over the side of it, the lithesome Madam Li running her fingers through his hair.

Frank. My Frank. I knew you were too good for me. Her heart broke a little bit more in her chest.

"I hope your room is to your liking, Mrs. Brennan?" Madam Li's voice purred like a tiger behind her, causing Alex to jump.

"Um, sure," she stammered, pulling the teddy down as much as possible. "It's great. You can just call me Alex." She paused and wrinkled her nose, uncertain how to address the elephant in the room. "Sorry I threw up on you."

Madam Li was sailing across the floor to the tea tables. Her elegant hand on the small of Alex's back swept her along with her as she did.

"Do not concern yourself in the slightest. We are delighted to have you and your beautiful children here, Mrs. Alex. Let us, you and I, have tea and get to know one another. I am honored Frank Brennan trusted us with his precious pearl."

Oh God, Alex thought, sliding into yet another gilt chair. *A tête-à-tête with Frank's old flame. Kill me. I lack the verbal skills to handle this. I'd rather talk to all the other mothers in the PTA.*

Alex sat on her hands while Madam Li gathered the voluminous arm of her ivory and gold kimono and poured for both of them.

"Ceylon tea. Drink," she commanded.

Alex obediently took a sip. "It's delicious. Thank you," she said awkwardly.

"Now eat cookie. Cookie will settle your stomach. Eat, eat."

Alex picked up the delicate confection and took a nibble, barely gagging it down. "Thanks."

Alex squirmed in her seat, trying to pull the impossibly short robe down enough to cover her bottom. It was no good. *I think one-third of my ass cheeks are hanging out.* She gave up fussing with the negligee and let her hands slump in her lap, twisting uncomfortably.

"How do you find our fair country, Mrs. Alex?" Madam Li fixed her with a dagger-like gaze.

"Well," Alex said, gulping the rest of her tea, burning her tongue in the process. Her stomach felt like poverty, and the hot liquid seemed to settle it enough for her to dare another bite of cookie. "Honestly, I saw one garden, fifty-seven reclining Buddhas, and the back of a panel van. Didn't really get much of a view."

Madam Li favored her with a small smile, her red lacquered lips arching like a bow. "Perhaps when this is all over, you will get to see my beautiful country from more than a whorehouse window and a panel van."

Alex froze, torn between hysterical laughing and ugly crying. *What is the appropriate reaction when your husband's former lover cracks jokes about your pseudo-kidnapping in her whorehouse over tea?* The two emotions fought for a fraction of a second before emerging as something between a sob and a snort.

"If this ever *is* over. I mean, if Frank . . . if . . . if I . . ." She broke off, unable to articulate the typhoon of feelings that were choking her.

Madam Li let out a snort of disgust. "Men. They understand nothing. They stomp through life, making messes and leaving us to clean up and worry. I will keep you safe here, Mrs. Alex. I do it not only for Frank Brennan, but because I, too, am a woman and have known what it is to love a man who is, shall we say, *complicated*?"

Her kind words felt like small daggers in Alex's chest. She tried to hold back the torrent, but it was useless. She burst into tears and began sobbing hysterically, incoherent words falling from her lips, her nose bubbling snot.

Fucking hormones. Baby, I thought we had a deal. I hate being pregnant. Frank, you asshole.

She grasped the edges of the tablecloth to wipe her face and blow her nose, then jumped in surprise as a cloud of Asian perfume washed over her and she found herself being cradled by Madam Li.

"Poor little pearl. You have a good cry. Good cry better than tea, I think, right now."

Against all reason, Alex sobbed against Madam Li's satiny robe, her tears finally drying and being replaced by something closer to anger than hurt. When there were no more tears left inside her, she sat up and unwound herself from Madam Li's arms.

"Better?" she purred down into Alex's blotchy face. "Here." She handed her an enormous silk scarf. "Blow your nose, little Alex pearl. Now we have had tea. We have had tears. No more tears. We move now from strength to strength."

"Strength to strength? I don't think I even have one strength, let alone two. Maybe I need more tea," Alex said, wrinkling up her nose.

"I have something for that, little pearl. But I think when dealing with a man like Frank Brennan, something stronger than tea is in order."

"I'm going to kill him, Madam Li."

A genuine smile lit up Madam Li's face. "That's a good girl. Don't let that man get your panties in knots. And please, call me Trixie."

"What did you say this was, Trixie?"

"Thai rice wine. A few sips won't hurt someone in your condition. Will calm you down."

Alex took another sip, feeling pleasantly warm and tingly, and admittedly a little drunk on an empty stomach. *She's right. One won't hurt. And besides, if I don't calm down, I'll stroke out, and me and this kid will be dead.*

"So tell me about yourself, Trixie."

"My story is typical. I started out as a back-alley girl in Rangoon, saved my pennies, moved to Bangkok, became businesswoman. I own several pleasure houses, three restaurants, and a chain of manicure shops."

"Wow. You really diversified." *Oh God, did I just say that?* Alex cringed.

"Yes, Mrs. Alex. Not all whores spend their lives entirely on their backs." Trixie winked at her. "Now tell me, who is Alex Brennan?"

Alex's mind went blank. "Me? I'm nothing. I'm nobody. I'm just a housewife from Detroit."

Trixie let out an elegant laugh. "A *nobody*? Frank Brennan's girl? Impossible. Try again."

Alex felt her face go red at the familiar way Trixie said Frank's name.

"Well, I mean, I have a degree from Wayne State. Creative Writing, pretty useless. I take kickboxing classes with Gwennie." She wrinkled her nose, thinking. "I used to teach, but I stopped when the babies came along. I try to write. Like, at least two thousand words a day. I'm a mom. And of course, there's Frank. He's a lot to deal with." She blushed.

"What do you write about?"

"Oh, nothing special. Little plays. Short stories. Like scripts, except I really only show Frank."

Trixie smiled at her. "No wonder Frank adores you. Scholar. Fighter. Mother. Writer. Lover. You *are* a pearl, Alex Brennan. Gritty inside, lovely outside."

Alex flushed and hurriedly drank the rest of her wine, although she blamed it on her oversharing. She wanted another drink but knew that was a bad idea. But she could *feel* that damn bed looking at her. She could see Frank rolling around on it, the elegant, fancy, long finger-nailed, satin-draped, non-Midwestern, non-housewife, non-sweaty, non-pregnant woman underneath him. Alex felt sick. *Wait. What did she mean, 'in my condition'?* She glanced down at the skimpy lingerie. *Am I showing already?*

"I'm kind of tired, Trixie, maybe I should . . ."

Trixie cut her off.

"Nonsense. You are not tired. You want to know if your husband was one of my clients. You are angry and hurt and want to ask but do not know how."

"No. I mean yes. I mean I . . ." Alex studied her thumb-nail like her life depended on it.

"Let me put you at ease. Yes, he was one of my clients. Once." Trixie leaned over and refilled Alex's glass. "Then he was my friend."

"Okay, sure. Great. Can I go now?" Alex mumbled, blinking back tears. *Fucking useless thumbnail. Fucking Frank.*

Trixie sat back in her chair and tilted her head, studying her, then sighed. "Frank was a double agent back then. G-man sent to infiltrate Russian mob in Thailand. He was trying to blend in, play the game. All the big players frequent establishments such as mine. So he came here, he and I engaged in some of the worst sex I have ever had, and as a professional prostitute, let me tell you, that's quite an accomplishment, Mrs. Alex."

Alex swallowed hard. *Well, there it was. At least she knew the worst now.*

"Then we decided we were more compatible as poker friends than as professional ones. From then on, Frank Brennan kept his appointments with me, and we played Texas hold 'em here at this very table instead of doing other things in my bed. He was *beyond* useless as a lover, let me tell you, more like a fumbling fifteen-year-old, but became a very good friend." She stared pointedly at Alex. "Do you understand now?"

Alex licked her lips and bit them, confused. "That doesn't sound like my Frank *at all.* He's a . . . a . . ."

"He's what, little pearl?"

"He's a volatile lover. Like a volcano covered in hair."

Trixie smiled then, her expression softening. "Of course. He was useless as a lover to me because he was holding a torch for you, do you see? How *delightful.* You must write this love story, Mrs. Alex."

"Wait, I . . . you don't understand. He didn't even *know* me. Back then. We only met ten years ago. In a Tim Hortons. I was eating a donut." *I am rambling. Why am I rambling? I am pregnant and drunk off my ass with a Thai whore. Help. Somebody help me shut up.*

"A man like Frank Brennan goes through life holding a torch for the love of his life. He was holding it for you before he even knew you. Fate guided him to you and your donut. You are a fortunate woman, Mrs. Alex. He is a good man, despite this unfortunate business."

"I know that." The wetness in her eyes turned her thumbnail into a kaleidoscope of tiny shiny thumbs, each of them chewed and chipped.

"Good. Now we leave this unpleasant business in the past where it belongs. Let's play poker."

"I don't know how to play poker, Trixie." Alex let out a shuddering breath and squared her shoulders. *Get your shit together, Winters.*

"Then I shall teach you. Better poker than my ping-pong ball trick." Trixie winked at her.

"Well, you could teach me that one, too." She grinned up at Trixie, a genuine smile now, her eyes beginning to spark again with mischief. "Frank and I have been married ten years now. Might liven things up."

"I will do no such thing until you have that baby you are carrying," Trixie said with a snort. "And yes, it is obvious. I am a madam in a whorehouse. I know exactly what pregnant looks like. Frank doesn't know, does he?"

"No." She shook her head. "I was waiting for the right time to tell him."

"Excellent. I hate to see men holding all the cards. That is your first lesson in poker. You will tell him as soon as it is possible, given the circumstances."

"No, Trixie, I can't. You don't understand how he is, how overprotective he gets. He gets crazy. And now all of this? I can't imagine how he'd react."

"Oh, I can guess." Trixie paused, as if she were choosing her words carefully. "Alex Brennan, you know your husband better than anyone. Except in this one matter."

"What's that?" *Please don't be a horrible sex revelation, please don't be a horrible sex revelation.*

"I know what he is like when he is around Alexei Morozov. I know how he behaves in unfortunate circumstances. I know what he is like when he is a double agent hell-bent on vengeance."

Alex gulped and stared at her wide-eyed.

Trixie leaned over, her voice low and haunting. "He is single-minded. He is dangerous. He thinks he has nothing to lose, and it blinds him. You must remind him, Alex Brennan."

"Remind him of what?" Alex whispered.

"That he has *everything* to lose."

"How do I do that?"

"You are Frank Brennan's girl. I'm sure you'll think of something. Something that will crack that vengeful façade of his. And I am certain he will not like it. And so now I ask you, Alex Brennan. What will *you* do? How does this love story end?"

Alex wiped her face off with the silk scarf and then stood, adjusting her teddy. She crossed her arms and bit her lip, studying the ceiling for a moment, and then she flashed Trixie a rueful grin.

"He pulled the rug out from under me. The least I can do is repay the favor."

"Excellent. I like you, Alex Brennan."

"You know what, Trixie? I like you, too," she laughed, astonished to find that she meant it.

CHAPTER EIGHT

Frank crept into the rear entrance of Madam Li's late that night, having taken a circuitous path through the dark streets to throw off anyone who might be trailing him. Satisfied he had not been followed, he slipped once more into the back door of Madam Li's. His tactical boots made no sound as he stalked the marble halls, searching for his family.

He found them in the only other room that rivaled Trixie's, one she normally reserved for heads of state. *God, I owe you Trixie. I owe you again.* He stood in the doorway, instantly recognizing the soft snores of his wife and kids in the dark. He crept across the room, the moonlight through the lattice windows illuminating Alex's pale shoulders, Gwennie's freckles, and Frank Jr.'s pot belly. Alex was sprawled on her face, and the children were twined around her as if they were at home in Michigan. He leaned down to kiss their heads and stopped suddenly. Alex smelled like a wino, and the kids were both wearing lace teddies. *What the fuck?*

A sound at the door whipped his head around. Trixie stood there, her ivory robes glowing in the dark. He crept back over to her and hissed tersely.

"What the fuck did you do to my wife, Trixie? And why are my children wearing women's underwear?"

Trixie pulled him into the hall and closed the door halfway.

"Frank, you asshole. She was totally unprepared for all of this. You threw that poor innocent girl in the back of a panel van and dumped her at a whorehouse, not knowing if you were safe." She smacked him across the face, her normally serene expression now furious. "*Pạyyāx̀xn.* Imbecile. Heartless man pig."

"Ow! Well, what was I supposed to do? Introduce her to Alexei? 'Hey Alexei, I faked my death and ran off because you were close to figuring out I was a double agent and my own country threw me to the wolves. This is my wife and kids, please don't kill them?' And what if he figures out who she *is*, Trix? You know what he'll do."

Trixie let out a snort. "Coward, *Khn k̄hî k̄hlād tākhāw.* You're just afraid to be honest with your wife. Chicken shit." Trixie gave the tip of his boot a savage stomp with her kitten heel, sending him stumbling back. "So because you are an idiot coward, I gave her a little rice wine. I let her cry, I let her drink, I taught her poker. Among other things." A rare smile passed over her face. "You'll see."

"Alex doesn't play poker," Frank hissed.

"She does now. And well. She won 14,000 baht off of me tonight at Texas hold 'em."

"She did?" Frank's face softened. "That's my girl."

"Yes, exactly. That's Frank Brennan's girl." She flicked him on the ear. "And you lied to her. Ass. Hmū, pig."

"Stop hitting me, Trixie. I didn't *lie*. I just . . . withheld things."

Trixie raised another hand to smack him, but he grabbed her wrist before she could.

"Enough. Listen, I need to get them up and ready to move. I found a guy to get them over the border. Tonight. D'eng is going to drive them to the meet. I can at least go that far. They'll be in the Philippines by dawn. Then I can clear my head enough to settle this once and for all."

"Oh no, no, no, Frank Brennan. You shut your stupid American mouth with your 'once and for all'."

"What do you mean *no*?"

"I know you, Frank. You get your family out of the country so you can do a suicidal warehouse explosion again. Only this time you might not walk away. No. They stay here with me. I want you tense, not suicidal. You finish this. This way you have reason to live. Three reasons right under your stupid nose."

"Goddamn it, Trixie." He ran a hand through his hair, slicking it back and closing his eyes, thinking. "Fine. They stay here." He turned to look back in the room at his slumbering family. "Please keep my family safe,

Trixie. They're all I have. If something happened to them . . ."

"I will, Frank Brennan. But not for you. For her. Her I like. She is worth five of you."

"Don't I know it," he said ruefully. He started back into the room, but Trixie held him back.

"Let them be. You come back tomorrow. Afternoon. Your little pearl needs some time. Let me get her on her feet, then you come see them. Then you go and finish this."

"Can I at least stay here tonight?"

"No," she said shoving him down the hall. "Make your own arrangements."

"Why? You have plenty of rooms, Trixie. Come on."

"Why, Frank? One, you attract trouble and I plan to keep my new friend safe. And two, it would hurt her to see you so casual about sleeping in my whorehouse. Stupid imbecile. Heartless monkey testicle."

Frank's face drained of color. "Does she know about us?"

Trixie laughed at him. "Yes, I told her everything."

"Everything?"

"Especially what a bad lay you were."

"I love you, Trixie."

"You shut your sweet-talking mouth, Frank. Get out. Come tomorrow. Kill that bastard Russian. Then kiss your wife's ass." She pushed him out the back door and slammed it in his face.

CHAPTER NINE

After a sleepless night, Frank retuned the next afternoon, freshly shaven and penitent. He'd traded the track pants and wife-beater for a pair of worn jeans and a black t-shirt after being teased relentlessly by D'eng. He kept the gold chain and windbreaker though—the first because it looked cool, the second because it disguised his love handles. Frank wandered the halls, looking for his wife, nervously adjusting the gun he had jammed in his belt. Finally, unable to locate her in the maze-like interior of Madam Li's, he knocked on one of the doors. One of Trixie's girls peered out from behind the cracked door, giggling nervously.

"Mrs. Frank?" he growled.

The girl giggled again, covering her mouth as she did.

"Peacock Room." She shook her head. "You in big trouble, Mr. Frank Brennan." Then she slammed the door in his face.

Shit. Real nice, Frank. Once again, you find yourself literally the only man in a whorehouse who doesn't want to be there.

The girl had directed him to a small salon where Trixie received private callers, named so because of the rich blue silk-swathed walls and ceiling. Frank strode back through the halls, made a left, a right, and another left, then paused outside the door to the Peacock Room, hoping to get the lay of the land before he ran headlong into what would no doubt be the fight of his life. *In and out, deal with this later, get out and kill that bastard.* He peeked around the doorframe.

Alex was sitting cross-legged on a sea of blood-red pillows, her hands draped over each knee, serene as one of the statues that flanked each corner of the room. She locked eyes with him, her hair falling over one side of her face like the sun rising on Bangkok's Grand Palace, the rich chestnut washed with a ray of sunshine that fell on her from the high transom windows. Frank studied her face for signs that she had been crying, searched for signs that she was angry. What he found instead was more than a bit unsettling. Alex looked like the wrath of god; vengeful, foreboding, aloof.

He swallowed hard and stepped into the doorway. Alex remained silent, and Frank's study now shifted to what she was wearing. Acid green teddy, plunging neckline, a wisp of a garment that ended halfway down her creamy thighs. Cascading out on either side of her were the ends of a silk robe, the same savage green but heavily embroidered with flame-red dragons. Situated as she was on the ocean of blood-red pillows, she looked like an eastern dragon in its lair. She shifted slightly, and as she did, a celestial chiming filled the room. Frank's eyes slid down his wife's body to her lovely ankles. Each was encircled with small bracelets encrusted with bells.

His breath caught in his chest at the sight of those ankles. *I should just drop to my knees and crawl across this floor and kiss her ankles and beg her to forgive me. She'll probably just kick me in the face. But I deserve that.*

He let out a small noise that sounded like a whimper.

Alex's eyes narrowed.

Oh, shit. Here it comes. But from where?

Alex didn't say a word. She just patiently stared at him. Frank felt his balls crawl back up into his body. *You fucking cowards, get back out here and help me,* he thought helplessly.

"That's quite the getup you're wearing, babe," he tried clumsily.

"That's all they have here, Frank," she said in a low, cool voice. "Underwear. You should see your children."

Frank blanched and resisted the urge to run. *Mobsters, drug dealers, gunrunners, freedom fighters with machetes. I'd rather any one of those, or hell, all of them, instead of one pissed-off Alex. I am a dead man.*

"Tell me they're not still wearing teddies," he stammered.

Alex shook her head, a tight, coiled motion. "Some of the girls ran out and bought them t-shirts. Wait till you get a load of what passes for American fashion in Bang-kok. Amazing. They can find clothes for the kids but not for the giant American housewife." Her eyes flashed at him, dark, liquid and dangerous as quicksand.

Frank finally broke under the weight of her distant stare.

"What do I do, Alex? Tell me what to do to make this . . ." he gestured between them, "better. Like it was. Tell me how to make this stop. Scream at me, yell at me, hit me. Do something, but don't shut me out. Please, babe, I can't do this without you. I can't do anything without you." He walked into the room on shaking legs and stopped at the edge of the pillows.

Alex tilted her head at him, then shifted her position, tucking her knees to one side, gifting Frank the small-est glimpse of the inside of her milky thighs, a paradise guarded by eyes like daggers. She licked her lips and slid her hair back behind her ear, the tattoo on her wrist flashing at him as she did.

"Tell me everything you never told me, Frank. Were you ever a Marine? Or was that a lie, too?"

Frank scratched the back of his head nervously, un-sure what to do with his hands. He shuffled his boots on the marble floor.

"No, that was true. But then I got drafted into special ops. From there, it was a short skip into covert assassin stuff. I did that for years."

"Of course," she nodded icily. "No big deal. Usual cor-porate ladder stuff. Do you mind telling me why you are dressed like Eurotrash in tactical boots?" That last part threw him off. *Wait, what about the whores and assassins? Why isn't she screaming at me? She screams at me about the gutters, for Christ's sake. She should be nuclear. What the fuck is going on?*

Unnerved now, he stammered, "It's the look, Alex. Arms dealers don't wear bowling shirts."

Alex rose in one elegant motion, wrinkling her nose at him. She crossed the sea of pillows and began circling him slowly, the bells on her ankles chiming out her disgust.

"Have you been *smoking*?"

Frank let out a short laugh, feeling relieved and then immediately terrified. *Why is she so calm? I need to get her screaming. Screaming Alex I can handle. This Alex, what is this?*

"Jesus Christ, woman," he barked, hoping to get her to snap back. "Would you let me do what I do? Everyone in Asia smokes. It's the national pastime."

"I don't want the kids to see you smoking. Frank Junior wants to do everything Daddy does." She crossed her arms over her chest and stared at him. *What was going on in that head of hers?*

"Fine, I also won't let him see me gut that Russian son of a bitch. You happy now?" he snapped.

She stared at him, her face unreadable, the silence stretching out between them. Finally she spoke. "Did you want something, Frank? Why are you here?"

Shit. Frank let out a deep breath and sank to his knees in front of her.

"It was only the scum of the earth, I promise. Arms dealers, drug dealers, that kind of thing. I wasn't killing presidents or children, babe. I'll tell you everything. Please just give me a chance."

She stalked back to her pillow perch and resumed her languid posture. "Oh, will you? How generous of you, Frank."

Frank scrambled for words, all the carefully composed speeches he'd kept on hand over the years vanishing under her intense glare.

"Okay, my last job. I have to go deep cover with these Russians. Alexei and his brothers. His dad. I mean deep, princess. I was actually running guns and other things, things I'd rather not get into. And then things went bad."

"How bad?"

"Some things happened about fifteen years ago, five years before we met. My own country disavowed me. Cut me loose. Said I'd blurred the lines. Some things went down in Detroit, things I do not regret doing, things I had no choice but to do. The Feds used that as an excuse to set me adrift. I think they just wanted out of it all and it was easier to sacrifice me than bring me in. I had to get myself out. I arranged it to look like I was dead, rigged a warehouse to explode. Took a whole organization with it. Trixie helped, and I cut and ran. Covered my tracks. Last I heard, Alexei and his guys were working Eastern

Europe and the eastern seaboard of the States. The Thai government ran them out. That's why I said no to the Outer Banks—it's their territory now. Also, it's where douchebags vacation. I thought we were safe here." He slid on his knees closer to her, pushing his way into the sea of pillows. She scooted back and froze him with a look.

"Are you even a consultant?"

"Well, I am. Just not vinyl siding."

"Then what exactly do you consult, Frank?"

"Security. Training. Transport. But nothing hands-on. Not a single thing since we met. I swear to God, Alex."

Alex sat quietly, playing idly with the bells on her ankles for a long time. The minutes ticked by, driving Frank slowly insane.

"Say something Alex, I can't stand this."

"Do you even love me? Or am I just part of your cover? That's what it was, right? That's why you came on to me that day. It was just a game with you."

"How can you even say that, Alex?"

Frank crawled on his knees over to her, reaching out for her hands. She let him take them in his, even as she held herself rigid and away from him. Raising her hands to his lips he kissed each one.

"Alex, that day in the Tim Hortons. What do you remember?"

She cleared her throat and looked over his shoulder, purposefully avoiding his eyes as she answered. "I was eating a donut and coffee. Alone like I'd been every day since my dad died. I just looked up, and you were there, smiling at me. And I didn't feel alone anymore." Her face clouded. "I don't remember much after that. It was a blur. The next thing I knew, we were married and we had the babies and it was like . . . it was like . . ." She stopped and looked at him. "It was unreal. It made no sense. You picking me like that. And now I know why. Because none of it was real, was it, Frank?"

Frank gripped her hands tight, too tight. "No, that's not how it was. I saw you, and it was like everything before *you* vanished. All of that shit ceased to exist. That's how it was for me, babe. I was sick to death of running—sick to death of myself and this horrible shit show I got trapped in. I saw you, and I knew I'd run far enough. And the rest of it, all of it ceased to exist for me."

Her eyes were hollow and gutted as she spoke. "The truth is, I have never thought I was good enough for you. Look at you, Frank." Her wrathful face became suddenly vulnerable, her voice soft and sad. "You're ridiculously handsome. You're so kind, so wonderful, even when you're being horrible. I always knew you were too good for me. I always worried you'd realize that one day and leave. I saw it in your face, the way you'd go all distant and blank. I told myself it would be okay, that wherever it was you went to when you shut me out that it was okay because you'd always come back to me. But now I find out you're some kind of double agent super spy with Russian mob enemies and secret madams and a driver with a name out of a Cold War spy movie. And what am I, Frank? *I'm nothing.* What is the point of me?" Her voice trembled, dragging out the last word into a sob.

"Jesus Christ, woman, have you been carrying this around for the last ten years?"

She nodded, biting her lip.

"Alexandra Winters, you beautiful idiot, look at me. I would kill everyone from here to Fiji just to listen to you bitch at me to clean the gutters. *Who are you?* You're my girl. My miracle. And you're far more than I deserve, princess." He looked down at her hands, swallowing hard. "Let me ask you this, Alex. Why me? Why did you kick that chair out for me? Why didn't you tell me to fuck off?"

She answered immediately, almost without pause. "Because you looked like home. At least, I thought you did. I think I was wrong."

"Baby, no! I *am* your home. And you and the babies are mine. The only real home I have ever known. You three are the only living proof that Frank Brennan isn't a colossal piece of shit."

She looked at him then, her brown eyes spilling tears, really looked at him, like she used to. "And you've been carrying *that* around for the last fifteen years." Her voice hovered between hurt and accusing.

Frank looked down at his hands, his answer little more than a breath. "Longer, even."

"And you never told me. You kept all of yourself from me, didn't you?" She slipped her hands from his.

"Alex, no . . . I . . . could I hold you? Please?" he whispered, desperate.

Her brow wrinkled at him in consternation, and she gave a small nod. Not much encouragement, but Frank took it. He wrapped his arms around her and pushed her back into the pillows, trying to make her hold him back.

"Can you ever forgive me, Alex?" he whispered in her hair.

"I don't know, Frank. I just don't know anymore."

Frank's heart plummeted. "I understand." His voice was hoarse.

"Do you, Frank? Do you really?"

More than you know, he thought while he clenched her to him, trying to convince himself that everything was going to be okay. *Even as I hold you, I can feel you slipping away.*

So he released her and sat back. *She looks so tired. She looks so hurt. I did this.* He ran his hands through his hair, ran them across his eyes, blinking, his throat tight.

"How long till you leave?" she whispered.

"I have this afternoon, then I have to go."

"How long will you be gone?"

"Three days, tops. Then we leave. Together."

She nodded stiffly. "Maybe. I'm not sure I want to leave with you."

Frank nodded tersely. "I deserve that. I get that." He cleared his throat. "Anything else I should know that's going on in that head of yours?"

Alex nodded and stared at the silk-draped ceiling. "I'm pregnant," she said softly.

Frank's face shifted from confused to elated to horrified in a fraction of a second. "That's it. You and the kids leave Thailand today. This instant. It's too dangerous."

"No," she said softly.

"Alex, I'm not going to argue with you. Not about this. Alex, why didn't you—"

"I'm not going to argue with you, either. I'm staying. You don't get to tell me what to do. Not now."

"Alex..."

"I'm tired, Frank. Go see the kids. I'll come find you later."

Frank rose from the pillows, leaving her sprawled there looking so fragile, so hurt, so distant. He walked silently from the room, his head bowed, wondering how on earth he'd ever manage to get her back.

You fucked up, pal. You should have told her on day one. You lied to her for ten years. It's no wonder she doesn't want you. You made her whole life a lie. You made every beautiful moment of the dream you've been living a nightmare for her. And the worst part is you can't even tell her why. She'd never understand.

CHAPTER TEN

\\\\\\\\\\\\\\\\\\\\\\\\\\\\\\\\\\\\

Alex sat motionless, listening to the sound of Frank's boots carrying him away from her, her legs wanting to run after him, her arms wanting to hold him, her voice yearning to scream for him to come back. She did none of these things.

The heavily swathed walls behind her parted, and she turned to see Trixie emerge from behind a concealed door. Alex let out a sob, and Trixie hurried to her side and gathered her in her arms.

"There, there, little one. Oh, my poor pearl," she cooed.

"That was the hardest thing I have ever done, Trixie," Alex sobbed. "I feel like a monster."

Trixie patted Alex's shuddering back, heedless of the fact that the sleeve of her priceless gown was now saturated with tears and snot. "You did well, my dear. Very well. I had no idea it was even possible to bring Frank Brennan to his knees. You are . . ." she trailed off.

Alex pushed herself upright and untangled herself from Trixie's arms, searching her lovely face for the rest of the sentence. "I'm what?"

"Terrifying, my dear." Trixie laughed, a high, sparkling sound. "You are absolutely terrifying."

"I am?"

"You are. And you are not a monster. You are his guardian angel, whether he knows it or not. You just gave him all the ammunition he needs to end this and come back to you."

"I know, but I just . . ." *I just hurt him more than he hurt me.*

"Listen, Alex. If you had sobbed or screamed, he would have just tuned it out. Disappeared behind that carefully controlled mask of his. By shutting him out, you have made him something more dangerous than the old Frank and someone far more vengeful than the Frank you married. You have made him something that Alexei Morozov should fear."

"What's that?"

"A lovesick Frank Brennan hell-bent on getting his wife back. I cannot think of a more terrifying creature than that."

Alex nodded. "I'm so scared, Trixie."

"I know." She smoothed Alex's hair back. "Rest. Nap for a bit. I'll have a tray of food brought to you in an hour. Then when you feel stronger, you can go see him and the children." She pushed Alex back into the sea of pillows, reached for an embroidered tapestry that lay to one side, and tucked her in like a child.

"Thank you, Trixie," Alex said, grasping her arm as she rose. "You're like some kind of angel."

Trixie laughed and kissed her forehead. "Of course I am. Haven't you ever heard of the hooker with the heart of gold?"

Alex stood outside the courtyard, peeking in to spy on her family unseen, their familiar cacophony of voices music to her ears. Frank was sitting with his back to her, his hair blue-black in the sunshine. Gwennie was throwing knives at a crudely drawn man on the wall. Junior was hopping excitedly back and forth on his chubby legs, knives clutched in both hands.

"Outstanding, cubbie!" Frank bellowed when the knife hit the man in the head. "No, no, Gwennie love, wait till your brother is clear. Your mom will kill me if you stab him. Remember, we're all going to be nice to Mommy because she's tired. No sassing her while Daddy is gone. I'm looking at you, Frank Junior."

"Aww, jeez, Dad. Gwennie fusses her more than I do," Junior protested.

"Move, Frankie. I want to throw again." Gwennie's voice was bossy and breathless.

"Daddy, she's hogging the knives."

Alex couldn't help but smile at their shirts. The ladies had selected what they considered the height of fashion from the market nearby. For Gwennie, they had chosen an oversized pink t-shirt that read "BRUNO'S DONUTS". Junior was wearing a similarly sized green shirt that hung down to his knees and read "ARMED ASSAULT FORCE ARMAGEDDON."

"Wait your turn, bud. Ladies first," Frank admonished his son. He turned then and looked at her, his grin fading briefly at the sight of her, then reappearing forced and strained.

"Hey, Sleeping Beauty has awoken," his voice a shadow of its former growl.

Alex crossed the room, determined not to throw herself into his arms. Instead, she sank down in the chair next to him as frostily as she could. "I'm sure I should be upset about this, but I'm all out of righteous outrage at the moment."

Frank reached over and laid his hand over hers. She waited for him to say something. He didn't. He just held her hand while they watched the children throw knives at the target. Two parents worrying over the most precious things in the world, children who were oblivious to the mess they were in.

"Frank, I . . ." Alex started.

Frank cut her off. "It's okay. I get it. It's fine. We can talk about it when I get back." He slipped his hand from hers and rose when a gaggle of Trixie's girls rushed into the room, a flock of silk-clad beauties, the chiming of their ankle bracelets like birdsong.

"Babies, babies!" they cried. "Time for baths!"

Junior and Gwennie each made one last savage throw with their knives, the gleam in their eyes eerily like their father's, then allowed themselves to be carried off by the delighted women.

Frank stood awkwardly across the room, hands jammed in his pants, his face twisted up in a crooked grin. *Say something, idiot, Alex thought. I have to say something to him before he leaves so he knows I love him. It's fine? What does that mean? Oh, God, I could never not love him. How can I tell him that? How can I let him know?*

"They are loving having the kids here," Frank said. "Maybe we could work out a permanent arrangement."

"Trixie says work here has entirely shut down because of your children, Frank. We stay here too long, we might put Madam Li out of business."

Frank gave her that tight forced smile again.

"When are you leaving?" *This is horrible. We're talking to each other like strangers.*

"Soon. I'll take care of this, I swear." His eyes were dark, and something gleamed there that Alex had never seen before. Something vicious.

"Are you really that tough, Frank?" she said, trying to make him smile, just once, before he left. It didn't work.

"Yeah," he said softly.

Encouraged, Alex tried again. "Did you really blow up an aircraft carrier full of patriot missiles?" She rose and took two steps toward him.

A small grin tugged at his lips, then died. "I see Trixie and you are becoming friends."

"She's nice. Weird, but nice. I think . . . I think . . . she's always been a good friend to you."

"You're a miracle, Alex. You always have been."

"Some miracle," she said, crossing her arms. "I was oblivious to the fact that I married an assassin."

"No, I meant you've always been my miracle."

Alex nodded stiffly, trying not to cry.

"Baby, come here."

Alex crossed the remaining distance between them and stood uncertain in front of her husband. Frank bent down and pulled a knife from his boot. The seven-inch blade gleamed wickedly in his outstretched hand, the leather handle worn and stained with time. He grasped her hand and wrapped her fingers around the grip, his eyes never leaving hers. "Keep this on you. At all times. Promise me, Alex." Everything about his face and his tone terrified her.

She swallowed hard and smiled at him. "Will you teach me to throw knives before you go?"

Frank shook his head and put her hand on his chest. "You don't need lessons."

He reached out, his fingertips caressed her lips, and then he was gone.

CHAPTER ELEVEN

L ater that night, after the children went to bed, Alex made her way to Trixie's office for company.

"Mind if I come in?" she asked. "I can't sleep."

"Come, come, Alex. You can help me with work while we wait this all out. Keep you busy." Trixie waved Alex into her rooms. She was sitting at her desk in front of her laptop, neatly ordered piles of paper surrounding her.

Alex threw herself into the chair across from her. "Work? Here?" She laughed at the absurd notion of working in a whorehouse while she waited around for her husband to kill a Russian. "I mean, I guess I could do some hand stuff." She raised her eyebrow sardonically at her new friend.

Trixie threw a sheaf of papers at her. "Smart ass. I do not mean that kind of work. Although there is quite a market for athletic American women with wicked tongues. You could make a killing." She reached over and patted Alex's hand. "Okay, little pearl?"

Alex nodded, "Yeah. This sucks."

"It does. Now, help me understand some of these foreign email requests I have for next week. I am not sure I grasp what they want from my ladies." Trixie's lovely face wrinkled up in concentration. "Here, like this one." She handed Alex a sheet of paper.

Alex scanned it. "Okay, so this guy wants some daddy porn."

Madam Li nodded and began making notes. "Ah, I see. And what is this 'Lolita' business?"

"I think he wants hair ribbons and baby doll dresses. It's a kink."

"Fine, fine. And this one?"

Another piece of paper. Alex studied it. "This one wants well, I'm guessing . . . general humiliation?"

Trixie rolled her eyes. "Then I will add to his joy and charge him double. And this one?"

Alex read the two-page email in silence, her face coloring. "This one just wants someone to try men's shoes on for him while he watches in a bathtub filled with whipped cream. He just took two pages to say that."

"Ugh. Another one? Such a mess to clean up after."

Alex reached over and took the last paper off the desk. "Wow. Personally, I'd reject this one, because I think he sounds like one of those German cannibals. But that's just me." Alex cringed and handed the paper back to Trixie.

Trixie wadded the paper up and tossed it into a bronze wastepaper basket.

"Consider it done. Now, enough work. Will you take tea with me in the courtyard?"

"It's like nine o'clock at night, Trix."

"There is no time in a whorehouse, Alex. We do what we want, when we want. Tea, and then I think moonlight massages for the both of us." She winked at her as she rose from her desk.

"I like the way you work, Trixie," Alex laughed.

"Shoo, shoo," Trixie chirped, pushing Alex from the room. "I have a few things to attend to. Go check on your babies, and I will send Chaem Choi to sit beside them until we are done. I will meet you in the courtyard in half an hour."

Frank looked up at Alexei. They were in a private room at Club Euro, going over the details for the drop.

"Piece of cake, man," Frank said, nodding. "I got this."

"Is good to have you back, my brother."

Alexei reached under his chair and pulled out another folder wrapped in red cellophane. Frank felt the bottom drop out a bit further.

"Take look." Alexei looked like a self-satisfied cat.

Frank didn't even look down at it. Instead he flipped it over and pushed it back to him.

"No. I told you no. This is the last job. "

"At least have look, Franchesko."

Fuck. "Fine." Frank ripped the cellophane off, and then reached into his boot for his other knife, the one with the wicked serrated double edge meant for gutting things. He slit the envelope open, then stabbed the knife down into the table. Alexei made tut-tutting noises with his teeth. Frank ignored him and began shuffling through the papers.

"You want me to go back to Moscow with you? Are you out of your goddamn mind?"

Alexei plucked the knife out of the table and, gripping it in one hand, tested the edge against the meat of his thumb.

"So sharp. Yes, I plan to retake territory lost to me after unfortunate incident with Red Lotus." He fixed him with his gaze. "You cost me more than just money, old friend. You cost me all of Russia."

Frank jammed the papers back into the envelope and pushed it back across the table.

"Tough shit. No." *I am in way over my head. I'm missing something here, something big. Fuck, fuck, fuck, what's going on?*

"Let me ask you this, Frank. Why so eager all of a sudden to quit?"

"What do you mean all of a sudden?" Frank snapped. "I've been off the grid for *ten years.* I'm semi-retired. This shit in Bangkok was a favor for an old friend. Why can't you let it rest?"

"You know why. I cannot have man of your caliber working for anyone else, including himself. You either work for me or . . ." Alexei shrugged. "And besides, you do recall deal you made fifteen years ago, do you not? Your life in exchange for Dmitri's daughter's life? Poor Frank, so sentimental. I never forget my deals, you know this. Or have *you* forgotten?"

Frank felt a cold bead of sweat make its way down his back. *That's the third time he's mentioned her. What does this Slavic piece of shit know about Alex? Something is off, something is very wrong here.* He licked his lips and made sure his eyes were dead and empty.

"I haven't forgotten anything." *I haven't thought of anything else since the day I walked into that Tim Hortons.*

Alexei smiled, teeth gleaming like mother of pearl.

"Good. So here is deal. You do job tonight. I shall tag along with my associates and make sure you do not get lost on way back." He raised one elegant hand to gesture at the goons silently drifting into the room, blocking the exits. Frank studied their young, unfamiliar faces. *This batch looks dumber and more ruthless than their fathers did.* "Then you and I get on a plane to Moscow, and I let you live and continue to repay me great debt you owe."

Fuck, fuck, fuck, Frank thought, feeling the entire situation tumbling away from him in a landslide. He was trapped, pinned, alone in a room outgunned and outmanned with Alexei and his goons on Alex's scent. *Think, Frank. How do I throw him off her scent? How do I get out of this room alive?*

He reached over and plucked his knife out of Alexei's hands.

"What if there was a third option?"

"Intriguing, Franchesko. I cannot fathom one for someone in your position."

"I can." He drove the knife back into the table, then rose, crossing the room slowly, eyes leveling the Russian goons, daring them to make a move. He picked up a chessboard, Alexei's personal set, and carried it back over to him, dropping it heavily on the table next to the knife, scattering the chessmen as he did.

"One game. Winner takes all. No fingers."

"Franchesko, you do not play chess." Alexei gaped up at him in astonishment.

"I spent a year in the hospital. For all you know, I have dedicated my life to chess since then. Or maybe you're right and I don't know a pawn from a rook." Frank shrugged. "It's your choice. Unless you think you can't beat me." Frank clenched his teeth together and nailed Alexei to his chair with his murder-war-no-remorse stare.

Alexei's eyes gleamed, his expression mirroring Frank's with one addition—greed.

"Your terms, Franchesko?"

"If you win, I stay in your employ until another building blows up around me. Or you put a bullet in my head. You pick."

"Tsk, tsk. And if you win?"

"I win, I walk. No fingers, no bullet, no job, we're square. I know you're a murderous piece of shit, Alexei, but even you wouldn't welch on a chess bet."

"I agree to your terms with one addition."

"Name it," Frank said, sinking into his chair.

"If I win, I decide your fate. Tonight."

Alexei's nimble fingers began setting the chessboard to order, spinning it and gifting Frank with black. Frank licked his lips. *Second move. I can still do this. Frank Jr., I hope you taught your thick old man well. My life depends on it, champ.*

Alexei floated one elegant hand over the board, dropping like a dagger to move his pawn to queen's rook three, flashing Frank a challenging look when he removed his hand from the piece.

Frank closed his eyes and tried to transpose the finely carved chessmen with Junior's pez heads, plastic saints, and dice. *No, wait. I know what to do. Holy shit, I know what to do.*

Frank reached out and moved his own pawn to white king's three.

Alexei's smirk faltered while he inclined his head. "I see you have been learning, old friend. Excellent." He moved his rook across the board to queen's rook two.

A bead of sweat appeared on Frank's temple. *Think.* He scanned the board. *Die to duck head three, Daddy,* he heard Junior chirp. He squinted and then saw the move. He shifted his pawn to king three.

Alexei let out a grunt of frustration and removed his jacket. He threw the immaculate garment on the floor, then removed the cuff links and rolled up his sleeves.

"Quit grandstanding and move, asshole," Frank spat.

Alexei's lips became a thin line when he moved his rook to queen's rook two. "Is joy to be challenged so, Frank. Been long time since someone truly challenged me."

Daddy, Daddy, Saint Francis to— I know what to do next, buddy, Frank thought. *Remind me to raise your allowance.*

Frank moved his bishop to queen's bishop four and sat back, arms crossed over his chest. "Your move, Morozov."

Alexei's hand was already moving his pawn to queen's rook three, a sudden smile on his face that Frank didn't like. *What am I missing? He knows something. Something I don't.* Frank scanned the board, but he could already see that he'd won. It was inevitable.

Frank moved his queen to queen's bishop three. *Nowhere to run now, asshole,* he thought. *I got you now.*

With no other move to make, Alexei moved his pawn to queen's rook four, a sour look on his face. Slowly, never taking his eyes off Alexei's, Frank moved his queen to capture the pawn.

"Checkmate," he growled. *Holy shit, Junior. Your old man just beat a Soviet near grandmaster. How about that?*

Alexei's lips twisted up in a cruel smile while he reached across the board to shake Frank's hand. Frank gripped it tight enough to feel Alexei's delicate bones grind together. The mobster did not react. Instead, he simply slid his hand from Frank's, stood, stretched, and began rolling his sleeves back down.

"Take him," he said quietly to his goons.

Frank jumped to his feet, the chair flying back as he did. He spun in a slow circle as the twenty new Russian goons moved in on him, brandishing knives, guns, and baseball bats.

"What the fuck, man? We had a deal!" he shouted at Alexei.

Alexei ignored him and threaded his cufflinks back into his cuffs. Frank struck out at the goon closest to him, managing to land a single blow before another goon took out the backs of his knees with a bat. A short, futile scuffle later, and ten of the goons had Frank pinned and bleeding on his knees.

Alexei bent over and picked up his jacket and shook it out, then slipped his arms into the sleeves.

"Take him to warehouse. Work him over and lock him up. I'll deal with him when I get back."

"But . . ." Frank said frantically, his mind spinning, looking for an out, "the drop, the deal. It's tonight. At least let me do that much," he pleaded. *Even another hour. I could get word to Alex, I know I could. I have to.*

Alexei bent down, his face a gleeful sneer.

"Stupid American G-man. This was *all* game. To see how fast I could make you dance, Frank Brennan. Oh yes, I know everything. There *is* no drop, no deal. There never was."

Frank's mouth dropped open, thunderstruck. Alexei laughed, the sound a knife in Frank's chest.

"You see, I am better chess player than you imagine." Alexei swept his arm out, knocking the board clear, chessmen landing like shrapnel across Frank's chest. "I let you win, idiot. If you were real chess player, you'd have figured that out." He nodded at one of the goons, who kicked Frank in the gut. Another kicked him in the back. "Did you really hope to use Fool's mate on *me*? I learned how to counter that two-move checkmate when you were still pissing in your diapers."

The room began to go dark around the edges. *No. No. This is not happening.*

"You walked right into my trap, Frank. From the moment you entered country with your family, I decided to make you pay for deceiving me all those years ago."

No. Frank began to struggle against the arms that pinned him until a blinding punch to the face broke his nose and aborted his futile struggle.

"Yes, yes, I know all about your family. I think," he said, picking up the heavy chessboard, "that I will go visit them. At Madam Li's. Your wife is lovely creature. You know what I like to do with lovely creatures. Especially ones who owe me debt of honor."

"She doesn't owe you shit, asshole," Frank spat, blood blinding his eyes. "She had nothing to do with the deal her father made, you sick bastard."

"Dmitri passed his debt on to her when he fucked up that drop in Detroit, Frank. Everyone who works for me knows my rules. And those two little ones? *So fragile.* You know, there is no nobility in being trusting and weak, Franchesko. I will be one to teach them that."

"No," Frank choked out. "No, Alexei. Not like this." *I never even got to tell her I was sorry.*

"Yes, Frank. Exactly like this," Alexei hissed before he raised the chessboard over his shoulder and slammed it upside Frank's jaw.

The last thing Frank heard was the raucous sound of the Russian's laughter. Then everything went black.

CHAPTER TWELVE

Alex strolled into the moonlit courtyard, feeling strangely at home. The children were asleep, with little Chaem Choi standing guard over them. The fragrant night air wafted through the courtyard palms, setting them stirring, heavy with lotus and lily.

As much as she wanted to enjoy the beauty of this marble harem, she couldn't. Not as long as she had a Frank-shaped hole in her heart. *I could forgive it, Frank, all of it, if I knew you really loved me. I would forgive you anything if you just gave me a chance to know the real you. If I could just know who you are and why you did what you did to me. To us.*

She threw herself on a chaise and buried her head in her hands, wishing she could go back to not knowing any of this. His occasional blank looks would be paradise now compared to the loss of him entirely.

"Is my lucky day. American flower blooms in Thai garden. "

The purring, heavily accented voice caused Alex to jerk her head up, eyes wide. She shifted on the chaise to look at the man lounging in the doorway.

Linen suit. Russian. Blond hair. Oh shit. Alexei. She considered her options, raced ahead to write the three likeliest scenarios, then discarded them all in terror.

Alex plastered an unconvincing smile on her face and stood. "Oh, I'm a new hire. Uh." She cleared her throat. "Me love you long time." *Oh God. What the fuck did I say?* She stood frozen, shaking, while he strolled over to her.

Alexei reached out with one long fingered hand and grasped a tendril of her hair, winding it around his hand.

"Wonderful. Just my type. What is your name, little flower?" he whispered, taking one step closer to her. Alex took one shaking step back, ankles chiming alarm.

Her mouth opened like a fish but she couldn't form any words. "I . . . I . . ." she whispered, mouth dry. *Oh God. The babies. My babies. Frank, help me. Think, Alex. What would Frank do?* Alex stared at the ground, unable to look up.

"You know what I think?" Alexei said, dropping her hair. "I think you're not one of Trixie's girls. You look too wide-eyed. Too sweet. No one has ever ridden you hard and put you away wet, have they, my dear?"

Alex's head jerked up as a surge of hormone-drenched adrenaline rocketed through her body. *Oh my God, is this what a momma lion feels like? I feel like I could kill an army of Russians. Thanks, kid, I needed that.*

Before she thought about it too much, Alex drew her arm back and drilled Alexei Morozov in the jaw, then spun around, kicked him in the shoulder, and watched him stagger to one knee.

"Oh yes, they have, asshole. I'm Frank Brennan's wife," she spat at him from between her teeth. *Fuck yeah, mommy-daughter kickboxing,* she thought to herself, dropping her fists to her hips. *And I'm a pregnant woman from fucking Detroit, bitch. I'm going to kick your ass all over Bangkok. God, they should bottle this pregnancy shit.*

Her hormonal bravado fell flat when Alexei reached into his jacket and pulled out a gun. Alex stumbled back while he climbed back to his feet, pointing it at her. Reaching into another pocket, he extracted a handkerchief and held it to his mouth.

"Not very ladylike, I'm afraid. About what I'd expect from Frank's girl."

"What do you want?" Alex stammered.

"I've come to collect on your father's debt, my sweet. A debt fifteen years overdue."

He drew a hand back and slammed it into her face, pistol-whipping her. Alex's eyes rolled back into her head while she felt her mouth fill with blood, and she struggled to stay on her feet. *My dad? Frank? What?*

She stumbled back farther away from the gun, running into a pillar. She gripped it behind her with both hands, bewildered.

"What are you talking about? My father is dead." Alex eyes searched the room for something, someone, anyone, but they were alone. *Where was Trixie? Oh God, no. Trixie, no.*

"I know, quite dead. But Dmitri was under contract to me when he died. And everyone who works for me knows. Your debts become your children's debts."

"I don't . . . I don't . . ." she stammered. "I don't understand."

Alexei's grin was a wolf's mask as he came to stand in front of her, the gun settling on her chest. "Oh, he never *told* you did he, your knight in shining armor? Your Frank."

Alex spit a mouthful of blood on his suit, feeling a small measure of satisfaction when he tried in vain to brush the stain off his immaculate linen.

"Don't talk about my husband, asshole."

"Never told you how your father's death was all his fault? Are you sure you don't want to hear story?"

"What the fuck are you talking about?" Alex hissed.

"Our Frank had been," Alexei raised one hand to curve his fingers into quotations, "'deep undercover' working for me for nearly five years. You have no idea how I enjoyed watching Frank Brennan dance. Letting him think he had me fooled while I fed him exact information I wanted Feds to have. He would vanish from time to time, when his people pulled him back in for debriefing. He always had cover story, but I knew. He disappeared just before I had some business to attend to in Detroit."

He reached out to grab her hair again, pulling it viciously. Alex swallowed a scream, afraid it would draw Trixie, or worse, the children. Alexei leaned forward and smelled her neck, his eyes closed.

"It should have been Frank that day, making the drop. But instead it was your father. Dmitri Winters, desperate for money to send his darling daughter to college. Desperate enough to come to me."

Alex moaned, low in her throat. *Dad. Oh, God. What did you do?* She struggled to escape Alexei's grip, even while he yanked her to him, savagely kissing her, trying to force his tongue between her lips. Driving one knee up, she kneed him in the groin while she bit his tongue, her own teeth jarring in her mouth when he smacked her head against the pillar.

"So much vigor, little Alex. What fun we will have." Alex wrenched one hand free and tried to claw his face, but he dropped the gun to pin her hand, forcing it up behind her back. "Your poor daddy just wanted to make enough money to send his baby girl to college. Pity."

"You son of a bitch," she screamed. "It was you who killed my father."

"Me? I did nothing. It was darling husband's fault. If Frank hadn't vanished for week, it would have been *him* at ill-fated drop, and your life would have continued on as boring and predictable as ever. But our Frank, when he heard what happened, went insane. When I told him I expected Dmitri's daughter to settle her father's debts, he nearly killed me. Killed three of my men, then vanished for another week. I found out later, much later, that he went to Detroit, to see you."

Alex's head was spinning with this new version of her life, one in which she was a pawn in some Russian mobster's game. "No, he never . . . Frank never came to see me when my dad died, he . . ."

"Shh . . ." Alexei whispered, smacking her again, then gripping her chin. "It would be a shame to wake babies."

Alex moaned in terror.

"He did go to Detroit, to that sad little cut-rate funeral chapel. Then he came back to me and confessed everything. Told me what he was and who he worked for and promised to be my particular pet if I would only let you go. I agreed, of course, because as I said, I find Frank delightful and useful. And wonder of wonders, you receive settlement from mysterious life insurance policy that afforded you the chance to go to college and eat your donuts and carry on as if nothing had happened. Because our Frank is sentimental fool."

"Frank? Frank did that? But then why—"

Alex's words cut off when Trixie appeared in the doorway, eyes flashing, lacquered lips a grim slash, a small revolver in her hand. Alexei spun around at the sound of her voice.

"You get your hands off her, you Russian pig fucker. Nobody touches my girls that way."

Alex took the opportunity to slip around the pillar. With one hand, she slid her robe up, grasping the knife, Frank's knife, that she'd fastened around her thigh with a red garter.

"She's not one of your girls, Trixie. Let this go," Alexei said, stooping to pick up his gun. He aimed it at Trixie coolly.

"No, she's my friend. And you hurt her." Trixie's thumb drew back the hammer on her revolver with a click.

Alex slid the knife from the garter on her thigh, using the distraction to move a few steps closer to Alexei while his back was turned to her. *Oh God, am I really going to do this?* She gritted her teeth. *I fucking well am. He murdered my father.* Her hand holding the knife shook.

Her breath caught, Trixie's eyes widened, and Alexei spun. Before she could even think what she was doing, Alex jammed the knife into his eye socket, wrenching it and his eyeball out.

A scream exploded out of her when he fell toward her, socket gaping. Throwing the gore-covered knife to the ground, she pushed him off her and scrambled back. Alexei spun, a horrible scream bubbling from his lips, his gun raised, trying to stand and aim at the same time, his free hand clawing at his own face. There was a dry click, followed by a look of dismay on Trixie's face when her revolver misfired.

Alexei spun around, his one enraged eye now searching for Trixie. Alex flew past him, throwing herself at Trixie, knocking them both to the floor as Alexei's gun went off. Alex froze and waited for pain, blood, anything. Nothing. She opened her eyes and saw a crimson stain across Trixie's hip, marring her ivory robes.

"Oh, Trixie, no . . ." she murmured, her hands immediately pushing at the gushing wound. Her head swiveled around. Alexei stood only a few feet away, rocking on his feet, blood dribbling down his face, his mouth drawn up in rage.

"You," he spat. "You will suffer."

Alex turned away from him back to Trixie, who was, strangely, smiling at her.

"Trixie, what do I do? Tell me what to do," Alex whispered.

"You Frank Brennan's girl. You know what to do," she whispered. Reaching into her sleeve, she produced another small gun, pearl-handled with silver scrolling. Alex slipped it from her hand.

She turned back to face Alexei, arranging her face into one of fear, even as she felt that adrenaline coursing through her again.

"Alexei," she pleaded, "please don't hurt us."

"Maybe I won't hurt you," he groaned, limping toward her. "Maybe I just *keep* you, princess. Forever, until you are truly sorry you took my eye. And I'll make sure Frank knows." He stopped, rocking back and forth unsteadily on his feet.

Alex's eyes widened when Gwennie and Frank Jr. appeared behind him on bare feet, stealthy as cats. Gwennie's face was indignant, and Junior was clutching his blankie and his lunchbox. *Oh God, no. Go back to bed. Get out of here, babies.*

Alexei was still monologuing, "As for children, I think they shall accompany us tonight back to Moscow. I have never had privilege of training up two children to be my personal bodyguards. I shall delight in raising Frank's orphaned children myself. What I will turn them into will make the Tokyo job look like tea party."

The words had barely left his mouth when several things happened at once. Frank Jr. threw his lunchbox filled with chessmen at Alexei's hand, knocking the gun from it. Gwennie exploded into a blinding spin, kicking Alexei, once, twice, three times in the back of his knees in a whirl of perfectly executed roundhouse kicks. Alex scrambled to her feet when Alexei hit the ground, his head slamming into the marble floor and his gun skittering to the side.

Alex strode over to where he lay, a gasping, senseless Cyclops, and she planted one bare foot on his chest.

"I'm nobody's princess but Frank's, asshole."

Pointing the gun at his head, Alex pulled the trigger and blew him away. Then she fell to her knees, arms outstretched as her children flew to her. She kissed them and hugged their squirming bodies, terror and relief and joy cascading down her face in tears.

Frank Jr. whispered in her ear, "Here, Mommy. For Trixie's booboo."

Alex looked down and saw he was holding out his blankie. Alex grabbed it and crawled back over to Trixie, pressing it into the wound to stop the bleeding, the children fast on her heels.

"Thanks, chief. Gwennie, I'd thank you if what you did wasn't incredibly dangerous and stupid. You two should have stayed inside."

Gwennie scowled at her, irate. "Daddy said he didn't want you fussed. That mean man was *fussing* you."

"God, you are your father's children," Alex sobbed. She looked down into Trixie's agonized face. "Now what? Tell me what to do, Trix. I don't know what to do."

"Too sleepy to think, Frank Brennan girl," Trixie murmured. "You think for me."

Alex bit her lip. "Can you walk?"

"I think so, little pearl."

"You got a secret way out of here?"

"Of course," Trixie said, coughing. "This is a whorehouse, Alex Brennan. Lots of secrets. I have a secret tunnel."

Alex spun around to her children. "Stop kicking the dead Russian, babies. Go get all the ladies. Tell them to take you to the secret tunnel. I will meet you there with Trixie. Go, now," she urged.

The children ran off, after Gwennie gave the dead Alexei one last savage kick.

"What will you do, Alex?" Trixie asked while Alex helped her up.

Alex threw Junior's blood-stained blankie down and ripped off her robe, using the sash to securely tie it to Trixie's hip.

"We need to make you all disappear. All of you. And that asshole's body."

"But how?" Trixie groaned when Alex slipped an arm over her shoulder and began helping her out of the courtyard.

"I'm going burn this motherfucker down," she answered grimly.

"But Frank will think you're dead," Trixie whispered, pale from loss of blood.

"I can't worry about that now. I'm worrying about you and the girls and the kids. One disaster at a time, Trixie."

CHAPTER THIRTEEN

"Frank, wake up." The voice seemed to come from a great distance, barely breaking through the pain in Frank's head.

"Frank."

Someone smacked him, sending the pain in his jaw soaring from blinding to excruciating.

"Stupid American asshole. Get up."

Frank cracked open one swollen eye and looked into the grinning face of his friend.

"D'eng," he croaked. "But . . ." He sat up and coughed out a mouthful of blood onto the warehouse floor. "How?"

"Look around you, Frankie. Look at all my sleeping Russian beauties." D'eng laughed and cast an arm around the darkened warehouse. Grasping his arm, Frank let D'eng help him on his feet.

"What the fuck, D'eng?" Frank choked out, incredulous. The entire warehouse floor was littered with unconscious Russian goons, and lying next to each of them were half-empty bottles of vodka.

"D'eng heard shit went down at the club. I saw them throw your fat ass in a van, followed them here." He grinned and helped Frank into a rusted folding chair near the wall, pausing to kick a Russian. "So I ran to the liquor store, bought a case of cheap vodka, dropped a roofie in each one and delivered it here, compliments of their boss for a job well done."

"You roofied the Russians," Frank said flatly.

"That's three hundred dollars in vodka alone, Frankie. You owe me."

Frank looked around at the scattered goons and laughed, gasping at the pain from what was likely a cracked rib. "How long are they out for?"

"Maybe six more hours. Long enough for their boss to find out how stupid they were to let Frank Brennan slip." D'eng laughed.

Frank's brain finally woke up. Goons. Boss. Alexei. *Alex.* He jumped to his feet and pushed D'eng to the door.

"Frank, you better take it easy. They worked you over good."

"No time for that, D'eng. Alexei is on his way to Madam Li's. He knows about Alex and the kids. What time is it?" Frank demanded while he jumped into the panel van.

D'eng jumped into the driver's seat, jerked the transmission into drive, and floored it, tires spraying gravel.

"Oh shit, Frank." D'eng looked over at his friend. Bloody, bruised, eyes like an apocalypse.

"How long, D'eng?" Frank growled. "How long since they threw me in that van?"

D'eng punched the accelerator to the floor, his eyes never leaving the road. "Three hours, Frank."

Three hours, Frank thought, *I'm too late*. He prayed every prayer to every god he could think of while D'eng navigated the Bangkok streets like a madman, but it was no use. The road to Madam Li's was barricaded off, crowds gathered to watch the firemen finish putting out the flames. There was nothing left. Nothing.

D'eng drove as close as he could, slamming the van into park. Frank leapt out and stumbled through the crowds, punching an officer who tried to stop him and forcing his way through the barricade. Madam Li's was gone. A crater in the middle of the city. Nothing remained but a few charred beams and wet, ashy debris that littered the streets.

Hands grabbed at him from behind, police trying to pull him back to the barrier. Frank heard D'eng yell and felt fists land, and knew his friend had bought him just enough time to fall to his knees and crawl closer to where he'd left his family. He could see it, just up ahead, peeking out from under a charred gilt table. The edge of a blanket, blood-stained and covered in scorched army men. He burnt his hands pulling it out, held it to his face and sobbed, wanting nothing more than to crawl into the smoldering flames and die with them.

D'eng's voice broke through the noise of his grief and the sounds of sirens and firefighters.

"I'm sorry, Frank. They're still finding bodies. No survivors. Someone torched the place, Frankie."

Alex. Gwennie. Frank Jr. Gone.

His words shocked Frank out of his stupor. He stood, clutching the blanket in one hand, fists clenched.

"How much longer will those sons of bitches be unconscious, D'eng?"

D'eng stared at Frank, the anguish on his face for his friend's loss shifting to confusion.

"How long?" Frank bellowed, clutching his shoulder and shaking him.

"Like six more hours, at least, Frank," D'eng sputtered. "Why?"

"I need twenty-odd cinder blocks. And a ride back to the warehouse. Then you and I are dropping every one of those Russian bastards in the Chao Phraya River. Then I'm going after Alexei."

"It won't bring them back, Frank," D'eng said, jogging behind him back to the van.

"No, it won't. But I'm doing it anyway," Frank spat, his eyes filling as he looked at the tattoo on his wrist, a scorching reminder he'd carry with him forever. "I want revenge. I want vengeance. And it's the only thing I can do for them now."

The bar was little more than a hole in the wall. The light from the street barely penetrated the gloom inside, and the low ceilings and dark furniture seemed to absorb the light that patrons at establishments like these usually came to escape. Drunks. Small time criminals. Big time thugs. Dregs. People who were, for whatever reason, dead inside. The walls were covered in a myriad of unheeded prayer flags and flyers for titty shows, and decades of spilled drinks and spilled blood created a patina that almost matched the dead look in Frank's eyes.

He sat at a table in the back corner. Everything from the set of his shoulders to the raw look in his dark eyes, down to the way he gripped the scorched children's blankie, flashed *danger, danger, danger* to everyone around him. The bartender and the waitress, by tacit agreement, kept the bottle he clenched in his other hand full, serving him with a deference they did not normally show the regulars.

The regulars whispered about him, laid odds on what he'd do once he got himself drunk enough to let go of that rag. The odds-on favorite was that he'd do nothing. People who are empty inside know a dead man when they see one. And Frank was dead. His body just hadn't caught up yet. If he saw the fistfuls of bahts changing hands over his fate, he didn't let on.

Frank was remembering. Alex. Gwennie. Frank Jr. So many memories, but in the grand scheme of things, not even close to a lifetime full. That time in kindergarten Gwennie beat up a little boy who wouldn't do sharing. Alex's sighs in that dark motel room the day they met. Frank Jr.'s pot belly and his goddamn blankie. No one to remember but him.

I shouldn't have given him shit about his blankie, Frank thought.

Alex nagging him to clean the gutters. Gwennie saying, "Daddy, tie my shoes." Frank Jr.'s serious little face while he tried to explain chess to his thick old man.

I did it all wrong. I thought that by giving them a normal life, I was protecting them. I thought by lying to them, I was protecting them. But in the end, it didn't matter one bit. I should have taken them away. I could have taken them away. I could have hidden them away and given them every single thing they ever wanted. I was selfish and greedy, and now they're gone. And that fucker Alexei vanished like a ghost. I could search the rest of my miserable life and never find him. And the worst part is that she died thinking I didn't love her. She never knew how much.

When his head hit the table he didn't even feel it.

"Mr. Frank! Mr. Frank! Wake up, Mr. Frank!"

Hands were plucking at him, twin voices like songbirds pecked at his alcohol-soaked brain. He tried to push them off, but his arms were too heavy, too weak. One of the hands pulled his head off the sticky table and pushed him back in his chair and held him upright. His eyes rolled in his head while he tried to focus them.

"Mr. Frank. You come now. VIP! Come, come!"

Frank flinched at the sunlight, peering with one bloodshot eye at the kaleidoscope of women plucking at him, watching as if from a distance as the hundreds of smiling faces shrank down to two. He shook his head to make sure he wasn't seeing double, then barked, "What?"

"Mr. Frank, we search everywhere for you. All of Bangkok. VIP, Mr. Frank! You come now."

His right hand scrambled for the bottle on the table but one of the songbirds was faster.

"No more drinky, Mr. Frank. You come now. She be so mad at you, you don't come now."

Frank wiped his face with the back of his arm, Junior's blood-stained blanket still clutched in one fist.

The girls. Twins. In matching t-shirts that read "See The White Mountain Forest of New Hampshire."

He looked back up at them. "You two Trixie's girls?" he asked.

"Yes, yes," they said in unison. "She say go find Mr. Frank before he burn whole city down. You come now?"

A small tremor went through him. He wanted it to be relief that his friend was alive and looking for him, but he knew better. It was jealousy and rage that Trixie was alive, and *they* weren't.

He forced a smile at the two girls and reached into his pocket. Withdrawing a handful of money, he shoved it at them. "Take it. Tell Trixie I said goodbye. You two run along. I've got business here."

The girls cast anxious glances at each other. The one on the right pushed the money back at him. "You come now. No business here. VIP, Mr. Frank. You have VIP visitors that need see you right now!"

The tremor returned. This time it felt like hope. Vengeance.

Trixie would know the only visitor Frank would want to see would be one who knew where Alexei was. And maybe, just maybe, she could tell him something about their last minutes that would make it easier for him to . . . He rose from his chair so fast, it shot back and bounced off the wall.

"Well, why didn't you say so?" he growled at the songbirds.

They twittered and backed away toward the door.

Throwing the fistful of cash at the bartender, he sneered, "Save my table. I won't be long."

They led him through miles of back alleys and twisted narrow lanes. Their little feet seemed to float just above the pavement while he staggered heavily after them, trying to think. Trying to focus. Up a flight of stairs into an anonymous tenement building, the hallways filled with children playing and drunks passed out and old women smiling, finally coming to a stop at the end of an endless hall. The girls looked at him and giggled again and rapped on the door five times.

Shave and a haircut.

A small voice inside rang out. "Two bits!"

Frank shook his head. *No, no. Get a grip.* He squeezed his eyes shut. It had sounded just like Frank Jr. *Two bits. No.*

His eyes flew open at the next voice, high-pitched and bossy. Frank pushed the girls aside and slid his hands up the door, eyes closed, his cheek coming to rest on the splintered wood. He waited and listened, unable to believe he wasn't dreaming.

CHAPTER FOURTEEN

Frankie, I'm telling Daddy when he gets here that you sassed Mommy. He said Mommy was tired and we were to mind her." Gwennie's voice was just as obstinate as ever.

"You tattletale. Then I'll tell Daddy you tried on the fancy ladies' underwear and kicked the dead Russian after Mommy told you to stop." Junior's voice was calculating and clipped.

Frank held his breath, unbelieving, and gasped when another voice floated through the door to him. A wry, amused voice, tart and sweet, like lemon meringue pie.

"Gwendolyn Winters Brennan, did you try on Aunt Trixie's underwear?"

Alex. Alive. All of them. Alive.

Frank ripped the door open so hard, he pulled the hinges from the frame. They fell with a clatter behind him when he burst through the door.

The two sweetest voices in the world rang out, "Daddy!"

Frank fell to his knees while his children clambered all over him, his hands clutching them even as his eyes sought out the one face he knew he couldn't live without.

Alex sank to the floor and pulled him to her. Frank buried his weary head in her chest, surrounded by the shifting mass of arms, legs, and excited chirps of his children. Threaded through that was the soothing voice of his wife and the sound of someone sobbing.

Wait, he thought. *Jesus fuck, that's me.*

"You're alive. You're all alive," he managed. "I thought . . . I thought . . ."

His head pivoted at the sound of Trixie's voice. She was limping out of the back hallway toward him, an ivory cane in one hand, surrounded by more of her girls.

"Yes, yes, Frank. Alex got us all out. Your wife saved my life."

Alex flushed and pulled away from Frank, rising to her feet and crossing her arms.

"Kids, get off your father. Help him up."

Gwennie and Junior began vigorously tugging on him, doing more to keep him on the ground than actually help him up. Frank pretended they were helping and stood on his own steam.

"You did *what*?" he asked Alex.

She scowled and shook her head at him. "Nothing. She's exaggerating."

Trixie flashed her a derisive look. "*Nothing*. She got all of my ladies out. Then she burned Madam Li's down so those filthy Russians wouldn't come looking for any of us."

"You what?" Frank choked out, his head swinging back to his wife.

"I was afraid Alexei's men would come looking," Alex muttered, flushing.

Frank looked, uncomprehending, from Trixie to Alex.

"But who . . . I mean . . . they found bodies . . . that's why I thought . . ."

Trixie laughed, and all her girls laughed with her, a chorus of songbirds that made his hung-over head hurt. "Oh, my basement was full of bodies. Don't ask, don't tell, Frank." Trixie winked at him, eyes filled with glee.

But Alex just stared at him, her face unreadable.

Frank ran his hand through his hair, trying to process what this all meant. *Alex. The kids. Alive. Alexei. This isn't over yet.*

"We need to get you all out of here," he said frantically. "Alexei is still out there somewhere. I couldn't find him. He . . ."

Trixie laughed again, but this time Alex joined in, her eyes sparking.

"Oh, you don't worry about Alexei. He bother you no more. Right, Alex?"

Frank looked mystified at his wife. A small, mischievous smile tugged at her lips when she shrugged.

"Babe, what did you do?"

"I blew him away," she answered coyly.

"You *what?*"

"She Mrs. Frank Brennan, all right. She stab him in his eye, then she blow head off," one of the little birds chirped.

Frank sank down into a nearby chair, his face painted with disbelief.

"She did, Dad! It was sweet! We helped!" Junior squawked.

"Frank Jr., shut it," Alex snapped.

"Frankie did nothing, Daddy, except throw his chess set at that mean man's gun and put his blankie on Trixie's booboo," Gwennie said, shoving her brother. "I was the one that kicked him so Mommy could shoot him. He was *fussing* her, Daddy."

Frank looked over to Alex, his face perplexed.

"Don't look at me. Wicked footwork, our Gwennie. And thank God for Frank Jr.'s chess set." She swallowed, and her eyes filled with tears. "He hurt my friend. And he hurt you. And he threatened our babies, Frank. And . . . and . . . I . . ."

Frank rose on somewhat steadier feet and pulled her to him, wincing when she wrapped her arms around him.

"Shh, princess. I know. We can talk about it later."

Frank used the flat of his hand to wipe the tears from her face, then traced his fingers carefully around her bruised eye and the fresh stitches on her split lip.

"Are you telling me you did something I, several governments, and a multitude of hit men couldn't do?" He lowered his forehead to hers, closing his eyes when he kissed the tip of her nose.

Alex slid her hands up into his hair. He was smiling at her.

"Don't worry, Frank. I won't make a habit of it."

Trixie clapped her hands together three times, and everyone jumped.

"Okay, okay. Enough fun time. Everyone out. Mrs. Alex and Mr. Frank need to talk. Come babies, the ladies and I will take you to the park." She rapped her cane on the floor in punctuation, and the room cleared in a blur. The door slammed shut, and Alex and Frank were suddenly alone.

Frank slid his fingers through Alex's hair. "Alex, I thought. I . . ."

She put one hand on his lips and silenced him. "I know what you did," she whispered.

"No, you don't know. I should have told you, but . . ." He trailed off. "Shit. I don't know how to do these things. I suck at this."

Alex kissed him softly on his lips. "At what?"

"Being a good husband."

Alex shook her head, eyes shining. "No, you don't. You're the best." She cleared her throat. "Alexei started monologuing before I stabbed his eye out. He told me everything about my dad. About you. About what you did for me before you met me."

Frank's eyes flashed up to meet her, desperate. "Alex, you have to understand. That day in the donut shop, I never meant to stay. I never meant to lie to you or fall in love with you. I went in there to apologize and give you the truth about your dad. I thought you deserved that much. But you knocked me sideways. You always do," he said, ruefully kissing her back.

"But what I don't understand is why?" Alex whispered. "Why would you make that deal with him? You didn't even know me."

Frank saw her swallow hard and her eyes cloud over. "Why *you*? Because you were just an innocent by-stander. You were just a kid. In this line of work, I've seen what happens to people like you who get trapped by people like Alexei. It twists them into people they were never meant to be. Makes them do things they would never otherwise do. And I couldn't have it on my conscience. I saw you from outside that shitty chapel, and I thought, 'Maybe I can save one. Just one.' I have never regretted the deal I made with Alexei. I just had no idea that when I saved you, I was saving myself, too." He tilted her chin up. "Ask me. Anything. I'll tell you whatever you want to know, from here on out. If you'll still have me."

Alex shook her head and kissed him again, long and slow.

"You're filthy, Frank," she whispered against his jaw.

"Am I?" he asked, his lips on her forehead.

Alex nodded.

"I think you need a shower, Mr. Brennan." Alex laced her fingers in his and pulled him down a dark hall into a microscopic bathroom. He pulled her shirt off even as she tugged his pants down, their clothes hitting the floor in a flurry of scrambling arms and stumbling feet. Laughing, Frank kicked the door closed behind him.

"Close quarters," he said, pulling her against him.

Alex pulled him backwards into the shower, her laughter sweet and light in his ears. He reached over and turned the nozzle, sending a torrent of cold water over both of them.

She pulled him down to the tub floor on top of her, her teeth tugging on his earlobe as she purred in his ear, "I can make them closer." Alex wound her legs around him while the cold water turned warm and steam began to fill the tiny room.

Frank's hand slid down her wet belly, slipping between her legs and making her gasp.

"That's a hell of a grip you have there, Brennan," she said in his ear.

"League bowling champ, four years running, doll." His mouth found her breast, and he kissed his way from one to the other, and then drifted back up to her lips.

"I'm not done telling you I'm sorry, Alex."

"I can think of better things for you to do with that pretty mouth, Frank." She ran a hand over his wet hair and slid it back from his face. "Whoever you are, Frank, a Marine, a vinyl siding salesman, an assassin . . ."

"Agent, babe. Words are important."

She slid his wet hair back down over his face and kissed him. "Double agent, or just a husband and father, I love you, Frank Brennan. Forever."

"I love you, too, Alex Winters Brennan."

"I know that now. Shut up and make love to me."

"Yes, ma'am."

———————

Night was falling over Bangkok. As it did, the bright lights of the city reflected off the windows of the hotel room where Frank had whisked his family away after getting Trixie and her girls settled in a better temporary situation.

Frank searched inside his mind for a word that encompassed what he was feeling. Gwennie and Frank Jr.'s snores were a discordant song that floated out of their private adjacent room. Below, the city chimed in with sirens and cars honking. He was sprawled on crisp white sheets in the most expensive hotel in Bangkok, arms and legs entwined with Alex, the nightmare of the previous days being erased by every moment she played with his hair.

She smoothed it back. Pulled it forward over his eyes. Back again. *Content. I feel content.*

He watched as an unsettled expression floated across his wife's face. "What?" he rumbled at her, pulling her closer.

"What do you mean, what?" she said into his neck.

He pulled back and looked at her. "That face. What is that face? I'm sitting over here perfectly happy, and you're scowling."

Her forehead wrinkled while she cast a hand across the expansive, luxurious room he'd settled them in.

"How can we possibly afford this, Frank? I mean, I know you're relieved that we're alive, but this is too much."

"No, it's not," he said, grabbing her hand and kissing it. "It's not *nearly* enough."

She pulled away from him and crossed her arms, scowling again. "You remember that when we're eating beans on toast for three months running, pal."

He sat up in the bed, and then took a deep breath. "I haven't told you *absolutely* everything."

She gritted her teeth and rolled her eyes at him. "Oh, so there's more than 'assassin hunted by Russians'? This ought to be good. Jesus, Frank, you're taking this whole complicated anti-hero business to a whole new level of absurd."

"Double agent. Stop calling me an assassin. It's insulting."

She stuck her tongue out at him. "Fine. Spill."

"So, a funny thing happened when I got disavowed."

"How funny?" She sat up and crossed her legs so their knees touched.

Frank looked up at her, grinning. "How about three hundred million dollars' worth of chuckles funny?"

"What do you mean?" she demanded, punching him in his chest.

"Well, during that last job, Alexei wired three hundred million into my dummy account for the arms deal that the government thought I was welching on. They disavowed me, Alexei tried to kill my ass, and I cut and ran. So suddenly, Frank Brennan is three hundred million dollars richer, through almost at no fault of his own."

"Shouldn't you give it to the government? It's dirty money, Frank!"

"Fuck those dudes. They tossed me to the bears. And after this last job, Jesus, it's nearly doubled that. Minus the island costs, anyway."

"What island?" she demanded.

"I used part of the money years ago to buy a small island in the Philippines. Nothing fancy. You wouldn't believe what maintenance costs." He studied his hands, his ears turning red under her gaze.

"Wait, back up. You own an *island*, Frank? An entire goddamn non-fancy island?"

Frank shrugged and blushed. "I mean, yeah."

Alex punched him in the arm.

"Ow, what was that for?" he growled.

She punched his arm again, softer this time. "You own a goddamn island, and you had me living in *suburbia*? What the fucking hell is wrong with you?" She pulled his head down to her and kissed him, biting his lip as she drew back again.

"Why do you have to be so rough, princess?" he whispered, pulling her back to him.

"You like it rough, Brennan. Explain yourself." She made a fist and drew it back.

"Fine, fine. Stop hitting me."

She lowered her fist.

"It's just that Gwennie loves soccer and, God help us all, kickboxing. And Frank Junior has his model airplane club and his chess club, and I *wanted* that for them. A normal childhood. I thought I was doing right by all of you."

"Fuck a normal childhood, Frank. They're *your* kids. They can learn to fly, like, real planes and spearfish and rappel off cliffs or something. Something double agent-y. It's not like we can go back to Detroit now, right?"

Frank shook his head. "No. That would be a bad idea. The Feds might catch wind. I'll send a crew in to get our stuff, put in on a ship. It'll be to the island inside six months. Torch the house."

"Torching things is kind of our thing now, right?"

He laughed. "But what about you? You won't be lonely?"

"Hmm . . . let me think about that. Private island-owning, kingpin former-assassin filthy-wealthy husband. I'll suffer stoically. Jesus." She pushed him back down on the bed and straddled him, kissing him so hard it took his breath away. "I love you. No matter what. But what will we do if Alexei's people find your island, Frank? Didn't you say he had goons?"

Frank wrapped his arms around her and held her tight to his chest. "You didn't think I got my own island by being a nice guy, did you Alex? I took care of that. There are no loose ends. No more Russians. Remember, I thought you and the kids were dead. I did . . . things." He squinted up at her, abashed.

"Things, huh?"

"Bad things."

"You're the best husband ever, Frank."

"No, I'm not. I'm a cold-hearted double agent."

"I stabbed a Russian in the eyeball and burned down a whorehouse. What does that make me?"

"My dream girl."

Frank rolled her over and slid his hands down to her waist, his lips following them, then settled his head against the small rise he felt there. Content.

"What are we going to call him or her?" she whispered.

"Frank Junior," he said firmly.

"We are not naming both of our sons after you, you sociopath. Or any of our daughters."

"It'll make things easier when there are five more of them. All little Franks. I won't have to tell them apart."

"What about a few Alexes mixed in, for variety?"

"I can live with that."

AFTERWORD

Alex stepped out of the low-slung white-washed house. The cool breeze off the South China Sea set the edges of the thatched roof rippling. Shielding her eyes with her hand, she scanned the shore for her family, smiling when she found them.

Gwennie was tacking in her little sailboat in the harbor, her fierce scowl apparent even from this distance, her freckles indignant punctuation marks against whatever was currently annoying her. Frank Jr. was huddled in the shade, white with zinc, frowning over a chessboard.

And her husband, Frank Brennan, the double agent/arms dealer/assassin/turned vinyl salesman/turned double agent/turned retired father and husband. He was tossing their youngest, Frankie Li, into the gentle waves at the shore. After each toss of the giggling toddler, he ran back to make another move on Junior's chess set, then sprinted back to the shore to toss his youngest daughter in again, missing the look of patient exasperation from his son, then bellowing out encouraging words to his daughter in her sailboat.

"Some retirement, huh, Brennan?" Alex called out. He tossed little Frankie Li back like a fish before he turned and fixed his wife with that rugged grin that still set her legs to rubber.

She walked slowly down the rickety boardwalk toward him, pausing to rumple her son's hair. Frank met her where the boards ended and wrapped his tanned arms around her waist.

"I should have thought of this years ago. Any excuse to keep you in a bathing suit year-round. You were right, babe, the suburbs sucked." He kissed her nose. "What's up? I thought you were working on a new story."

"Well, I was, but I got a very important email and I can't respond to it because my millionaire husband won't spring for Wi-Fi and I have the equivalent of 1990s dial-up in this shack." She kissed him back, long and lingering. "I'm going to take the boat over to the next island where they have civilization and use theirs. Back in a couple hours, cupcake."

"Mind if we all tag along?" he growled.

"Sure." She bent and picked Frankie Li up, smoothing her jet-black hair back from her face. "Maybe we can even Skype with Trixie Li so she can see how her goddaughter is growing. Technology, Frank. It's a thing."

"Important email, huh?" he said, waving Gwennie back in to shore.

"Yep." She winked at him.

"Spill, princess."

"Well, you know that story I was scribbling on?"

"The one about the action hero or the one about the assassin?"

"Neither. This one was about two married people who go on vacation and get caught up with the Russian mob in Bangkok. They keep secrets from each other, almost lose each other, and then somehow live happily ever after."

He grinned at her. "Oh, that one." He tucked her hair behind her ear. "Frank Jr., we'll finish our match tomorrow. Saddle up, son."

"I sent it to an agent back in the States. I decided that it couldn't be scarier than facing down a Russian mobster in a whorehouse. And she loved it. She says a studio wants to buy it."

Frank took Frankie Li back into his arms, letting her scramble up onto his shoulders. He pulled Alex to him, his hands sliding to where her stomach had begun to just barely swell above her bikini bottoms.

"Did you hear that, Frankie Li and Frank III? Your mommy is going to be famous. So they want to make it into a movie?

"I don't know. Some action hero franchise called Armed Assault Force?"

Frank shook his head and shrugged.

"I've never heard of it either, aside from Junior's t-shirt. She said something about wanting it for the sequel to the first movie. Apparently they want to make some changes to the story, so I have to talk to the agent in real time, not via smoke signals. Something about machetes and freedom fighters." She rolled her eyes.

"Outstanding, princess. I love to watch you soar. What's the story called?"

"*Bangkok Vengeance.*"

He pulled her back to him for another kiss, Frankie Li pulling his hair and squealing as he did.

"Catchy title."

"I thought so."

Dana McSwain grew up on the shores of the Great Lakes in the shadow of the Rust Belt. A graduate of Kent State University, she lives in a 106 year-old house in Cleveland, OH with her family and two dogs. Possessing a near encyclopedic knowledge of special effects-heavy blockbusters, bad TV, and a deep and abiding love for the intricate story lines of professional wrestling, the universe of Frank Brennan and Alex Winters is her love song to all things tropey and over-the-top.

danamcswain.com
Facebook: @danamcswain
Instagram: @danadmcswain